KNOT OF FEAR

BRYAN CASSIDAY

Bryan Cassiday
Los Angeles
ISBN 9781737628262
Published in the United States of America
First Edition: October 25, 2022

BOOKS BY BRYAN CASSIDAY

Threads (Scott Brody Thriller 4)
Electric Green Mambas (Scott Brody Thriller 3)
Horde (Zombie Apocalypse: The Chad Halverson
Series Book 6)
Ice in the Blood
Crime Blotter USA
Murder LLC (Scott Brody Thriller 2)
Bolt (Scott Brody Thriller 1)
Riptide of Fear
The Payout
Force of Impact (Ethan Carr Thriller 3)
Dying to Breathe (Ethan Carr Thriller 2)
Countdown to Death (Ethan Carr Thriller 1)
The Bus Stops Here—and Other Zombie Tales
Two Moons Rising
Alien Assault
Comes a Chopper
Zombie Apocalypse: The Chad Halverson Series 1–5
Helter Skelter
The Anaconda Complex
The Kill Option
Blood Moon: Thrillers and Tales of Terror
Fete of Death

Chapter 1

Sitting at a table on the sidewalk at the bustling Third Street Promenade in Santa Monica, Ivy thought she heard one of the men at a nearby table say, "The final option is murder, but only after the baby is born."

Murder, a figure of speech, she figured, not paying much heed, taking a pull on her latte. Or was she hearing things? She was under a lot of stress. Every day was a new crisis. Plague, famine, war, and death filled the days' headlines. They all made the virtual world her husband Orion Kingston owned attractive, a haven where you could escape the misery of modern daily living.

It was her business to sell real estate in his metaverse, Rabbit World. He envisioned it as a Disneyland-like playground suitable for the whole family.

Pushing thirty-two Ivy was five eight with a slender figure. The daughter of a newspaper magnate, she had a mien of self-conscious nervousness. She felt her father's wealth had nothing to do with her and she didn't like talking about it. The apple had fallen far from the tree, she decided. Unlike her father, who was brimming with chutzpah, she lacked belief in herself. She suffered from anxiety attacks and had a psychiatrist.

The guy who had spoken about murder was facing away from her in a grey hoodie, his back hunched. She could hear a lot of chatter from other nearby tables on the patio, making it difficult for her to be sure of any dialog she was hearing.

Wanting to feel with it, she was eager to try out the new virtual reality headset her husband had brought home from work so she could see what Rabbit World looked like. The more she knew about VR, the better she could market it to the public. She believed the metaverse was the future, and she wanted to be part of it, even if she didn't completely understand it.

She was waiting for her friend Liz Zigler to return from the ladies' room.

As if on cue, Liz appeared at their table. At five four, with bobbed chestnut hair, she was a bit on the plump side—unlike Ivy. Liz liked to wear hiking boots to show how tough she was. About Ivy's age, Liz was taking courses in martial arts to help her survive in the big city. She liked to brag about her expertise in taekwondo.

Born and raised in Twin Falls, Idaho, she had come to LA two years ago to escape her abusive mother who used to slap her around when she tied one on. Not knowing what she wanted to do with her life, Liz roamed the streets of LA seeking to find purpose in her life. The legions of homeless people and drug addicts she saw depressed her. She felt the world was doomed and would end soon.

"They need to clean their restrooms more often at this restaurant," said Liz, sitting down opposite Ivy.

Ivy smiled briefly, brushing back her blonde bangs. "Their latte is pretty decent," she said, holding up her cup.

Liz searched Ivy's face. "Are you OK? Are you still having marital problems with Orion?"

"We argue, is all."

"About what—if you don't mind my asking? I'm not married. I want to know in case I decide to change my mind and take the plunge."

"Sometimes he makes me feel like his employee instead of his wife."

"Because?"

"Because he owns Rabbit World, the VR company I work for as a real estate agent."

"I forgot. Yeah, I can see where working for your husband might cause a problem."

"Usually, it's not an issue. Maybe I'm imagining it. Being married to the boss can have side effects."

"Like meds, huh?"

"Except meds are good for you."

"And marriage isn't. Is that what you're saying?"

"All I'm saying is, marriage can be tough sometimes."

"I'll make a note of that."

Ivy pulled a face. "I'm not an expert on the subject. Sometimes it drives me crazy."

"Being single can drive you crazy, too. Like me. I start talking to the walls when I'm alone too often."

"Been there, done that."

"You look pale."

"I'm not getting enough sleep. I keep waking up at night and can't get back to sleep."

"Have you been to a doctor?"

"No. It's just insomnia. It'll go away."

Ivy watched Hoodie stand up and leave the restaurant with his companion, a squat muscular guy in his late twenties wearing a black T and sepia cargo pants. The squat guy glanced at her as he left with Hoodie. In his early thirties, the guy had a shaved head and was wearing a mask thanks to the lingering Covid pandemic. He had an equine, pallid face with eerie-looking large blue eyes.

Ivy had never seen him before. As for Hoodie, she still couldn't see his face, as he kept it turned away from her.

Chapter 2

Ivy drove her silver Tesla to her pink Mission Revival house in Brentwood that had a red tiled roof.

Standing in her well-appointed living room, she donned the virtual reality headset and the cybergloves Orion had brought home for her. The headset fit too snug. She had trouble breathing. She wasn't looking forward to wearing the contraption for any length of time.

She wasn't keen on the fit of her cybergloves, either. They constricted her movements. Not a good way to start her journey into Rabbit World.

She had to buy clothes for her avatar before she introduced it into the virtual world. She bought a simple loose purple dress and put it on her avatar.

Her dressed avatar walked down the street exploring it.

This was fun, she decided. It was like visiting a new country. She saw buildings lining the street. Clothing stores, gaming stores, furniture stores. She knew avatars had to buy furniture for the houses they purchased from her in the virtual world.

Out of nowhere two male avatars charged her. The one with his hair cut in a mullet was wearing a black hoodie and blue jeans, the bald one a blue hoodie and black jeans. Save for a weird half smile, their faces had the static, expressionless, inhuman look of dolls, with outsized blue irises. Smooth-faced, the two looked to be in their late twenties or early thirties.

Grabbing her they tore off her dress, threw her savagely to the sidewalk, leapt onto her, and raped her. Laughing, they fled.

Overcome with fright, her heart pounding in her ears, Ivy pulled her avatar to its feet and smoothed its rumpled dress, which the rapists had torn and rucked up to its hips.

Ivy tried to process what had just happened, staring into the headset, unseeing.

Traumatized, she finally pulled herself together and tore off her gloves and headset.

Feeling violated, she staggered to her sofa and fell down on it, her face ashen.

What the hell happened?

Was this the nightmare world she was supposed to sell to the public? she wondered. Why would anyone want to enter Rabbit World, let alone buy real estate there?

True her body hadn't been violated. But she felt violated, nonetheless. The very idea that someone would want to assault her terrified her. What was she supposed to do?

It wasn't like she could call the cops. She had no bruises on her body, no proof she had been assaulted. She didn't even know if it was considered a crime to be virtually assaulted. If it wasn't, it should be.

She decided to call Orion. After all, Rabbit World was his creation. If anybody knew what to do, it should be him. She dug her cell phone out of her purse and called him.

"I've been assaulted," she blurted into her phone, as soon as he picked up.

"What?" said Orion, taken aback.

"I was assaulted by two men in Rabbit World."

Orion paused. "Start from the beginning. What happened?"

"I put on the virtual headset and the cybergloves and entered Rabbit World. Right after I bought some clothes for my avatar and dressed it, I was gang-raped on the sidewalk," she said, her voice breaking.

All in all, she was proud of the control she was managing to assert over her raging emotions.

"Wait a minute," he said. "*You* were gang-raped or your avatar?"

"My avatar."

"Was your avatar wearing clothes when it was attacked?"

"It was dressed with the new clothes I bought. It was raped right after it came out of the clothing store. Why?"

"A naked female avatar could've aroused the two attackers."

"Don't tell me you're blaming me for their attack."

"I'm trying to find out the facts."

"Should I call the cops?"

"No, no. Don't do that."

"Then where do I file a report against the two assailants?"

"You weren't hurt, were you?"

"You mean, physically?"

"Right."

"I didn't fall down and hurt myself while I was wearing the virtual head gear, if that's what you mean."

"You have no proof that a crime took place? No bruises on your body, nothing of that sort?"

"That doesn't mean I wasn't assaulted."

"The point is, you didn't get physically hurt."

"I was traumatized," said Ivy, becoming angry. "How is inflicting emotional pain not a crime?"

"I'm looking at it like a cop would."

"Are you saying that because the assault happened in the virtual world, it didn't really happen?"

"That's how the cops and the law would look at it, I'm sorry to tell you."

"You're saying I should do nothing?" she said, incredulous.

"In this case, it's best for you to forget the unreal assault ever happened. No harm, no foul."

"I feel violated. An assault is an assault, no matter where it takes place. How is it not a crime?" she said, her voice fraught.

"The best policy is to drop it and forget about it."

"Best policy for who? Not me." Ivy mulled it over. "Are you worried about the bad publicity Rabbit World will get if I report the attack to the cops? Is that it?"

"Of course not. No way. Not me."

Methinks she doth protest too much, thought Ivy.

"Your well-being is all I care about," Orion went on. "Making a spectacle of yourself at the police department reporting an assault that didn't really happen will only succeed in trashing your reputation. Is that what you want?"

"I want some kind of justice. The men who own those avatars that attacked me should be punished."

"But it didn't really happen."

"Then why do I feel so violated?" she said, sobbing.

"Calm down and think this through. You'll see, it's best to keep this between us."

"You mean, it's best for Rabbit World if we keep it between us."

"Don't you see? You can't prove anything happened. The cops won't do anything, if you tell them. You're gonna come off as a kook."

"You want me to pretend it never happened. Is that it?" she said, raising her voice.

"The cops can't do anything. What are they gonna do? Bust a couple of male avatars?"

"Somebody owns those avatars. The owners should be punished."

"I know what they're gonna say. They'll say nothing happened. They never laid a hand on you." Orion heaved a long sigh. "Maybe you should see your psychiatrist."

"You think I'm crazy?" she said, indignant.

"He can calm you down. That's all I'm saying."

Ivy stewed. "Are you gonna allow these attacks to continue in Rabbit World? If I don't report this, there will be more attacks—*worse* attacks."

"Nothing happened. Think of it as a movie or a nightmare. And forget it."

"You wouldn't say that if *you* were the victim."

"I have to get back to work, Ivy."

"Don't you have any laws or rules in Rabbit World?"

"None. It's about freedom. It's about doing what you want but can't do in the real world."

"Like assaulting people."

"Concentrate on selling real estate in Rabbit World. You don't have time for doing anything else."

"Why do I want to sell real estate in a nightmare world?"

"Nightmares aren't real," said Orion, his patience worn out. "Nothing happened. Rabbit World is a happy place. Remember that in your sales pitch."

"A happy place for rapists," said Ivy, her voice brittle with outrage.

Orion hung up.

Chapter 3

Alone in her living room after the assault, Ivy felt uncomfortable. She eyed with fear the headset she had flung onto the sofa. She had to get out of the house.

She bolted out the front door, hurried to her Tesla, climbed into it, and drove out of the driveway at speed, her eyes frantic. The driver of a plumber's van passing on the street honked in warning, as she backed recklessly out of her driveway, impatient to get away from her house. Spotting the van she slammed on her brakes. Her tires screeched to a halt, inches away from the oncoming van.

She had to calm down, she told herself. All she needed now was to get into an accident.

Sitting in the driver's seat, she took three deep breaths, steadying her nerves.

Calmer after a fashion, she backed out of her driveway and drove away from her neighborhood.

She didn't even know where she was going. All she knew was she had to get out of her house, the location of the assault. Who could she confide in? The cops? Orion told her to stay away from them. Maybe he was right. She had no bruises on her body, no signs of rape. And, as far as she knew, an assault that took place in virtual reality wasn't considered a prosecutable crime. *Even though it was a crime.*

She decided to drive to Liz's apartment.

She hung a right on Wilshire Boulevard and headed west. She glanced in the rearview mirror at a black Dodge Charger that turned after her. The reason she had checked it out was because its engine was making a commotion that got on her nerves.

Her hands froze on the steering wheel, as she discerned the driver and his passenger. She did a double take. The two faces behind the windshield looked like those of the avatars that had assaulted her in Rabbit World. The pasty faces had the same eerie doll-like appearance and seemed too large for their bodies.

How could it be? she wondered, her pulse racing. Avatars weren't human. They couldn't exist in the real world. And yet there were two of them following her in their Charger. She couldn't wrap her head around it.

Maybe it was a trick of her imagination. Maybe she was seeing avatars everywhere she looked because of the trauma induced by her assault in Rabbit World. She glanced away from the rearview mirror. Maybe the avatar faces would disappear after she looked away. She eyed the traffic in front of her then glanced into the rearview mirror again, hoping the avatar faces wouldn't be in the Charger this time.

They were still there with that weird half smile they had worn when they assaulted her.

She wanted to scream.

Terrified, she sped up, trying to put distance between her and them. They gave pursuit, accelerating to follow her, their eight-cylinder Hemi engine throbbing with power.

There was no way she could outrace the Charger, decided Ivy, her fear-wide eyes locked on the rearview mirror, watching the Charger barreling down on her rear. She would have to try evasive tactics. She cut her steering wheel, hung a sharp right, her tires screeching in protest.

She sped down a narrow street bordering a park then hung a left at the next block. She eyeballed her driver's-side mirror.

No black Charger in sight.

She must have lost it, she decided. She hung a quick left to make sure.

Her heart was beating so fast she thought it would explode any second. She told herself to get a grip.

She got her bearings and resumed her journey to Liz's.

Fucking avatars driving a car? Oh sure. Like anybody would believe her, she decided.

She must have been imagining it. She cut her eyes to the rearview mirror. The black Charger was gone.

She parked in a public parking garage and walked four blocks to Liz's apartment, which never had any street parking spaces available in front of it.

She punched out Liz's number on the speakerphone in front of the security door of the three-story, Spanish-style, avocado stucco apartment house. Liz answered and buzzed her in.

Ivy took the elevator to Liz's floor, got out, walked to Liz's door on unsteady feet, feeling lightheaded, and knocked on it.

Liz answered the door, wearing a white T, khaki cargo pants, and a backpack.

"I just got back from my walk," she said, reaching toward her backpack. "What happened to you?" she said in alarm. "You're white as a sheet."

Ivy clutched her forehead. "Can I sit down? I feel like I'm gonna pass out."

"Sure, sure. Come on in."

Ivy made her way through the cluttered living room past a bicycle lying on the floor. The minute she reached the sofa she collapsed on it.

"I'll get you some water," said Liz, retreating to the kitchen.

She returned to the living room, handed Ivy a glass of bottled water, and flung off her backpack.

"What's with the backpack?" said Ivy, accepting the water.

"My motto is, be prepared for anything. Including the apocalypse. Which is overdue."

"I didn't know you were a prepper."

"These days how can I not be?"

"Is it that bad?"

"Are you kidding? The Four Horsemen of the Infocalypse are here."

Ivy shook her head in confusion. "Infocalypse?"

14

"Terrorists, money launderers, pedophiles, and drug dealers. The four horsemen. They're already here. They've taken over the world. The Infocalypse is when the real news can't be distinguished from fake news. It signifies the beginning of the end.'

"I had no idea you were into that."

"Enough of me. What the hell happened to you?"

Chapter 4

Ivy took a pull on her water. "I don't know where to start."

One of the springs in the sofa must be broken, she decided, because she felt it digging into her left buttock.

"I'm dying to know," said Liz, sitting next to Ivy on the sofa, all ears.

Ivy gathered herself.

"Orion thought I should know more about Rabbit World, so he gave me a headset for me to experience it firsthand," she said.

"You never did VR before? You must not be a gamer."

"I'm not."

"That explains it," said Liz, nodding.

"Anyway, I put on the headset and the cybergloves and entered Rabbit World. I bought a dress for my avatar, dressed her, and walked onto the sidewalk. And bam! Two thugs assaulted my avatar, tore her clothes, and gang-raped her."

"Jesus," said Liz, her mouth agape.

"I threw the headset off in horror. I can't get it out of my mind."

"Something like that. Wow. You need to report it."

"Report it to who?"

"Did you tell Orion?"

Ivy nodded yes. "He told me not to tell anyone."

"You gotta tell the cops."

"He told me it's not a crime."

Liz stared at her. "I never thought about it. I guess he's right. If committing murder in the virtual world was illegal, gamers would all be thrown in the joint every time they killed an enemy when they game."

"How can he be right? I was assaulted. Violated. I'm still suffering from it," said Ivy, her hand shaking as it clasped the glass of water.

"It's the Infocalypse."

"Is that all you ever think about?"

"When you can't tell the real world from the fake world, how do you know what's true? This is how the Infocalypse messes up our minds."

"Are you saying I wasn't really assaulted?"

"That's not what I'm saying. I'm saying being assaulted in the virtual world is no different from being assaulted in the real one."

"That's my point."

"And I take your point. I'm on your side. You need to file an official report of this. Don't paper it over like Orion wants. Otherwise, the thugs will rape you again the next time you enter Rabbit World, because they know you won't do anything about it."

"Where do I file this official report?"

"Hmm. That's the question," said Liz, scratching her chin. "Maybe you should sue."

"Sue who? I don't know who owns those two avatars that attacked me."

"You could sue Rabbit World."

"It's owned by Orion. Why would I want to destroy my own husband's reputation? Anyway, just because he owns the real estate doesn't make him responsible for everything that happens on it."

"I'm telling you, girl, you have to do something. You can't take this lying down. For sure, they'll attack you again if you do nothing."

Liz had a point, decided Ivy.

"I agree, I have to do something, but what?" said Ivy, racking her brains for an answer.

Liz snapped her fingers. "I got it. You could take it to the press. They'll publish your story."

"Orion doesn't want anyone to know I was attacked. He's worried about the bad publicity for Rabbit World."

"Is bad PR all he cares about? What about you? Doesn't he care about you? You're his wife, for Chrissake."

"He believes I wasn't really harmed. No harm, no foul."

"Maybe your body wasn't harmed. But what about your mind?"

"It gets worse."

"You're scaring me, Ivy."

Ivy hung her head.

"I might be losing it," she muttered.

"Losing your mind?" said Liz with concern. "I don't believe it. You're as smart as anyone I know. Whip-smart, that's you to a T."

"While I was driving here, I saw two men in a black Charger who looked like the two avatars that assaulted me. They were following me."

"An avatar driving a car?" said Liz, shaking her head with disbelief. "You must've imagined it."

"Maybe."

"Of course. You were upset because of the assault, and you imagined you were being attacked all over again."

"I'm telling you, there were two avatars in that car chasing me. They had the same doll-like, big faces with spooky grins of my attackers."

Liz held Ivy's hand. "Avatars can't drive real cars, honey. They can only drive virtual cars."

"Are you calling me a liar?"

"Of course not. You're overwrought. You're seeing avatars all over the place."

"I know what I saw," said Ivy, withdrawing her hand from Liz's and crossing her arms over her chest.

Liz paused in thought. "Have you talked to your psychiatrist?"

"You think I'm going nuts?" said Ivy, wondering, despite herself, if Liz might be right.

"You suffered a traumatic event. It could trigger psychological problems. What harm would it do to consult your psychiatrist?"

"Orion doesn't want me to tell anyone about it. I shouldn't even have told you, but I had to tell someone. It's eating away at me."

"What you tell your psychiatrist is confidential between you two. You don't have to worry about anyone else finding out about it, including Orion."

"I guess it couldn't hurt to make an appointment."

"Good."

"But what can a shrink do to punish the rapists? They have to be brought to justice."

"Maybe you should take justice into your own hands, since nobody's gonna help you."

"How?"

"Find the rapists and punish them."

"How am I supposed to do that?"

"I don't know. I'm not tech savvy. There must be some way of finding out who the avatars belong to. Orion must know. Ask him."

Ivy shook her head no. "He told me to drop it and forget it happened. It's bad PR to let people know I was attacked at Rabbit World."

"He cares more about his virtual world than about you," said Liz, frowning.

Ivy stood up. "I feel better after talking with you. A little tired—" She yawned.

"Because you're stressed out."

Ivy walked to the door, her gait unsteady.

"Do you want me to call a paramedic?" said Liz, watching her.

"No. I'll be all right," said Ivy, opening the door and leaving.

Chapter 5

Ivy drove back to her house in her Tesla, glancing often in the rearview mirror, worried she would pick up the two avatars hanging a tail on her again. Liz hadn't convinced her she had imagined it.

So far so good. She didn't see the black Charger behind her.

Then she cringed. She noticed in the rearview mirror a black car accelerating and gaining ground on her, its chugging, intimidating silhouette looming behind her. Apprehensive, she widened her eyes as she made out the two pasty-faced avatars staring at her with their eerie half smiles fixed on their lips.

She couldn't be imagining it. They were right behind her.

Gasping, she hung a right off Wilshire Boulevard, running the red light. She had to get away from them.

Swerving, her hands shaky on the steering wheel, she didn't know what to do. She picked up on them pursuing her in the rearview mirror again.

She hung a sharp right, followed by a left. A cacophonous symphony of car horns blasted by drivers infuriated by her cutting them off followed her.

Eyes popping, she furtively checked the driver's-side mirror. She didn't see the Charger behind her.

She breathed easier. She must have shaken the tail. She drove back to her house, but not without checking the rearview mirror on and off for the Charger the entire journey.

She pulled into her driveway and noticed Orion's silver metallic Porsche Turbo S cabriolet parked there. Good, she decided. She needed to talk to him. She parked behind his car.

Climbing out of her Tesla she checked all around her for the black Charger. She didn't see it roaring down her street. As she strode to her front door, she kept craning around, expecting the Charger to burst into view any second.

Christ, she was losing it, she decided, her nerves frayed.

She ducked into the house. She shut and locked the door behind her.

Dressed in his Silicon Valley uniform of blue jeans, a lime T, and white sneakers, Orion was standing in the living room, flipping through a copy of *Wired*. The Stanford grad had a smooth, almost boyish face with long black hair.

He had an arrogance to him that she had misinterpreted as self-confidence when she had first met him. She was attracted to self-confident men. Maybe they reminded her of her father. She learned only later that Orion was full of self-doubts that he concealed with his supercilious demeanor. It was a protective shell he wore around him.

"What happened?" he said, looking up at her.

"We need to talk," she said.

"That's why I came back home," he said, tossing his magazine onto the round cherrywood coffee table in front of him.

"I'm being stalked."

"A stalker?" said Orion in surprise.

"Two guys—the avatars that attacked me—are stalking me."

"You're still upset by that. I understand."

"No, you don't understand. They were stalking me in a black Charger."

"You mean, in the real world?" he said, bewildered.

"They followed me twice today when I was driving."

"It makes no sense. Avatars can't drive real cars."

"It was them. I recognized their creepy doll faces."

"You're upset. You need to calm down," he said, putting his arm around her back and trying to console her. "You're seeing things."

"I'm not seeing things. They were there. They tailed me in a black Charger."

"Have a seat and relax. I'll pour you a drink," he said, and retreated to the sidebar.

He poured Sancerre into two glasses.

Chapter 6

"I've got to report this to the cops," said Ivy.

Orion rounded on her. "They'll think you're crazy if you tell them. Think of your reputation. You don't want to be known as a kook, do you?"

"I saw those two thugs stalking me, I tell you."

Orion handed her a drink. She shook her head no.

"Suit yourself," he said, replaced her drink on the sidebar, and took a pull on his wine. "They're stalking you, you say?"

"I know it must sound crazy. I couldn't believe it either."

Orion angled to the picture window and gazed past the scarlet bottlebrushes growing in their front yard. The neighborhood road was deserted.

"I don't see any black Dodge Chargers outside," he said.

"I lost them."

He ambled back toward her. "I realize you're under a lot of stress because of your incident in Rabbit World—"

"Incident? It was an assault," she said, folding into herself, holding her arms across her chest and rubbing them. "The two of them must be punished."

"You need to understand the metaverse. It's about freedom. Like the Internet used to be when it first started. The Internet has changed. It's too controlled. That's why we invented the metaverse to take the place of the Internet. In the metaverse people are free to do what they want."

"Like commit rape."

"Unfortunately, there are bad apples in every basket. It's the price we pay for freedom."

"It doesn't sound like freedom to me. It sounds like anarchy. People assaulting each other whenever they feel like it. That's not my idea of freedom."

23

"Just tell yourself it didn't happen. That's the best thing to do. Look at you. There's not a scratch on you. You weren't physically harmed. In the end, nothing happened to you."

"Nothing happened to me except I was violated."

"Forget about it," he said, raising his voice in irritation. "No good can come of pursuing the matter."

"I'm not letting those scumbags get away with this."

"You'll destroy my company if you don't let this go. Nobody will invest in Rabbit World if they think they'll be assaulted when they enter it."

"You should tell that to the thugs that attacked me."

Orion confronted her, face flushed. "I'm not gonna let you trash my company. I didn't work all my life to make my dream come true just to have you destroy it with your accusation. Drop it, I say."

"I can't do that."

"Then I'll do everything I can to stop you."

"I can't believe you. You're my husband. You should be on my side. Instead, you're attacking me."

"All you have to do is drop it. That's all I'm asking of you. The bad PR will sink Rabbit World, if you tell anyone about this."

"Can't you find the IDs of the two who attacked me and kick them out of Rabbit World? What's so hard about that?"

"I told you, the metaverse is about freedom. Nobody is required to give their IDs to join Rabbit World."

Ivy couldn't believe it. "No IDs mean no accountability."

"I repeat, nothing actually happened to you. It was all in your mind in a world that doesn't exist in reality."

"Is this your way of saying you're not gonna help me find these two pervs?"

"I'm not gonna trash my life's dream. It took me too long to get to this point to throw it away just like that. There's nothing more to say."

He stalked out of the room, spilling wine from his glass in his agitation.

How could she track her assailants if she couldn't find out their names? wondered Ivy. It was clear Orion wasn't going to help her find them.

Orion popped back into the living room. "How do I know you're not making all of this up? How do I know you even used the VR headset?"

"Because I told you I did. Why would I make up something like that?"

"Maybe you want attention."

"How could you believe that?" she said, fired up.

"Were there witnesses?"

"I was here alone when I put on the headset."

"Figures," he said, as if to himself.

"What's that supposed to mean?"

"It means, we have to take your word for it that you entered Rabbit World with your headset."

"Why would I make up—"

Orion withdrew, shaking his head.

Chapter 7

It was becoming apparent to Ivy she was on her own. If she wanted to find justice, she would have to do it herself. Which meant punishing her attackers.

She wasn't about to let them scare her away from her job selling real estate in Rabbit World. If she lived in fear of them, she would never return to Rabbit World to do her job. Then again, why would she want to sell real estate in Rabbit World if it was a crime-ridden jungle where nobody who entered was safe?

What if she sold real estate in Rabbit World and the new landowners were attacked as she had been? Would she feel guilty for brokering the sale?

On the other hand, why was it her duty to make sure Rabbit World was safe before selling real estate in it? No real-estate agent could be held accountable for every crime that took place on property they sold.

That said, she still bore the responsibility of fighting back against her attackers. Letting them get away with what they had done to her would embolden them to attack her again. The attackers needed to be punished. But how?

She thought about it and decided to call a PI. She used her smartphone to search for a local PI on the Internet. She chose the Internet detective Scott Brody and called him for an interview.

The better part of a half hour later, he drove onto her driveway in a Mini Cooper and parked behind her Tesla. She greeted him at the front door, as he walked up the flagstone path that led from the drive.

Six two and muscular, he wore stonewashed jeans and a sky blue polo. He was wearing Ray-Ban shades in the bright California sun.

He didn't look very friendly, she decided, letting him in with a tight smile. It was hard for her to smile ever since the avatars had attacked her. She didn't feel at ease with strangers, especially men.

"Have a seat, Mr. Brody," she said, gesturing toward her living room.

"Just Brody, Mrs. Kingston," he said, removing his sunglasses and hooking one of the bows on his polo's neckline.

"Just Ivy."

Nodding, he sat down on a leather recliner.

"Do you want some iced tea?" she said.

"Sure."

"Sugar and lemon?"

"Fine."

Ivy retreated to the kitchen, poured iced tea from a pitcher into two glasses, returned to the living room with the two glasses, and handed one to Brody.

"Do you know anything about the metaverse?" she said, sitting on the sofa opposite him.

"Not a lot," said Brody, rattling the ice in his chilled glass and staring at the cubes.

"I was assaulted by two avatars in the metaverse."

He looked up from his glass and gave her a puzzled look. "Is that possible?"

"It is, I'm afraid. It was a very traumatic experience," she said, wincing at the memory etched in her mind with blinding clarity.

"Did you tell the cops?"

"No."

"Why not?"

"My husband told me not to."

"I don't get it. Why would he tell you that?"

"The attack happened in Rabbit World, which is owned by Orion."

"Your husband?"

"Right."

"I don't understand."

"He doesn't want me to report the attack because of the bad PR it would bring on Rabbit World. He's afraid publicizing the attack would scare away potential real-estate buyers."

"I see."

"What could the cops do, anyway? It happened in the metaverse. It didn't happen in the real world of LA."

"But you were in LA when it happened. Right?"

"I was wearing the headset here in my home, so the answer is yes."

"Have you gone to the hospital?"

She shifted restlessly in her cobalt blue velour pantsuit on the sofa. "I don't think you understand. I was attacked in the virtual world, not here in my living room."

"You weren't attacked here," said Brody, puzzled.

"I was, and I wasn't."

Which elicited additional confusion from Brody.

Chapter 8

"Let me explain," said Ivy. "My body was standing here, but I was wearing that headset"—she pointed with distaste at the headset lying on the opposite end of the sofa where she sat—"when I entered Rabbit World, where I was attacked by two avatars."

"*You* in the flesh were attacked by two avatars?"

"Let me be clear. My avatar was assaulted by two male avatars."

"Ah," said Brody, understanding. "Then you didn't suffer any physical harm."

"Right."

"Which is why the cops wouldn't do anything if you reported this."

"You have to understand, I wasn't physically hurt, but I was traumatized during the attack," she said, her voice breaking.

Brody nodded yes with concern. "What exactly do you want me to do?"

"I want you to find the two avatars and teach them a lesson."

"Before I can do anything, I have to know who they are."

"I can't help you."

"You didn't recognize them?"

"No."

"Could they have been complete strangers?"

"They could have been anyone."

He swallowed a mouthful of his iced tea.

"I can't very well find them if I don't know who they are," he said. "Is there some way to identify the owners of avatars in the metaverse?"

"Beats me. I'm not tech savvy. I'm a professional realtor. My husband Orion says the owners of the avatars in Rabbit World are anonymous and can't be ID'd."

"I'm no expert on the metaverse."

"Nobody is, at this point. It's a new frontier where you're free to do what you want."

"Hmm. Like the Wild West."

"What about *my* freedom?"

"What?"

"I was attacked in Rabbit World. How can *I* be free if I get attacked when I set foot there?"

"Maybe you should carry a piece for self-protection."

She looked puzzled. "I don't know if they allow guns in Rabbit World."

"Why not? You said everybody is free to do what they want."

"It would have to be a virtual gun. Not a real gun. I doubt you could kill another avatar with a virtual gun."

Brody nodded. "Even if a virtual gun could kill an avatar, the owner of the deceased avatar wouldn't die as a result."

"I'm not so sure. The owner could die of a heart attack, if you ask me. My attackers traumatized me and almost put me in the hospital."

Brody raised his eyebrows. "True," he conceded.

"I'm afraid they'll attack me again, if I don't retaliate. Since the cops won't help, I have to turn to someone like you. I'm terrified to go back to Rabbit World," she said, glancing anxiously at the headset.

"Have you thought about suing these guys?"

"I can't sue anyone till I know their names. Your job is to find out their IDs. And you'll need to do it fast."

"Why? Just stay away from Rabbit World till I find out their names."

Ivy held her head down. "It's not that easy."

"Why do you have to return to Rabbit World so fast?"

"I haven't told you everything."

"Go on," said Brody, his visage intent.

Ivy collected herself and looked up at him. "The two avatars stalked me in a black Dodge Charger while I was driving my Tesla."

Brody cocked an eyebrow. "I don't understand. How can avatars drive cars?"

"I swear, I saw them following my Tesla."

"You mean, in Rabbit World."

"No. I mean, in the real world."

"Are you sure you saw this?"

"I saw them following me *twice*."

"Are you sure they weren't the owners of the avatars?"

"They didn't look like normal people. They were avatars. Their faces were humanlike, but not human—if you know what I mean."

"How can that be possible?"

Ivy shook her head in confusion. "All I know is, I saw them stalking me."

"What do avatars look like?"

"These two look sort of like dolls or modeling statues. Their big pale faces are blank like statues, except for a creepy half smile on their lips. And they have big eyes," she said, making circles around her eyes with her hands, like she was looking through binoculars.

Orion entered the living room and picked up on Brody. "Who's this?"

"He's Brody, a PI," said Ivy.

"Why do you need a PI?"

"Because you told me not to go to the cops."

Orion glowered at Brody. "Get him out of here."

Chapter 9

"No problem," said Brody, getting to his feet. "I was getting ready to go."

"Stay where you are," said Ivy.

"I want him out of here," said Orion. "I told you to drop this and forget about it."

"I'm not letting those two thugs get away with attacking me."

"Get out of here," Orion yelled at Brody.

Brody didn't move.

"I'm not done with him yet," said Ivy.

Brody stood still.

"You're not wanted here," Orion told Brody. "Get going."

Brody stood his ground.

Orion stalked over to him and shoved him. "Get out of here. You're trespassing. Go."

Brody staggered backward a few steps, stopped, approached Orion, and shoved him back.

"I'm working for her, not you," said Brody.

Orion stumbled backward, windmilling his arms, and fell on his butt.

"Shit," he said, and jumped to his feet.

"Stop it, both of you," said Ivy, bolting to her feet.

"He assaulted me," said Orion, aggrieved. "You saw him."

"You started it."

"It's my house. I have every right to defend my house from intruders."

"He's not an intruder. I invited him here."

"Well, I'm inviting him out."

"Do you have something to hide?" Brody asked Orion.

"What?" said Orion.

"Why don't you want your wife to find out who owns the two avatars that attacked her?"

"If news of this attack got out, it could destroy my company—if it's any of your business, and it isn't. You need to leave before I sic the cops on you. This is my house."

"He stays," said Ivy. "It's my money that bought this house."

"Why are you bothering with this clown? There's nothing he can do to help you."

"Well, *you're* not gonna do anything. That's for sure."

Orion glared at her. "I'm not gonna stand by and watch you destroy my business. You were attacked. It was a fluke. It's not gonna happen again. So get over it and give this thug the bum's rush," he said, pointing at Brody.

"If I didn't know better, I'd think you're glad I was attacked," said Ivy.

"That's a cheap shot. And you know it. I'm starting to think you imagined the whole thing to get attention. I have nothing more to say."

Orion stalked out of the room.

"Did you get the license tag of the black Charger that tailed you?" Brody asked Ivy, who was staring with indignation at Orion as he departed.

She cut her eyes toward Brody. "I can't recall it. I was terrified. All I could think of was escaping."

"If it happens again, be sure to get the tag. If we can't get the IDs of the avatars from Rabbit World, we can track the owner of the Charger. Something tells me the owner of Rabbit World isn't gonna cooperate with us," said Brody, glancing in the direction of Orion's exit. "It's like he's going out of his way to block you."

"I'm not gonna let him get away with it. I'm getting the names of those two thugs with or without his help."

She sipped her iced tea, felt the ice cubes click against her front teeth. She hadn't realized how thirsty she was.

Brody set his drained iced tea glass down on the coffee table. Two melting ice cubes clinked together in the glass.

"If you see the Charger tailing you again, give me a call," he said.

"You're taking my case?"

"As long as you're OK with my rates."

"I am."

They walked to the front door.

"I'll try to find the identities of the two thugs," said Brody. "Other than that, I'm not sure what I can do. They didn't break the law."

"Somebody better make a law."

"Until that time, I can't arrest them. Nobody can."

"I'm not giving up. They picked the wrong person to mess with."

Ivy sounded determined, but inside she was scared to death. She feared being attacked again. Refusing to put on the headset and staying away from Rabbit World wouldn't keep her safe, because, as impossible as it seemed, the avatar pervs had escaped into the real world.

She watched Brody leave through the front door.

The notion that she was going nuts kept nagging at her. Avatars driving a car in the real world? It made no sense. Could her traumatized mind have imagined them riding in the black Charger?

Maybe Liz was right, decided Ivy. Maybe she should see her psychiatrist.

Ivy wasn't going to give up, though. She was going to do everything she could to find the IDs of her attackers. Whether or not the avatars had been in the Charger, the fact remained they had assaulted her.

Her cell phone chimed in her purse. She took the call.

"Hello," said the amused male voice. "Are you afraid?"

"What?" said Ivy.

"You should be. Nobody can help you."

"Who is this?" demanded Ivy, annoyed and confused.

"Are you afraid to tell the cops?"
"About what?"
The man laughed and hung up.

Chapter 10

Ivy wanted out. She had no control of her life as it was spinning out of control. She couldn't resume her job. She felt like she was scamming people, hawking real estate in a hellhole where violence and anarchy were the order of the day.

And now she was seeing avatars chasing her in a car.

Maybe her job was driving her nuts. Maybe the only way out of her dilemma was quitting her job and trying another one.

But she felt like she owed Orion to continue her realtor work at Rabbit World. She would be letting him down if she quit. It was his start-up, and he wanted to make it work. She wanted to help him succeed so he could have his IPO next week. Which didn't change the fact that she felt uncomfortable selling real estate in nowhere land. Worse than uncomfortable. She felt violated after being assaulted there.

She couldn't stand the idea of putting the headset back on and entering the nightmare called Rabbit World. What godawful thing would happen to her the next time she entered? Would she be tortured and dismembered by sadists? Hanged by the neck and whipped? Dragged through the streets chained to a tailgate?

Or was her imagination running amok, conjuring monsters where there were none? She had to admit she had an overactive imagination.

She stood in front of the picture window and watched Brody's Mini pull out of the driveway and leave. Was she sending him on a wild-goose chase hunting two avatars that existed only in her imagination?

She retreated to her sofa and plunked down on it.

Orion entered the living room and looked around.

"I'm glad that clown's gone," he said. "What do you expect to accomplish hiring a PI to track a couple of avatars? What a colossal waste of time."

Ivy flared up. "It's my time to waste."

"You want Rabbit World to fail, don't you? That's the only reason I can think you're doing this."

"No, I don't want it to fail. I want to help you succeed, but what happened happened."

"In your mind."

"It happened in virtual reality. If that's considered my mind, so be it. But what happened there was as real to me as if it had happened in reality."

"If you really want me to succeed, you won't tell anyone about the attack," said Orion, offended.

"I'm not going to the cops, if that's what you mean."

"I mean, them and the media."

"I don't know anyone in the media."

"And you shouldn't have told that PI whatshisname."

"He's discreet. He's not gonna rock the boat."

"All the same—"

"I'm not letting them get away with what they did to me," said Ivy, seething. "He's the only one I could think of that could help me. You're not gonna help me. I don't know who else to turn to. There aren't any laws regarding virtual attacks. I'm finding it out the hard way."

"Settle down. Let it go. I'll see what I can do."

"What can you do?"

"Just tell yourself it didn't really happen. Because that's a fact. *It didn't really happen.* It only happened in your mind."

"It happened in two other guys' minds, too."

Orion shrugged. "That doesn't change the fact it didn't happen in reality."

As he left the living room, Ivy's cell phone chimed in her purse. She took the call.

The caller hung up.

Chapter 11

In his apartment in West LA, Brody phoned Ivy.

"Where did you see the two avatars tailing your car?" he asked.

"Let me see," answered Ivy. "On Wilshire near Westwood Village, I think."

"Near Westwood Boulevard?"

"I guess."

"You're not sure?"

"I was upset at the time. They were trying to kill me, for Chrissake. Do you look at road signs when people are trying to kill you?"

Brody pricked up his ears. "How do you know they were trying to kill you? Did you see guns in their hands?"

"Uh—I can't recall. They weren't chasing me to tell me I won the lottery, that's for sure."

"But you can't be sure they were trying to kill you, can you?"

"Yes, I can. In fact, I am *certain* they were trying to kill me."

"Just a feeling you had, huh?"

"If someone assaulted you and then chased you in their car, would you think they wanted to apologize?"

"Point taken. But I'm trying to determine whether the guys in the Charger were packing."

"What difference does it make? Maybe their plan was to run me over when I got out of my car."

"Do you have proof of that?"

"What kind of proof?" said Ivy, nettled.

"I'm showing you how a lawyer would tear your story apart on the stand if you brought charges against your two assailants in the Charger with the evidence you've shown me so far."

"I didn't contact a lawyer. I contacted you. What gave you the idea I'm gonna press charges against these thugs?"

Brody paused. "That's what most of my customers do. They hire me to get evidence against the offending party."

"I don't give a damn about evidence. I want their names. I thought I made it clear to you there's no law covering what they did to me in Rabbit World. Therefore, why would I go to a lawyer or court?"

"OK. What time were you driving down Wilshire near Westwood when the black Charger hung a tail on you?"

"Uh—I can't remember exactly. Around one p.m., I think."

"I'll check it out."

"I'm sure they've left by now."

"What's the license tag number on your Tesla?"

She told him.

"I want to see if there are any private CCTV security cameras in the area," he said. "Bye."

"I don't see what good—"

Brody terminated the call, left his apartment, retrieved his Mini, and took Wilshire Boulevard to Westwood Village.

Chapter 12

As usual, the traffic was heavy in the area bordering UCLA.

Halted at a long traffic light on Westwood Boulevard, he inspected the buildings in the vicinity, trying to pick up on any security cameras trained on the road from neighboring high-rises.

Spotting a CCTV camera jutting from the second floor of a high-rise, he hung a right and drove into the building's underground parking garage.

He parked his Mini next to a black BMW, climbed out of his car, and took the elevator to the main floor, where he headed toward the security guard's desk.

"Hello," said Brody. "Could I take a look at your CCTV tapes of Wilshire Boulevard?"

"And who are you?" said the uniformed guard, a middle-aged guy with a potbelly and a lobster face who was sitting behind a desk. "Those tapes are private property," he added, cocking his chin toward Brody.

"I'm an insurance adjuster. There was an accident here earlier today, and I want to verify what our claimant told us is true. Your security camera tapes would help me do that."

It wasn't that Brody didn't believe Ivy had seen avatars chasing her in a black Dodge Charger, but he had doubts. He wanted to assuage his doubts. Maybe she was so upset after the assault in Rabbit World that she started seeing things. The CCTV tape could bear out her story.

The guard nodded. "I was in a hellacious four-car accident last week. I had to get all the proof I could lay my hands on to prove I wasn't at fault. I'm lucky I didn't get whiplash," he said, rubbing his neck. "I guess I could let you look at the tapes. It's just a bunch of cars tooling down the street."

He got up from his seat and led Brody to the security office, where he let Brody in.

A multitude of screens for CCTV cameras covered the wall in front of the console. The guard sat down in front of the console and found the screen that overlooked Wilshire Boulevard.

"What time was the accident?" he said.

"Around one o'clock in the afternoon."

The guard rewound the tape till he found one o'clock.

"Start at 12:50 p.m.," said Brody, looking over the guard's shoulder at the CCTV screen mounted on the wall. "She's not sure of the exact time."

"Sure," said the guard. "What kind of car was she driving?"

"Silver Tesla," said Brody, and told him the license tag.

They watched the monotonous traffic jamming Wilshire.

While the guard watched for the Tesla, Brody kept his eyes peeled for the black Charger that could be tailing it. Fifteen minutes later he yawned as he continued watching the CCTV screen.

"I don't see any accident," said the guard. "Are you sure this is where it happened?"

"That's what our claimant says."

Brody had spotted a couple of black Chargers, but they weren't behind silver Teslas. He decided he should keep watching the tape till at least 1:30 p.m.

"It's hard to make out a lot of the license tags on cars because of the cars surrounding them," said the guard.

Brody nodded, his eyes glued to the screen. He wasn't even looking at tags, he was watching for a black Charger behind a silver Tesla.

"Freeze it," he said, becoming alert.

"What? I don't see an accident."

"I think I see her car."

The guard froze the image, at a loss.

"Can you zoom in on that black Charger behind the silver Tesla?"

The guard complied.

Brody couldn't make out the Charger's tags. They were obscured by other vehicles surrounding the Charger.

"It's got a California tag," said Brody.

"The first number looks like an 8, though it's hard to see all of it," said the guard, scrutinizing the grainy image on the screen. "I guess it could be a *B*. The rest of the tag is blocked by another car."

"Not a whole lot of help," said Brody.

"Do you know the license tags of the vehicles involved in the accident?" said the guard, craning his head around to eye Brody.

"No. I wanted to see your video to see if it had recorded the license tag on the Dodge Charger that rear-ended my client's car."

The guard scratched the scruff of his neck. "I don't see an accident."

"It must've happened farther down the road. Could you zoom in on the windshield to see the face of the driver in the Charger?"

The guard zoomed in.

The driver's face remained in the shadows. Brody couldn't tell if anybody was riding shotgun thanks to the glare of sunlight obscuring half the windshield.

"Run it forward in slow motion," said Brody. "Maybe the rest of the license tag will be revealed."

The guard did so. "I'm not seeing the rest of the plate."

"And I can't make out the driver's face."

"What was it? A hit and run?"

"Uh, yeah."

"Bummer. Maybe the driver was uninsured and didn't want the cops to fine him."

"Could be."

"One of those uninsured drivers hit me last month. Pain in the ass. My insurance wouldn't pay me a thing. And

42

I couldn't sue him because he said he was out of work. So broke he didn't even have a bank account. You can't squeeze blood from a rock."

"I hear ya."

Brody wasn't listening. The video didn't prove the existence of an avatar driving the Charger, though it did bear out Ivy's story that a black Charger had been behind her. All he had was her word that the driver was an avatar. Which, frankly, was hard to believe, decided Brody.

He was of the opinion that Ivy could have imagined an avatar behind the Charger's wheel with her overheated emotional state triggered by her victimization in Rabbit World.

The video didn't prove anything, he decided, other than the existence of the black Charger that had been driving behind Ivy. Which didn't necessarily mean its driver had been tailing her. Maybe the guy was just headed in the same direction as her.

"How many California tags start with an 8 or a *B*?" said Brody.

"A couple million or more, I'd say," said the guard, shrugging.

"Like I thought. Not much help. Could you send the tape of that car to my e-mail address?"

"I'll send you a copy."

Brody gave out his e-mail address and left the office, pondering his next move.

Chapter 13

Wearing jeans and a stressed denim jacket Ivy was walking down the Third Street Promenade when she saw a pair of sneakers she liked in the shoe store she was passing. She stopped and peered in the display window at the sneakers.

Out of the corner of her eye, she noticed two men following her with weird pasty doll-like avatar faces. Their saucer eyes intent on her, they were walking with other pedestrians on the promenade.

She gasped in fear.

She wheeled around and hurried away from them. She glanced behind her.

They were stepping up their pace in pursuit.

Her rapid heartbeat battering her rib cage, she darted into the mall in an attempt to lose them. She had to get help. But who would help her? The avatars hadn't done anything to her on the promenade.

She ducked into a clothing store, tore her cell out of her purse, and called Orion.

"Hello," said Orion. "I'm at my office."

"They're chasing me," she said, keeping her eyes peeled for the two avatars.

"Calm down. Who is?"

"The two avatars."

"Ivy," he said in a reproachful voice.

"I tell you, I saw them on the promenade stalking me."

Orion hung up.

"Hello?" she said into a dead phone.

She couldn't believe he had hung up on her. Who else could she call? she wondered, peeking out the picture window in search of the avatars. She didn't want them to corner her in here. She wouldn't have an escape route. She saw only one exit.

She called Liz.

Liz picked up.

"Liz, you have to help me."

"Ivy, what happened?"

"The two avatars are stalking me on the promenade. Can you come here now?"

"Shouldn't you call the cops?"

"The pervs haven't done anything to me yet. They're just following me so far."

"Where are you?"

"I'm in the mall on the promenade."

"All right. I'm heading your way. Try to find a cop or security guard and hang around him so the creeps won't try anything."

"Hurry," said Ivy, and put away her cell.

Grinding her teeth she approached the display window and glanced past the mannikins standing in it. She swiveled her head to and fro, casting around for the avatars in the three-story mall. Could she have lost them? she wondered.

She froze when she spotted them emerging from the elevator. She thought they saw her.

She had to do something. She looked around for a security guard. There was never a cop around when you wanted one, she decided.

She saw a guard at the other end of the mall. She exited the clothing store and made a beeline toward him. She could feel the avatars following her. Terrified they would catch up to her, she dashed toward the guard.

She buttonholed the black thirtyish uniformed guard who had a friendly face. He was strolling through the mall.

"Those two men are chasing me," she said.

He gazed behind her. "Which two men?"

"The two with the weird doll faces," she said, staring at him with beseeching eyes.

He frowned. "I don't see who you're talking about."

She slewed around.

They weren't there. They must have seen her making for the guard and hightailed it.

"I don't see them anymore," she said, puzzled but relieved nonetheless.

"Doll faces, you said?"

"I know it sounds weird, but their faces look like avatars."

The guard nodded in understanding. "Masks. They wear all sorts of masks these days."

He could be right, she decided.

"If you see them again, let me know," he said.

She didn't stray far away from him as she window-shopped at the various clothing boutiques. Waiting for Liz she kept checking the reflections in the display windows to make sure the two avatars weren't closing in on her from behind.

She wished Liz would hurry up and get here.

Chapter 14

Dressed in jeans and a black T, Orion was sitting behind his desk putting down his cell phone in his Century City high-rise office. A VR headset lay on his desk blotter in front of him. An aquarium stood against one of the walls. In his late twenties wearing jeans and an oyster white seersucker blazer, Jeff Riley was sitting opposite him. Riley had a no-nonsense face and was tapping an impatient tattoo on the desktop with his right fingers.

"Who was that?" said Riley, nodding at Orion's mobile.

"My wife," said Orion.

"She sounded upset."

"She's OK," said Orion, not wanting to talk about it.

"I don't like being interrupted by phone calls."

"Like I said, she's my wife. I accept all of her calls."

"Let me remind you, we're talking business," said Riley, ticked off.

"I'm listening," said Orion, getting testy.

"What's your answer to my proposal?"

"I already told you my answer. It's the same as yesterday. No deal."

"I don't understand your decision. Do you think my consortium can't afford to buy real estate in Rabbit World?"

"I'm sure they can afford it. That's not the problem."

"Then what?"

"I don't plan on having casinos in Rabbit World."

"Why not? Our casinos make tons of money. We want to invest in your startup by developing real estate there. You should be pleased."

"No gambling at Rabbit World."

"What do you have against gambling?"

"I know people who have lost their shirts gambling."

47

"That's their problem for not gambling responsibly."

"I told you no yesterday. I haven't changed my mind. No casinos in Rabbit World."

Riley struggled to bottle up his anger. "This is your last chance. I'm not gonna make another offer to buy real estate in Rabbit World."

"Fine. Our meeting is over."

"I'm not leaving till I have a deal."

"You're wasting your breath."

Riley shot to his feet. "How can you turn down an offer as good as this one?"

Orion crossed his arms over his chest. "Easy. My mind is made up."

"You're gonna regret turning down our offer."

"Is that a threat?"

"The boss doesn't take kindly to being rejected."

"I don't take kindly to being threatened."

Riley stroked his chin in thought. "Are you doing something illegal in Rabbit World?"

"Whatever gave you that idea?"

"I'm trying to understand why you're so picky about who you sell real estate to."

"We don't want to attract the wrong kind of crowd to Rabbit World."

"What's wrong with attracting gamblers? Capitalism is all about taking risks and making money. That's what gamblers do. What's the problem?" said Riley, yanking on his Rolex's watchband.

"I don't want gangsters in Rabbit World."

"Gangsters?" said Riley, incredulous.

"Where there's gambling there are gangsters."

Riley shrugged. "Maybe in the old days like when the mob created Vegas. I guess that's what you're referring to. Bugsy Siegel and those wiseguys. Nowadays it's not like that. Things have come a long way since then. Everything's legit."

"Where there are gangsters, there is crime."

"Gambling's not a crime. Nobody's forcing people to gamble. They're free to do what they want. What they want to do is gamble. We give them what they want."

"Fine. Let 'em gamble somewhere else." Orion glanced at his wristwatch. "I have a meeting I have to attend in five minutes."

"Fuck us, *fuck you.*"

"I will not tolerate threats in my office," said Orion, fuming.

"We didn't get to be the number one casino by backing down. Messing with us is not a good idea."

"Are you trying to take this to the next level?"

"You don't want to find out. Make the right decision, and you won't have to worry about it."

"I'll make whatever decision I want. Now get the hell out of here."

"Tossing me out of here isn't gonna solve your problem. Think what you're doing."

"I know exactly what I'm doing. I'm not letting you bully me."

"There's no bullying here. We're making a business deal. Everybody wins. Everybody makes money. Everybody's happy."

"You're not getting into Rabbit World, no matter how much money you have."

Riley stalked to the door. "The boss doesn't like being treated like dirt."

"If he can't take rejection, he's in the wrong line of work."

"When you refuse one of his offers, you have no idea what he's capable of."

"He tries anything on me, I call the cops. Beat it."

Chapter 15

After Liz showed up at the mall, Ivy took her to a pizza parlor on the promenade, checking behind her fitfully to make sure her two assailants weren't stalking her.

"I'm glad you're here," said Ivy.

Liz was wearing jeans, hiking boots, and a backpack.

"I came here as soon as I could," she said.

"Why do you always wear that backpack?"

"It's my go-bag. The apocalypse could happen any time, and I'm gonna be ready for it."

"You and the apocalypse."

"Don't scoff. These avatars you're seeing stalking you could be the beginning of the end. Humans invent their own doom. That's how the apocalypse begins. VR is man-made. Creatures escape from it and kill all of us. This is scary."

They sat at a table on the patio and ordered a cheese pizza with iced teas.

Liz unstrapped her backpack and hung it over the back of her chair before she took a seat.

"That guard I was with when you met me helped me," said Ivy. "He scared them away."

"Did he see them?" said Liz, adjusting her wire-rim spectacles.

"Yes."

"That proves they exist."

"Of course, they exist. Did you think I was making them up?" said Ivy, drawing back from the table.

"No, no. I mean, others might think you're imagining these avatars stalking you. Let's face it, it sounds unbelievable."

"He said they were wearing weird masks. That's why their faces looked strange."

"Then you don't have proof that your two stalkers are avatars."

"What constitutes proof?"

Liz snatched a breadstick from a glass and munched it. The tattooed twentyish waiter served their pizza.

"Maybe if you took a picture of them," answered Liz, as the waiter retreated.

"That wouldn't prove they're avatars."

Sensing the avatars were watching her, Ivy whipped her head around, seeking them out. She didn't see them.

"What's wrong?" said Liz.

"I thought they were watching me."

"I'll watch your back. If I see them, I'll yell. You need to calm down."

"You have no idea what it's like," said Ivy, and took deep breaths.

"Living in fear isn't gonna help."

"Me? You're the one that thinks the world's gonna end any minute."

"But I don't live in fear. I'm prepared. I know what I'm gonna do when it happens, so I'm not afraid. I've got my bug-out bag. I'm ready to take off when the end comes."

"What are you saying?"

"I'm saying, be prepared like me. Know what you're gonna do if you're attacked again. Then you won't be scared of your own shadow."

Ivy thought about it. "OK. Makes sense. But I still don't like the idea of being stalked by two escapees from another world."

"Maybe the guard was right. Maybe they're just two guys wearing masks. A lot of people continue to wear masks because they're afraid of Covid."

"Are you saying you don't believe me?" said Ivy, annoyed.

"I'm saying maybe you're mistaken about avatars stalking you. You gotta admit it sounds far-fetched."

"What are the chances two guys stalking me are wearing masks that look like the faces of the avatars that attacked me in Rabbit World?"

"I see what you mean. Something's hinky," said Liz, and took a bite of her pizza wedge, which was dripping mozzarella. "Then again, your stressed-out emotions might be influencing your perception of the two people stalking you."

"Huh?"

"Maybe your two stalkers don't really have the faces of the avatars that assaulted you."

"They do. I'm sure they do. I thought you were my friend. Don't you believe me?"

"I believe two guys could be stalking you."

"Thanks a million," said Ivy, bitter irony in her voice. "At least, say you believe I was assaulted in Rabbit World."

"I do believe that. Which is why you could be seeing avatars wherever you look."

"Not everywhere." Her eyes wide with apprehension, Ivy scoped out her surroundings. "I don't see them now."

"Maybe in another week this will all be a bad memory."

"Not if those two pervs keep stalking me."

"It's time to report them to the cops. But don't say the stalkers are avatars. They'll think you're making it up."

"I don't know," muttered Ivy, twisting her mouth. "Orion doesn't want me to go to the cops."

"That's not right. If your life's in danger, you need to tell them."

"If I go to the cops, I'll have to tell them about being attacked in Rabbit World. Orion doesn't want the bad PR that would result."

"Leave Rabbit World out."

Ivy couldn't make up her mind. "The problem is, so far the stalkers haven't done anything illegal."

"Stalking someone is illegal."

"Is following someone considered stalking, in the eyes of the law?"

Liz pulled her smartphone out of her backpack and logged onto the Internet.

"According to the Department of Justice, and I quote," she said, "'the term *stalking* means engaging in a course of conduct directed at a specific person that would cause a reasonable person to fear for his or her safety or the safety of others or suffer substantial emotional distress.'"

"Then they're stalking me."

"If you aren't suffering substantial emotional distress, I don't know who is," said Liz, looking up from her smartphone at Ivy.

"That's for sure."

"Have they said anything threatening to you?"

"They haven't said anything."

"It would help your case, if they issued threats against you."

"They fucking assaulted me in Rabbit World. What more do you want?"

"You said Orion didn't want you to tell the cops about it."

"Exactly. That's why I better not go to the cops," said Ivy, becoming agitated. "What are they gonna do anyway? Give me a police escort? Only big shot politicians get that. You know that's not gonna happen."

"There must be something you can do."

"I'm open to suggestions. I just hope they con't try to kill me next time."

"You think they would do that?" said Liz, aghast.

"Especially if they think they can get away with it."

"But what would be the point?" said Liz, and sipped her peach-flavored iced tea.

"I wish I knew. Why did they attack me in Rabbit World? None of it makes sense."

Liz glanced at her wristwatch.

"I gotta run," she said, standing up. "I have an appointment at my martial arts class."

"All right."

"Are you gonna be OK?"

"Sure," said Ivy, and surveyed the promenade for any sign of the avatars stalking her. "I don't see them anywhere. Are you parked in the parking garage?"

"Yeah."

Ivy stood up. "So am I. I'll walk back with you."

She left enough cash on the tabletop to cover their meals. She looked furtively around her.

"You're making me jumpy," said Liz, as they set out for the parking garage.

"Now you know how I feel."

Chapter 16

From her Tesla's driver's seat Ivy watched Liz drive out of the multilevel parking garage. Now that she was alone, Ivy feared the avatars would show up again to harass her. A deserted parking garage was the perfect place for an assault. She shivered, thinking about it. She had to beat it.

She fired her Tesla's engine and drove out of the parking garage, keeping her eyes peeled for the two stalkers.

She pulled onto the boulevard and braked to a halt at the intersection. She didn't see the avatars. She hoped she had lost them. She would be glad if she never saw their goofy, sinister faces again.

The light changed, and she was on her way.

Until a car ran the light and plowed into her in the intersection.

The force of the impact whiplashed her neck. Luckily, she had remembered to buckle her seat belt.

Her initial shock was followed by rage at the idiot who had run the light.

Massaging her neck she clambered out of her car to exchange information with the driver of the sedan that had slammed into her passenger's-side door. Fitful honking punctuated the air. She inspected the crumpled sedan. A black Tesla, she noted. She peered into it at the driver's seat.

There was no driver.

Had the driver scrammed before she had gotten out of her car? she wondered. She didn't see how he could have moved that quickly. She inspected the rest of the vehicle's interior for any passengers. She saw none. The car was empty. She hadn't seen anyone exit the car.

At least nobody was injured, she decided. But where had the driver gotten to? She surveyed the area.

Rubberneckers were beginning to gather on the sidewalks and stare at her.

"Did you see where the driver went?" she asked them. Nobody answered.

She withdrew her cell phone from her purse and punched 911 to call the cops.

Drivers were having trouble navigating the intersection, honking their displeasure.

A squad car arrived at last and blocked traffic. Wearing wraparound shades, a uniformed thirtyish cop climbed out of his vehicle and approached her. He sported a mustache that looked like it was made of plastic above his harelip. She read his last name Barnes on his breast pocket.

"Are you the one who called 911, ma'am?" he asked with a slight Texas accent.

"Yes."

"Are you hurt? Do you need a paramedic?"

Wincing, she massaged her neck. "My neck's a little sore. I think I'm OK. That car came out of nowhere."

"What happened, ma'am?"

"I was going through the green light and this guy ran a red light and crashed into me," she said, gesturing to the abandoned sedan embedded in her car's right side.

"And where is he?" said Barnes, studying the sedan.

"I don't know."

"Was the driver a man or a woman?"

"I don't know."

"You didn't get a good look at them?"

"I didn't see them, period."

"Are you saying it was a hit and run?"

"I never saw the driver."

"I don't see him in his vehicle. Where could he have gone?"

"I can't tell you where he went because I never saw him," said Ivy, scratching her head in puzzlement.

Barnes poked his head into the Tesla and inspected the dashboard. He pulled his head out.

"Could it have been a driverless car that hit you, ma'am?" he said.

"I guess. But a driverless car with no passengers? It doesn't make sense."

"I know. This particular car can drive by itself, though. Therefore, it could be possible there was no driver."

"Somebody must have programmed it."

"True."

"But why would anyone program a car to drive around empty?"

Barnes circled the car, opened the passenger's-side door, and opened the glove compartment, searching for the car registration. The glove compartment was empty.

He pulled his head out of the car and inspected the crowd of rubberneckers.

"Did any of you see who was driving this vehicle?"

Nobody answered.

"Did anyone see what happened?" asked Barnes.

"The silver car had the light," said a middle-aged guy with a blond combover, wearing jeans and a paisley button-down shirt. "The black car ran the light and crashed into her."

"Did you see the driver of the black car, sir?"

"No."

"Did you see anybody get out of the black car after the accident?"

"No. It was a driverless car. When I looked at it, I could see that the driver's seat was empty."

Barnes strutted over to the man and got a statement from him.

First she's attacked by avatars, and now a driverless car rams into her, decided Ivy. What the hell was going on?

Barnes returned to her side.

"A freak accident," he said, shrugging. "I'm impounding the black Tesla, since there's no ID in it."

An accident? Ivy wondered. What were the chances a driverless car with no passengers would plow into her? On the other hand, what other explanation was there?

"What if it was deliberate?" she said.

"How could it be deliberate?"

"Maybe somebody was operating the car remotely."

"Why would they do such a thing?"

"To get back at me for something. Or to scare me off."

"Are you saying someone used a driverless car to terrorize you?"

"Why not? It's possible, isn't it?"

"I suppose. But I would need more to go on than sheer speculation—which is all you have now, unless you can name names."

Oh, yeah, Officer, a couple of avatars are stalking me. Ivy thought how stupid that would sound. The cop would think she was nuts. *Are you on LSD, ma'am?*

"I'm trying to get my head around it," she said.

"I'm gonna run the car's license tag," he said, inspecting the rear plate. "Be right back."

Ivy couldn't wait to find out who the black Tesla belonged to, especially if she knew the owner.

Barnes returned from his squad car.

"It belongs to XBY Systems, a Delaware corporation," he said.

"Are you notifying them of the accident?"

"That's not my job."

"Whose job is it?"

"Yours, since you want their insurance to pay for damage to your car."

"I'll tell my insurance company to contact them."

"That's up to you."

"Aren't you gonna search the car for fingerprints? Maybe the owner left his prints behind," said Ivy, annoyed that Barnes was about to leave.

"We don't have the manpower to investigate every accident. We only investigate the ones where people get injured. Nobody got hurt here. End of story. We need to get this intersection cleared. Did you call a tow truck?"

"I'm doing it now."

Barnes returned to his squad car.

She had no other options. She called her insurance, filled them in, and told them to send a tow truck to separate the two damaged cars. They didn't sound happy when she gave them the details of the accident, including the fact the other car had no insurance—and no driver to boot.

Chapter 17

Ivy called an Uber after watching a tow truck remove her banged-up Tesla from the intersection. She took the Uber back to her house.

Unsettled by the accident, she called Brody in her living room.

"I just had an accident with a driverless car," she said.

"Sorry to hear it," said Brody.

"The problem is, I'm wondering if it was really an accident."

She heard static on her cell phone.

"What do you mean?" he said.

"Did you hear that?"

"Hear what?"

"Static on the phone."

"No. It must be on your end."

"This is a bad connection. Can we meet somewhere?"

"I know a café on the beach on PCH near the Santa Monica Pier." He gave her the address.

"All right. I'll grab an Uber and meet you there in twenty minutes."

Ivy wondered if she was being paranoid thinking someone was listening to her phone because she heard static on the line. Too many weird, inexplicable things were happening to her. Maybe they were kicking her imagination into overdrive.

She hired an Uber and met Brody at the beachside café he had suggested. She smelled the mouthwatering aroma of hot dogs and hamburgers cooking on the grill as she crossed the parking lot to the café. Next door to the café a shop rented bicycles that stood on the sand in irregular rows.

Wearing jeans and a grey polo, Brody was sitting at a white round metal table on the café patio. He stood up and motioned to her.

She approached the table and sat down.

"Want me to order something for you?" he said.

"Just a Diet Coke."

Brody retreated to the counter and ordered a Diet Coke and a regular Coke. He returned to Ivy with their drinks.

"What's this all about?" he said, sitting opposite her.

"A driverless car crashed into my Tesla near the promenade."

"Accidents happen."

"The car had no driver and no passengers in it."

"No passengers? You didn't say that before."

"I thought somebody might be listening on my line when I called you earlier."

Brody drank his Coke. "Why do you say that?"

"Too many strange things are happening to me."

"Driverless cars aren't that strange anymore."

"It had no passengers. So why was it driving around?"

"Hmm. Did you get the owner's name?"

"The cop at the accident said it was some Delaware corporation called XBY Systems."

"Is that what the registration said?"

"There was no registration. The car's glove compartment was empty. He traced the license tag to find the owner."

"A Delaware corporation. I hate to say this, but it's probably a shell company. Half the companies in Delaware are shells, since they don't have to publicize their owners."

"I'm even more suspicious. A driverless car owned by a shell company crashes into me right after I see two avatars stalking me. What are the chances?"

"You saw two avatars stalking you?" he said, cocking an eyebrow.

Ivy nodded yes. "At the mall."

"Did anyone else see them?"

"A security guard. He said they were two guys wearing masks."

Brody chewed it over. "How did your accident occur?"

"I was at an intersection. The light turned green, and I drove into the intersection. The driverless car ran the light and crashed into me."

"A car driving around with no papers. That's gotta be illegal. Have you ever heard of XBY Systems?"

"Nope."

"I can try to find out who owns them, but I'm not optimistic. I've seen too many of these shell companies in my line of work. You'd be surprised how many of them there are. A lot of them are used by criminals to launder money."

"I can't understand what this company has to do with me."

"Maybe nothing. Maybe it was just an accident. What do you expect with a driverless car?"

A gull screeched and wheeled overhead, searching for food on the beach. Chattering teenage girls wearing swimsuits pedaled bicycles on the asphalt bikeway past the café, followed by a teenage boy riding a skateboard. The odor of cocoanut suntan oil wafted into Ivy's face.

"Just bad luck for me, huh?" she said. "Being assaulted and having a car accident."

"I said *maybe*. I can see why you might think otherwise, though. That's a lot of bad luck for one day. It's possible someone was controlling the driverless car remotely."

"And deliberately crashed it into me?"

"He could've been operating it with an app on a cell phone."

"Then he must've been nearby in order to know when to have his car run the red light and hit me."

"If it *was* deliberate."

Ivy sipped her Diet Coke. "Have you managed to find the names of the two avatars that attacked me?"

"I got a partial license tag on their Charger from a private security camera overlooking Wilshire, but not enough to identify the car's owner."

Ivy yawned. "I'm getting worn out from so much excitement. I need some rest."

She whipped her head around when she heard someone call her name. A smiling girl was greeting another girl in the parking lot, as they crossed to the sidewalk, where a street vendor was selling slices of fresh pineapple and papaya in his fruit stand. One of the girls must have had the same name as her, decided Ivy.

Her visage intense, Ivy scanned the beach for the two avatars. She didn't see them. She was wound up tighter than a rattlesnake preparing to strike, she decided and told herself to relax.

"That's a good idea about the rest," said Brody, watching her. "Meanwhile, I'll look into this XBY Systems and see if I turn up anything interesting."

They parted company.

Chapter 18

Ivy heard someone walking in her bedroom. She opened her eyes and found herself lying on her bed surrounded by avatars that were standing looking at her with their creepy doll eyes.

At least she thought she was on her bed. She realized she was lying on her back on an operating table. The avatars reminded her of aliens from outer space she had seen in sci-fi movies. The avatars were wearing scrubs and surgical masks. They were going to operate on her, she decided with horror.

One of them was holding a hacksaw. A brunette with bulging green eyes was holding up a hypodermic needle, studying the needle tip as she squirted fluid from it.

At least they didn't want her to have an embolism when they injected her, Ivy decided absurdly, watching the needle tip.

The whole scene was absurd. What were they going to do? Dissect her while she was alive to find out what made her run? Even as it was amusing, the thought chilled her blood.

Avatars don't run the world. Humans do. If there's any dissecting to do, we're gonna do it, she thought.

She tried to scream, but the scream stuck in her throat.

She had to get out of there.

She tried to get off the operating table.

She couldn't budge. Her body was frozen. Had they injected her with drugs to immobilize her? Terrified, she wondered what she could do to escape.

The avatars crowded in on her, bowing their heads toward her, buzzing like bees, inspecting her like she was an unknown specimen.

She felt like she was suffocating, as they tightened their circle around her, cutting off her air.

What did they want with her? she wondered. Were they going to operate on her and transform her into one of them? The thought horrified her. She didn't want to be one of them. They were unfeeling creatures that weren't alive—more robot than human. She was human. She wanted to stay human. Could they operate on her and turn her into one of them?

She didn't want to find out.

She was having more and more trouble breathing. Didn't they realize they were killing her, sucking away her air? Or was that the point?

With all the energy she could muster, she jackknifed into a sitting position on the operating table.

She realized she was alone on her bed in her bedroom, gasping for air, her throat dry.

She scoped out the bedroom. No avatars anywhere. Just a nightmare.

Her face soaked with sweat, she got out of bed in her peignoir and padded in her bare feet downstairs to the kitchen, intending to get a glass of water.

The two avatars that had assaulted her in Rabbit World were standing near the aluminum sink smirking at her, ogling her with their freaky blue eyes.

One of them made a motion with his hand like he was masturbating.

"Get out of here before I call the cops," she screamed.

The other one started to take his pants off.

"No," she screamed.

The nightmare ended for real this time.

She sat up in bed staring in fright at her empty bedroom. She hadn't gone to the kitchen, after all.

She got out of bed and padded to the bathroom. Standing at the porcelain sink, she ran the cold water and splashed it on her face, trying to wake herself up.

She peered at her weary face in the mirror. She pulled down her lower eyelids with her forefinger and examined her eyes.

Was she turning into an avatar? she wondered.

The usual color in her face was missing. Had the avatars finished their operation on her transforming her into one of them?

Impossible. It was a dream. In the dream they hadn't even started the operation. How could they have finished it?

She threw more cold water on her face.

She flung open the medicine cabinet and inspected her pill bottles. What should she take? A sedative? No. She didn't want to fall asleep again. She had a lot of pills. Not every answer could be found in a pill bottle. Pills could cure only so much. What did she want?

She wanted the two avatars that had gang-raped her in Rabbit World to be punished.

Taking meds wouldn't punish them. She wasn't going to take any meds. She slammed the mirrored door shut.

Avatar. What was an avatar anyway? It was a strange-sounding word. It didn't even sound English.

She returned to her bedroom, withdrew a dictionary from a bookshelf in the whatnot, and looked up the definition of *avatar*. In Hinduism an avatar was the manifestation of a deity in corporeal form. But virtual reality had nothing to do with Hinduism, decided Ivy. In computer terminology an avatar was a symbol standing for and manipulated by the user of the computer.

Ivy didn't believe in Hinduism. She didn't believe the two avatars that had assaulted her were Hindu spirits incarnate. In truth, she didn't believe in much of anything. Except maybe money. You couldn't live without it. How was she going to sell real estate in Rabbit World if she was too afraid to set foot in it again?

Things couldn't go on like this. Otherwise, she couldn't make a living. It was true she had a large inheritance, but she wanted to go back to work. She didn't want to be known as a trust fund baby. She wanted to work.

Instead of running away from the two avatars next time, maybe she should confront them. Did she have the courage to do so? she wondered. Running away from them wasn't going to solve anything. On the other hand, it might save her life.

Chapter 19

Brody answered his cell phone in his apartment that doubled as his office.

"This is Orion Kingston," said the caller. "I want to hire you."

"Wait a minute. Aren't you Ivy's wife?"

"What of it? Can't you take on more than one case at a time?"

"Not if there's a conflict of interest," said Brody, wondering what Orion's angle was.

"I know you're working for Ivy. It doesn't bother me."

"It might bother *her*."

"This has nothing to do with her."

"Let me decide. Is this about her assault?"

"No."

"Then what?" said Brody, his curiosity piqued.

"A guy called Jeff Riley, who represents a consortium, is trying to buy property in my Rabbit World metaverse. I told him no. He got upset and threatened me. He might try something."

"Are you talking about something illegal?"

"That's right."

"Why did you refuse Riley's offer?"

"Why do you need to know that?" said Orion with a trace of annoyance.

"I'm trying to understand what the problem is."

"His company has a bad rep. It's rumored they're funded by dirty money. They operate casinos. I don't want casinos in Rabbit World."

"Why don't you report Riley to the cops? Threatening someone in California is illegal."

"Calling the cops is gonna draw publicity. I don't want bad publicity for my company."

"I know." Ivy had already told him about Orion's aversion to bad PR, decided Brody.

"What?"

"Nothing."

Brody didn't think it was any of Orion's business what Ivy had told him. He never told anyone what a client told him in confidence.

"Can you take my case?" said Orion.

"What exactly do you want me to do?"

"I'm convinced Riley is gonna trash my company in revenge."

Brody got an idea. "Is Riley's company called XBY Systems?"

There was a pause.

"Why are you asking me that out of the blue?" said Orion.

"Just a hunch."

"I never heard of XBY Systems. Do you know something you're not telling me?"

"I'm searching for details. That's all. I need as many details as possible when I take on a case. What's the name of Riley's company?"

"Casino Gem Planet LLC. What's this XBY Systems you're talking about?"

"I wish I knew. I can't find anything about them."

"Why did you bring them up?"

Brody cleared his throat. "A shot in the dark."

"Let's get one thing straight. You *are* a private investigator. Correct?"

"What's your point?"

"*Private*, meaning discreet."

"You've been reading the dictionary or something?"

"I want to make sure you understand that nothing of what you find out for me or any action you take for me will be revealed to anyone."

"I'm not gonna write a tell-all book with James Patterson, if that's what you're worried about."

"This is serious. Somebody could get killed."

"Wait a minute—"

"I'm just saying."

"What's this about killing?"

Orion heaved a sigh. "You have a dangerous job. Right? PIs have contact with rough characters who don't shy away from committing acts of violence."

"Understood. I never backed down from a fight. But I don't go looking for one either."

"We understand each other."

"If you want me to rough up this guy Riley, I'm not your man. There are other guys that handle that kind of thing, and I can put you in touch with one."

"That's not what I want."

"What exactly *do* you want?"

"You have to promise me you'll keep to yourself everything I have told you and will tell you. Don't tell any of it to my wife."

"I'm not doing anything that will harm her. She's my client."

"My case has nothing to do with her."

"There's one thing I don't get. Why do you want to use the same PI that your wife is using? There are plenty of other PIs in LA."

"You look like you can handle yourself. Were you in Special Forces?"

"Ex-SEAL."

"I knew it was something like that," said Orion cheerfully.

Brody heard Orion slap his knee.

"That doesn't mean I work people over," said Brody.

"Of course not," said Orion with a slight chuckle.

The chuckle concerned Brody. Maybe Orion wasn't understanding him.

"Let me explain," said Orion. "I need someone with a pair between his legs. Understand?"

"What I don't understand is what you want me to do. Stop beating around the bush."

Orion chuffed. "I thought you'd never ask. I suspect Riley or one of his thugs will try to sabotage my server and force Rabbit World to crash and go offline. I can't afford to let that happen. I'm having an IPO next week."

"Where's your server?"

"It's in an office in West LA."

"Hire a security guard and post him there. What do you need me for?"

"I want you to catch Riley in the act so I can threaten him with exposure to gain leverage over him and stop him from trying to sabotage Rabbit World."

"Can't you hire a rent-a-cop to do that?"

"No, no, no," said Orion, losing his patience. "I don't trust those guys to keep anything secret."

Brody thought about it. He didn't see any conflict of interest by working for Ivy and Orion on different cases. And he needed the money.

"You're OK with me working on another case at the same time?" he said.

"You mean, my wife's?"

"Yeah."

"I'm OK with that."

"If I find out your case has anything to do with her, I'll have to drop your case, since she hired me first."

"Agreed."

Brody had a sixth sense about this case. Something didn't feel right about it. He had had the feeling before on previous cases. The trouble was, more often than not, it turned out to be on the money.

"I can't stand guard over your server 24/7," he said. "I got other work to do."

"I have a security guard manning a CCTV camera watching the server's office. If he sees a stranger trying to break in, he will call you."

"I might not be able to get to the server in time to protect it."

"The guard has orders to delay them until you get there to help."

"The cops could get there faster."

"I told you, no cops."

"OK. It's your party," said Brody with misgivings.

Chapter 20

Brody opened his laptop on his desk in front of his apartment's window. The afternoon sun was highlighting the desktop and the motes of dust swirling above it.

He got on the Internet and searched for Casino Gem Planet LLC. It was another Delaware corporation that didn't list its owners. It owned two casinos in Las Vegas. Other than that, Brody couldn't find much about it.

His cell phone vibrated in his trouser pocket.

"Hello," said Ivy.

"What's up?" said Brody.

"I'm thinking about confronting my attackers."

"That could be dangerous. Are you sure that's a good idea?"

"I don't want to live my life in constant fear of them."

"If you're gonna confront them, I suggest you carry a gun."

"Do you think they would dare attack me in real life? After all, rape is a crime in the real world."

"I don't know what they're capable of. You should be prepared for anything, though."

"In the real world if they rape me, I could end up pregnant with their baby. Oh, Jesus. It would be a monster. Or I could end up bruised and bleeding." Her voice became halting. "And maybe even dead."

"I understand your concern."

"Can you imagine the horror of having a monster baby, half human and half avatar? It would be like something out of *Rosemary's Baby*. Childbirth would probably kill me. Please don't let that happen to me."

"I won't."

"Am I losing my mind, seeing avatars in the real world?"

"You're upset, is all," said Brody, lacking conviction.

Frankly, she sounded like she was losing it, he decided.

"Do you know where I can get a gun?" she said.

He wondered if she was in any condition to carry a gun. In her disturbed state, she might shoot herself.

"I can give you one," he said, not keen on the idea.

He scrolled down the page to Casino Gem Planet on his computer screen.

"Did you find out anything about the XBY Systems company that owns the car that crashed into me?" she said.

"There's nothing on the Internet about them."

"I think my husband mentioned them once."

"In what context?"

"I don't recall."

"What about Casino Gem Planet? Have you ever heard of them?" said Brody, staring at his laptop screen.

"Uh, I'm not sure. Sounds sort of familiar. I think he might have said something about them, too."

Brody tapped his fingers on his desktop. "I feel I should notify you that I'm working for your husband as well as for you. I'm telling you because he knows I'm working for you."

"What?" said Ivy in confused surprise. "To find the IDs of my two attackers?"

"No. His case has nothing to do with yours. Otherwise, I wouldn't have agreed to take it."

"Taking it isn't a good idea."

"If I find out his case has anything to do with you, I'll drop it. I'm not gonna tell him anything about what you're doing."

"I dunno. It sounds wrong."

"If your two cases overlap, I'll drop his, I promise. You were my first client. I owe you that much."

"What's his case about?"

"I can't tell you. Just like I didn't tell him anything about your case."

"Uh . . . I guess it's OK, if you keep quiet about our cases."

"He did tell me he doesn't know anything about XBY Systems."

"I can't understand why they're out to get me," she said, disconcerted.

Brody shrugged. "You can't rule out that it was what it looked like. An accident."

"A driverless car runs the light and crashes into me? I don't buy it's an accident, especially after seeing those two pervs stalking me earlier."

"I'll keep digging. I'm not optimistic. These shell companies can be hard to crack because they're so secretive."

"In the meantime, bring me a gun."

"I would advise against confronting these guys. We need to know more about them. They could be serious bad news."

"Are you any closer to finding out who they are?"

"It's difficult. I did some research. Rabbit World doesn't require visitors to use their real names when they purchase avatars. Anonymity is prized there."

"So the avatars can commit crimes and get away with them."

"I don't know what Orion's reasoning is for protecting identities in Rabbit World. Crimes committed in the metaverse aren't considered prosecutable—as you found out, unfortunately. So why hide everybody's ID?"

"Orion is obsessed with freedom. Maybe he thinks people are more free if they act anonymously." Ivy paused. "Bring me a gun ASAP. I don't feel safe when I'm out alone."

She hung up.

Brody had a spare SIG P365 semiautomatic pistol locked in a gun safe in his closet. He retrieved the safe, unlocked it with a four-digit code, and removed the pistol.

He had sanded off the serial numbers on the piece. It was untraceable.

If she didn't know how to shoot a gun, he would train her when he gave it to her.

Recalling Ivy had said her husband had mentioned XBY Systems, Brody typed *Kingston* and *XBY Systems* in the search bar.

One entry mentioned them together. XBY Systems was helping fund Orion's Rabbit World. Why would they send driverless cars to harass Ivy? wondered Brody.

Chapter 21

While Brody was training Ivy how to use the SIG P365 in her living room, he got a call on his cell phone and answered it.

"This is the guard at the Rabbit World server. I'm watching the CCTV and seeing three strangers in front of the office. Mr. Kingston told me to call you if I sense trouble."

"OK," said Brody. "I'll be right there." He put away his cell and faced Ivy. "I gotta run. You OK with the piece?"

Ivy looked at the SIG nestled in her hand.

"I guess," she said with a meek smile.

"Remember to release the safety and jerk back the slide to chamber the first round. Then you're good to go," he said, standing with his back to the front door, getting ready to leave.

"I hope I don't have to use it, but I'm getting tired of running."

"If you don't want to confront them by yourself, call me."

"I need to have it out with them, whoever they are."

"It could be dangerous."

"I realize that. When I meet them, I'm gonna make sure it's a crowded area where a lot of people can see me when I'm with them."

"Good idea. But be careful."

"You really think they'd try something in front of a crowd?"

"Probably not. But they might try to kidnap you and assault you elsewhere."

"I never thought of that," said Ivy, worrying her lower lip.

"I wish you'd call me when you meet them."

"What if you're busy?"

"Hopefully, they'll be afraid to try anything in the real world for fear of getting caught. Maybe they live out their rape fantasies in VR so they don't try it elsewhere, because it's not illegal in VR."

"Well, it should be. I can't do my job because of those creeps."

"If they try something in the real world, you can always call the cops. They may not have jurisdiction in VR, but they do here."

She contemplated the piece in her hand. "I might just shoot the two bastards."

"Only in self-defense. Otherwise, you'll be the one doing time."

Brody jerked open the door and bolted to his Mini parked in the driveway.

Chapter 22

Brody drove south to the office that housed Rabbit World's server in West LA, just north of Culver City.

He parked next to a navy blue Jaguar F-Type in the underground parking garage.

He didn't know what to expect in the office, but to be on the safe side he prepared for a firefight. He clambered out of his Mini's driver's seat, strode to the trunk in the rear, popped the trunk lid with his key fob, and inspected the pasteboard box loaded with SIG P365 magazines.

He stuffed handfuls of magazines into the deep pockets of his khaki cargo pants. He withdrew his SIG from its ankle holster, jerked back the slide, and jacked a round into the spout. He holstered the SIG.

Deciding he didn't want to leave any prints in the office, he donned a pair of sheer black leather driving gloves that lay in the trunk.

He locked the Mini, found the elevator, and rode it to the top floor. The elevator door hummed open. Holding the door open he craned his neck into the hallway and saw nobody present. He stepped out of the elevator, withdrew a rubber wedge from one of his cargo pockets, and inserted the wedge under the door to keep it from shutting. He didn't want anyone to use the elevator while he was checking out the server office.

He produced his cell phone and called the guard.

Nobody answered.

Not a good sign, Brody decided. Why wouldn't the guy answer unless he was in trouble?

Brody stooped down, withdrew his SIG from his ankle holster, withdrew a sound suppressor from another cargo pocket, and screwed the suppressor onto his SIG's muzzle. He released the safety. He checked the numbers of the offices on a sign at the top of the wall across from the elevator, found out where the Rabbit World office was located, and stole down the corridor toward it, gun in hand.

He picked up on a door hanging ajar and realized it was the door to the office he was seeking.

He slowed down and crept toward the door, gun raised.

On the qui vive, he poked his head into the office.

He saw the feet of a supine man sticking out from behind a metal desk. Brody tensed. The grey trousers had a black stripe running down each leg. A guard's uniform, decided Brody.

He edged into the office, searching for movement, his pulse racing.

Rows of desks with computers on them lined the office. He saw two other bodies slumped in chairs in front of desks with computers on them. A twentysomething lanky guy dressed in jeans and a white T with an image of Mickey Mouse silkscreened on its chest bowed forward with his forehead pressed on his computer's keyboard, the black plastic bow of his spectacles broken where a bullet had split it and entered his temple.

A roly-poly blonde pushing thirty with a pasty complexion sat immobile in her chair, her head tilted forward onto her chest, her hazel eyes vacant, a bloody bowl-shaped section of her forehead lying like a section of cocoanut on her desktop.

As he neared the motionless guard, Brody saw blood on the guy's torn shirt where a bullet had punctured his heart.

Brody stiffened when he heard movement in an adjacent room. He heard talking.

As he stole toward the sound, he saw someone enter the hallway from a room, gun in hand, facing him.

It was a Hispanic guy with a two-inch-long scar grooving his forehead above his right eye.

Without hesitation Brody double-tapped the guy's upper body mass. Wearing jeans and a black Windbreaker the guy crumpled with a feeble groan, his heart bursting.

Brody had heard the guy talking. There should be at least one more in the adjacent office—unless the dead intruder had been talking on his cell phone when Brody had overheard him. Brody remembered the guard had mentioned three strangers.

Brody worked on the assumption there was at least one other person in the office.

Brody bolted to the office door, which hung open, revealing a thirtysomething guy wearing coveralls inserting a flash drive into a computer on the desk. Armed with a silenced pistol, he picked up on Brody and squeezed off a shot.

Not in time.

Brody had already let loose two shots into the guy's upper body mass. The guy was on his way down as he fired at Brody, his errant slug whizzing past Brody's ear.

Clad in a grey polo, a fortyish guy with cropped hair hiding behind the desk popped his head up along with a silenced pistol in his hand and fired at Brody. Caught off guard, Brody ducked back out of the office into the hallway, firing two unaimed shots as he retreated, and all but tripping over his own feet as he backed up.

He wondered how many intruders were here, his heartbeat jackhammering.

He had put down two, which left only one—as far as he knew. Unless there were others he couldn't see from where he stood. He scoped out the main office and saw no one moving. The office where the gunman was hiding must be the room where the server was located. There could be more bogeys accompanying him, ones the guard hadn't seen.

Not only were these intruders armed, they had sound suppressors on their pistols. Pros, decided Brody. They had broken into the office, planning to use their guns all along. The guard must have tried to stop them on his own. Maybe he didn't know the intruders were armed.

81

Orion didn't want to involve the cops, which meant Brody had to take care of this himself. He couldn't call for backup.

"We got him trapped," Brody called into the main office, eying the front door. "He can't get by us."

He wanted the intruder to think Brody had a partner and had the advantage in firepower.

"Give up, and we'll let you go," Brody told the intruder.

"You expect me to believe that?" said the intruder, crouched behind a desk.

"My client doesn't want the cops involved. He says to let you go if you agree to forget everything."

"What's in it for me?"

"Your life. What more do you want?"

Brody poked his head into the doorway. The intruder fired at him. The bullet struck the doorjamb, splintering it. Brody pulled back behind the wall, stumbled on the body in the hallway, but regained his balance.

"Throw your piece into the hall," he said, face sweaty.

"What makes you think I'm surrendering?"

"You have no other choice. You're trapped."

"I got friends coming to help me."

Brody figured the guy was lying, but he didn't want to wait to find out. He needed to flush the guy out before anyone else arrived.

"Ain't that a coincidence," said Brody. "So do I. I bet my friends get here before yours."

"Can you take that chance?"

"You'll be dead by the time your buds get here."

"This is bullshit," said the intruder, sounding antsy.

Brody figured he had the guy rattled.

"Tell me who you're working for, and we'll let you go," said Brody.

Silence.

A wooden chair flew through the doorway, crashed into the corridor wall opposite it, slid down the wall, and landed with a thud on the floor three feet in front of Brody with one of its legs broken. Brody started.

Bullets filled the doorway, followed by the heavyset intruder, who burst into the hall, gun in hand. As he swung one of his long ape arms around the doorframe to fire at Brody, Brody fired two slugs into the guy's head. A blood-streaked fragment of occipital bone shot from the back of the guy's skull and painted the wall with a red splotch where the bone hit, as he crumpled to the floor on rubber legs.

Brody bolted into the server's office and scoped out his surroundings, sweeping the area with his gun. He saw no one. The computer on the desk was running, as a flash drive inserted in one of the USB ports blinked. Words on the monitor said 70 percent complete.

Brody figured the intruder had inserted the flash drive, which was infecting the server with a virus. He whipped out the flash drive. The computer screen froze. He pocketed the flash drive. He didn't know enough about servers to know if he had saved this one from contamination by the virus or malware or whatever was in the flash drive.

He patted down the corpse that lay sprawled in coveralls next to the desk, but found no ID.

He darted into the hall and checked the two other corpses for IDs. He found nothing in either of the stiff's pockets, not even a wallet nor a cell phone. How did they communicate with their boss? They must have been on radio silence during the mission. Their boss was paranoid about getting ID'd.

Definitely pros, decided Brody. Riley's men? If so, there was no proof of it.

Chapter 23

Brody fished his cell phone out of his trouser pocket and called Orion.

"Three bogeys hit your Rabbit World office," said Brody.

"What? Right now?" said Orion in surprise.

"I'm standing here with them."

"Who sent them?"

"I dunno."

"Ask them."

Brody eyeballed the corpses. "It's a little late for that."

"What are you talking about? Make sense. I want to know who they're working for."

"They're dead."

"Shit."

"I had no choice. They were all armed with silenced pistols. I took them out."

"What are their names? Maybe I know them."

"I have no idea. They're pros. They had no IDs."

"Shit. And shit. What about the guard?"

"They blew him away. Along with a couple of your workers that were in the office."

"What the hell were the burglars doing there?"

"They inserted a flash drive into your server. Some sort of virus, I bet."

"Holy Christ."

"I unplugged it before it finished. It was like 70 percent complete. The server might be OK. I'm not a techie."

"Riley's thugs, maybe."

"Should I call the cops?"

"No way."

"What do you want me to do?"

Orion blew into his phone's transmitter in dismay. "Let me think. I'll send some of my computer geeks to inspect the server."

"What about the stiffs?"

"We have to ditch them. I don't want the cops to know about this."

"I know. Bad PR for Rabbit World," said Brody, reading Orion's mind.

"*Bad* is an understatement. It would be catastrophic. My IPO next week would be a flop if word got out about this."

"How do you explain away six dead bodies?"

"Nobody must know about this."

"What about the dead guard?"

"Uh—I'll tell his company he went AWOL."

"And your two dead workers?"

"Uh—let me think—Arrange a car accident for them. Can you do that?"

"I know people who handle . . . Don't you even want to know their names?"

"Uh—no. It's better that it comes as a surprise when I hear about the accident."

"You need to remove all of the stiffs. The cleaning staff will find them when they come in to do their job."

"Can you take the bodies out of there without drawing attention?" asked Orion.

"That would be illegal."

"Come on. We're all adults here. Laws get broken every day, and nobody does a thing about it."

"I don't handle this myself, but I can get in touch with a cleanup crew that does. And they'll arrange the car accident for your two workers."

"It has to look like an accident."

"It will."

"What about the bullets in their bodies? Do you think I'm stupid?"

Brody glanced at the blonde slouched at her desk with her forehead missing. A through-and-through kill shot through the back of the head. "Not all of the bodies have bullets in them."

"And the ones that do?"

"The bodies will be incinerated in the accident. If there are any bullets left in the wreckage, the cleanup crew will remove them."

"All right. Do it."

"It's not gonna come cheap."

"I don't give a damn what it costs," said Orion in a burst of anger. "I'm not risking my company's rep because of a bunch of hooligans hired with dirty money. Riley and his Mafia hoods are doing everything they can to sabotage my company."

"I'll give the cleaners a call."

"And don't say a word of this to anyone." Orion paused. "What are the fuckers gonna try next?" he added, as if to himself.

"It depends how desperate they are."

"Is there any way you can find out who hired these three goons?"

"I can try tracing their guns. I'm not making any promises. Pros don't use traceable pieces."

"Do whatever you have to. I'll bet the farm Riley's consortium is behind this. I'll send the money to you via Zelle. You pay these cleaners, or whatever they are, with cash. I want nothing to connect them to me. And, Brody?"

"Yeah."

"Keep your mouth shut. You understand? Talk to no one about this."

Orion hung up.

Brody put through a call to CPR, Cleaners of Personal Refuse, a company that discreetly removed corpses.

Chapter 24

While he waited for the CPR team to arrive, Brody inspected the stiffs to see if there were any identifying marks on them.

He noticed the guy wearing a grey polo had a tattoo extending under his sleeve down his arm. Brody stooped and lifted the polo sleeve to reveal a tattoo of a bone frog. He recognized it. The bone frog represented a fallen comrade among SEALS. The guy was a SEAL, or maybe he used to be a SEAL like Brody.

Could government Special Forces be involved in this break-in? wondered Brody. If so, why? Brody had no desire to run up against the government. He couldn't think of a reason they would try to infect Orion's server with a virus. However, he couldn't discount them.

Bone Frog might have left the SEALS and joined Riley's consortium because he needed a job. In any event, Bone Frog was trained for violence and was adept with weapons. Brody figured all three of these intruders were. Without the advantage of surprise, Brody might be the one lying dead on the floor instead of them.

Brody inspected Bone Frog's Glock 17, which lay on the floor near Bone Frog's hand. As Brody had expected, the serial number had been sanded off. He figured the same would be true for the two other intruders' weapons.

He laid the Glock on the floor, leaving it for the CPR crew to clean up, and approached the stocky guy in coveralls who lay in a heap on the floor. The guy had three dark green dots tattooed an inch apart from each other in the shape of a triangle just below the intersection where his thumb met his forefinger.

Brody was familiar with the tat, which stood for *mi vida loca*. My crazy life. Many cartel members bore the tat to indicate they were outside the law.

Brody picked up the guy's Ruger 3830 9 mm Luger with a Viridian laser from the floor, searched for the serial number, and found none. Another cold piece. He placed it on the floor.

While he was looking for the other intruder's piece, he heard a knock on the main office door and froze, his heart in his mouth. He eyeballed the dead bolt lock. He hadn't locked it.

He would have a lot of explaining to do if someone found him in a blood-splattered room full of bullet-riddled corpses.

He stood six feet from the door. He wondered if he had enough time to reach it and lock it before the visitor entered. He thought about reaching for his SIG, but he didn't want to shoot an innocent bystander who had nothing to do with the break-in.

He couldn't dally. He had to make a decision. If he dashed to the door to lock it, the visitor might hear Brody's footsteps and wonder why Brody had locked him out. So what? decided Brody. There was nothing the guy could do about it, and he would have no idea who had locked the door.

Brody heard the doorknob turn. He sprang to the door, slammed it shut, and locked the dead bolt.

"Ow," said the visitor. "What the hell did you do that for? You could've broken my wrist."

Brody said nothing.

"Brad, is that you?" said the visitor. "Very funny, you prick. Were you the one who blocked the elevator door from closing? What are you guys doing in there? Playing hide the salami?"

Brody said nothing.

"I knew it. I just wanted to know if either of you want a drink. I'm on a coffee run to Starbuck's. On second thought, get it yourself. I'll send you the hospital bill for my broken wrist."

Brody exhaled with relief when he heard footsteps retreating down the hall.

He hoped CPR would get here soon. They were experts at their job. When they were done, they would leave the office spotless. Not even a cadaver dog would be able to tell stiffs had been present.

Brody's cell phone vibrated in his trouser pocket. He took the call.

"The creeps are stalking me," said Ivy.

"Where are you?"

"I'm gonna confront them," she said, and hung up.

Brody cursed under his breath. How could he help her if he didn't know where she was?

Somebody tapped gently on the door.

Brody tensed. He hoped it wasn't the guy on a coffee run. Brody approached the door.

"CPR," he heard someone mutter in the hall.

Relieved, Brody unlocked the door, cracked it, recognized the crew, and let them in. A group of six men and women entered lugging six rolls of carpets and cleaning equipment. Two more brought up the rear, rolling vacuum cleaners in front of them.

"You've been busy," said the bald middle-aged guy who led the way into the office, surveying the blood-splattered office. "Where are the two who were in a car accident?"

"Sitting at their desks," said Brody, glancing at the dead office workers.

"Got it."

"You know what to do. Lock the door behind me," said Brody, as he stepped into the hall and shut the door.

Chapter 25

Ivy was at the Los Angeles County Museum of Art near the La Brea Tar pits enjoying their exhibit of modern American paintings when she saw the two pervs stalking her. They were standing the better part of thirty feet behind her, staring at her with their pupil-less doll eyes, not even pretending to be eying the artwork around them. They seemed to be laughing at her with their lopsided smiles.

Her first instinct was to make a run for it, as her pulse raced and her adrenaline surged when she caught sight of the two thugs.

She couldn't believe they would try anything here with so many museum patrons milling around. She didn't know what to expect.

She managed to suppress her urge to flee, remembering she had Brody's SIG P365 in her purse.

They probably wanted her to flee in fear, she decided. It turned them on to see her scared. Part of the sick kick they got from stalking her.

She couldn't tell if their faces were masks, as the guard at the mall had said. They were definitely strange. From where she stood, they looked plastic thanks to their smooth sheen and ghostly pallor. She figured they could be masks. After all, many people were afraid of catching Covid and continued wearing masks, even if they were vaccinated.

Despite her fear, she walked calmly out of the museum to an outdoor café, ordered a latte, and sat down at a table on the cement terrace. She snapped open her purse and peeked inside to make sure her pistol was there.

She didn't believe the creeps would try anything on her as she sat in a public café. But then again, avatars couldn't exist in the real world, and yet here two of them were making a beeline for her.

"Gotcha," the taller one said, taking a seat at her table. "I'm Ed."

Sporting a brunet mullet, he wore a black hoodie and blue jeans.

"I can't believe you didn't run away when you saw us," said the other, who had a shaved head, sitting beside Ed. "I'm Joe."

Joe wore a navy blue hoodie and black jeans.

Their faces were frozen in place with half smiles on them. Ivy couldn't see how the masks were attached to their faces—if they were masks.

"You can take off those stupid masks," she said. "They don't scare me."

"What masks?" said Ed, exchanging glances with Joe.

"Why are you stalking me?" demanded Ivy.

"You must be imagining it," said Ed.

"I'm not imagining anything. I've seen you two stalking me."

"You have an overactive imagination."

"I didn't imagine you assaulting me in Rabbit World."

"You're right. You didn't imagine that."

Ivy couldn't believe they were admitting it. "Why did you assault me?"

"Because we could," said Joe.

"We can do anything we want in the metaverse," said Ed. "Everything is allowed. There are no laws prohibiting you from doing anything. Everybody is free."

"That doesn't give you the right to attack me," said Ivy. "What about my rights? Did you ever think of me or anyone beside yourselves?"

"You don't understand the metaverse," said Ed. "Everything is free. There are no laws. We do whatever we want."

"This isn't the metaverse. We have laws here. I'll call the cops if you try anything."

"Did you tell the cops we raped you in Rabbit World?"

"No."

"Why not?"

"Because they can't do anything about it."

"You should tell them anyway."

Ivy couldn't figure out why they wanted her to tell the cops.

"Why do you care one way or the other?" she said.

"If you don't tell the cops, everybody will think you were asking for it."

"What?" she said, indignant.

"And they would be right," said Joe. "You *were* asking for it. You're a prick teaser, and you know it. Wiggling your hips like a whore and yelping in heat. What do you expect?"

"I don't have to listen to this bullshit."

"Don't get stressed out," said Ed. "You could have a breakdown—or worse."

"Worse?"

Ed paused for effect. "Suicide."

"I don't know what kind of sick game you're playing, but it's not working."

"We don't want you to commit suicide because of the shame you feel for being assaulted."

"What?" said Ivy, taken aback. "I don't feel shame. You're the ones who should feel shame."

"When you're free like us, you don't feel shame. That's what we've been trying to tell you."

"Leave me alone."

"We don't want you to kill yourself for being ashamed of teasing us into raping you, shaking your hot ass in our faces."

"Tease? You gotta be kidding."

"You were flaunting your body, bending over and sticking your bubble butt in our faces. How did you expect us to act?"

"I wasn't flaunting anything. I was walking down the street. I have nothing to be ashamed about. Stop trying to put this on me."

"If the shoe fits, wear it."

"How could anyone get turned on by my avatar?" she scoffed.

"Your pussy has a grip like a vise," said Joe.

"How would you know?"

"If you join us in the metaverse, you won't feel guilt or shame," said Ed. "You'll be free of all social and moral restraints."

Ivy shook her head, incredulous. "No thanks."

"Don't you want to be free to do whatever you want?"

"I don't want to join a place where people attack each other without consequences."

"Then you must not want to be free."

"I *am* free."

She couldn't understand why they wanted her to join Rabbit World. She didn't see how it profited them unless they were working for Orion, which made no sense. But who else would benefit from her joining Rabbit World? Who did the avatars represent in the real world?

Ed laughed. "You *think* you're free, but thinking doesn't make it so. You're enslaved by laws and outdated moral codes. We're Big Tech. We're the future. We don't obey superstitious moral platitudes."

"What do you obey?"

"Nothing. Honestly, you can't do much of anything in the real world. Join the metaverse, and you'll enjoy a whole new experience—the experience of total freedom."

"Come, be one of us," Joe told her.

She got the weird and disconcerting feeling they were telling her to get naked. She shook off the feeling.

"So you can assault me again?" she said. "Do you think I'm an idiot?"

"I think you want to be free like us," said Ed. "If you were honest with yourself, you would admit it."

"Why do you insist on lying to yourself?" Joe asked her.

"You're the ones who are lying to me," she scoffed.

"We're disabusing you. You're so brainwashed you don't even realize you're a slave."

"I can't believe you guys. You gang-rape me and ask me to come back to the metaverse so you can do it again. You got some gall."

"You call it *gall*. We call it *freedom*."

"You're a bunch of outlaws who have no respect for other people. You're goddamn animals who think you're better than everybody else."

"Animals? We're Big Tech. We're the future. We're the next step in man's evolution."

"I call you animals, because all you care about is yourselves."

"Not unlike you."

"Animals," Ivy hissed.

"You call us animals because we're free? I don't understand."

"I don't want to talk about this anymore," said Ivy, crossing her arms on her chest.

She couldn't reach her gun in this position, she realized.

Chapter 26

"What you want is immaterial," said Ed. "We're not finished with you. We've only just begun. We want you to be one of us. The first step is to cleanse your brain of false ideas."

"You should be flattered we chose you of all people, Ivy," said Joe.

"You say you want me to be free, and in the same breath you say what I want is immaterial," said Ivy. "How does that make sense?"

She uncrossed her arms and lowered them to her sides, wary of an attack. These creeps weren't apologizing in any sense of the word. In case they came at her, she wanted to be able to reach her gun in her purse, which lay in her lap.

"When you're free like us, you don't have to make sense," said Joe. "That's part of the beauty of Rabbit World."

Alice in Wonderland, decided Ivy. A place where nothing made sense. Absurdity was the rule. *'Twas brillig, and the slithy toves did gyre and gimble in the wabe.*

"You're in the real world now," she said, "and things make sense here. None of that Dormouse nonsense you're spouting about doing whatever you want."

"Things make sense here? You think?"

"You know what I mean. We have laws to prohibit people from assaulting each other."

"That's the problem with the real world. It's not something you should brag about."

"It's better than the absurd chaos where you come from."

"It's not absurd chaos. It's freedom. Read Sartre's *No Exit* and tell me with a straight face your world's not absurd."

"I'm not talking ivory tower philosophy. I'm talking the real world. We have laws here to protect the innocent. You have nothing but anarchy in your metaverse."

"Do you like feeling pain?"

Ivy resented the remark. "Of course, I don't. Is that some kind of threat?"

"In the metaverse we don't feel pain."

"What are you? The walking dead?"

"Come, join us, and free yourself from your world of suffering," said Ed.

"It's not all about suffering. We have good times, too. Except when you two are around."

"We know you want to join us. Why not admit it?"

Ivy sipped her latte. It was losing its taste. And it wasn't just the drink. It was the conversation that was leaving a bad taste in her mouth.

"I admit you two are full of shit," she said.

"Why are you so frightened of becoming an avatar? There's nothing better in the universe than freedom. In the metaverse we are free. In the so-called real world you are shackled by fear."

"I'm not afraid of you," she said, hoping they believed her dissembling.

"We can hurt you, you know," said Joe, with that idiot smile on his lips that made it sound all the more ominous as though he would enjoy doling out pain to her with a car battery hooked to her nipples with alligator clips.

Another threat, she decided, her heart pounding so loud she feared they could hear it slamming against her rib cage. She didn't want them to know she was afraid of them.

She shot to her feet, intending to leave.

"And we can hurt your husband," said Ed.

"What?" she said, taken aback

"You heard me.".

"Leave my family out of this," she said, furious they would threaten her family as well as her.

"We're serious. Join us, or you will continue to suffer."

"If you try anything, I'm calling the cops," she said, backing stiffly away from the café table, clenching her purse with white knuckles.

She wasn't going to pull out her gun unless they launched an attack. She doubted they would in a public concourse, but if they thought they could get away with anything they might try it. They knew they could get away with anything in the metaverse. They might get into their heads that they could do the same in the real world.

She backed into someone. She startled.

She wheeled around to face him, on the verge of whipping out her pistol, when she saw an elderly man wielding a cane as he hobbled behind her.

"I'm so sorry," she said.

"Look where you're going," he snarled, and shambled away, frowning.

She strode out of the museum concourse, glancing behind her fitfully to see if Ed and Joe were stalking her. She didn't see them.

Chapter 27

With her car at the body shop for repairs, Ivy drove a rented Volvo back home, not without checking her rearview mirror every five minutes to see if the black Dodge Charger was tailing her. She parked in her garage next to Orion's silver metallic Porsche, half of which she had paid for.

The heiress of an egomaniacal newspaper magnate, she never lacked for money. What she lacked, according to her psychiatrist, was belief in herself. On the other hand, her psychiatrist was full of himself, no matter how wrongheaded his analysis, she decided.

Walking into her house she met Orion in the living room.

With his unlined face he looked ten years younger than his forty years.

"I can't sell any more real estate in Rabbit World," she said.

"What are you talking about? Why not? You're my wife. I want you to be my real estate agent."

"I can't in good conscience sell real estate in such a dangerous and crime-ridden location."

"How can you say such a thing? It's not crime-ridden. And you can't get hurt in the metaverse, because you aren't physically in it. Your avatar is."

"Those two avatars are stalking me. They threatened me and you at lunch."

"You had lunch with avatars?" said Orion, staring at her, his boyish face creased in disbelief.

"That's what I said."

"Ivy, avatars don't exist in the real world. They exist only as symbols in the metaverse. They're not human. They represent humans."

"Are you calling me a liar?"

"You're stressed out after that attack in Rabbit World. I understand. But it didn't happen. You didn't get assaulted. Only your avatar did. You need to drop it and get on with your life."

"Did you hear me before? Not only did they threaten me, they threatened *you*. You need to be on your guard."

"This is ridiculous. It can't be happening. You must be suffering from PTSD." He strode to the sideboard and poured a scotch. "You need a drink."

"They want me to join them," she said, waving off the drink.

Orion tossed back the scotch.

"What do you mean, 'join them'?" he said, furrowing his brow.

"I'm not sure. That's what they said."

"It makes no sense."

"They want me to become an avatar."

"Oh, yeah? And how the hell are you supposed to become an avatar? Do you realize how crazy you sound?"

"They're the ones that said it. Not me," said Ivy, flapping her hand in frustration as she paced around the room.

"OK, I'll play along. Why do they want you to become an avatar?" said Orion, pouring himself another drink.

"They said I would be free if I join them in the metaverse."

"You're already free. We live in the USA."

"They said there are no laws in the metaverse so I could do whatever I want when I become one of them."

"What did you tell them?"

"I said no, of course."

"OK. Well, I don't see anything threatening in asking you to join the metaverse."

"They want me to become an avatar."

"So they want you to have an avatar and use it in the metaverse. That's all. You must have misunderstood them."

"I'm telling you, they wanted me to *become* an avatar."

99

"You can't *become* an avatar. You use an avatar to represent you in the metaverse. You don't understand the terminology."

"You're the one that doesn't understand. They *are* avatars. They want me to be an avatar like them. If I don't, they'll harm me."

Orion drummed his fingers on the sideboard. "You didn't call the cops after these guys threatened you, did you?"

"No."

"Good," said Orion, relieved. "Don't tell the cops anything about this. I want Rabbit World's IPO to be successful next week. No crazy PR about avatars threatening people."

Ivy glowered at him. "You make me sound like a wacko."

"You must have PTSD. You'll get over it. Don't worry. Just don't tell anyone about this."

"Stop patronizing me. They could come after you next."

He walked over to her and held her. "Nobody's coming after me, and nobody's coming after you."

"Those two creeps give me the willies. They think they can do whatever they want. We're not safe with them out there."

"We *are* under attack, but not from avatars. Somebody broke into our office and tried to infect the Rabbit World server with a virus."

"What?" said Ivy, locking eyes with him, her eyes wide.

"It just happened."

"Who did it?"

"I don't know yet."

"Do you think they're gonna come after us?" she said with concern.

Orion wiped his brow. "I don't think so. They want to destroy Rabbit World."

"But you're the owner. What's to stop them from coming after you?"

"There's a big difference between sabotaging a server and assaulting people. But . . . ," he trailed off.

"What were you gonna say?"

"Nothing."

"Do you think this is connected to the avatars' attack?"

"No. Get that attack out of your mind. You're becoming obsessed with it. It wasn't real."

"They're not stalking *you*."

He took a pull on his scotch.

"What did the police say about the break-in?" she said.

"I—uh—didn't tell them."

She did a double take. "What? Why not?"

"Bad PR would trash my IPO next week. If it became public knowledge that Rabbit World has enemies, my IPO would tank. If I report the break-in to the cops, the media will get wind of it, and that's that."

"But the break-in was illegal."

"I'll take care of it."

"What's to prevent them from trying again?"

Orion snorted. "They're not in any condition to try again."

"What's that supposed to mean?" she said, bemused.

"Never mind. I'm taking care of it. I never should have told you. You're too stressed out as it is."

"You would be too, if it happened to you."

"I'm going to the office to make sure everything is OK after the break-in," he said, and strode out the front door.

Ivy heard him start up his Porsche in the garage. The 640 hp engine rumbled to life.

Watching him through the picture window back out of the driveway, she produced her cell phone and called Brody.

Chapter 28

"I confronted the avatars," said Ivy.

"What happened?" said Brody. "Are you OK?"

"I'm OK, but being with those pervs unnerved me. Just talking to them gets to me."

"Did they try to assault you?"

"No. They actually told me to tell the cops about the assault in Rabbit World. Can you believe it?"

"Like they were daring you to go to the cops about it? They were goading you in order to make themselves feel superior, figuring you were too scared to go to the cops because you're afraid the two rapists would attack you again in retaliation."

"Is that what they were doing? I couldn't make sense of it."

"Where did you meet them?"

"At LACMA."

"Could you tell if they were wearing masks?"

"They weren't wearing masks. They admitted it. They're avatars."

Brody paused on the line. "Did anyone see you with them."

"Other patrons? I dunno. Is that important?"

"They could verify these guys are avatars."

"You still don't believe me?" she said, outraged.

"I'm not saying that."

"Then why do you want to know if anybody else saw them with me? What difference does it make who else saw them?"

Brody changed the subject. "I could check the security cameras at LACMA. Where did you meet them?"

"At the patio restaurant."

"Good. There must be video footage of you and them."

"So what?" she said, annoyed. "What good is it?"

"I want to see these damn avatars, so I can get some idea what we're dealing with."

"They're animals. You should've heard what they said to me," said Ivy, becoming agitated at the memory, fidgeting.

"Did you tape-record it?"

"Uh, no. I didn't think to."

"That's OK. It took a lot of guts for you to confront them."

"I want them to leave me alone."

"Did you get the impression they will?"

Ivy shook her head no. "They're gonna keep stalking me. I'm convinced of it. They didn't apologize. Just the opposite. They relished degrading me, calling me a whore, and blaming me for their attack."

"Do you have any idea who they are?"

"Actually, they told me. Well, their first names. Ed and Joe."

"It's a step in the right direction. Maybe we're getting somewhere. Did their names ring a bell?"

"No."

"Hmm. You must not know them, or they wouldn't have risked telling you their names."

"Of course, I don't know them. I don't know any avatars."

"I mean, the avatars stand for real people. They're the ones I'm trying to ID."

"I don't think these avatars stand for anyone but themselves. They're not puppets in the metaverse being manipulated by humans like other avatars."

Brody paused a beat. "That's hard to believe."

Ivy waved her hands in frustration. "Nobody believes me."

"I do believe you're being stalked."

"Do you think I'm nuts like Orion does?" she said, taking umbrage.

"Not at all. We need to know more information before we can figure out what's really going on. Let me think. If you meet them again, be sure to tape-record your conversation in case they threaten you again. You can report them to the cops for making threats."

"I don't plan on meeting them again. It accomplished nothing. I didn't get the impression I frightened them away by confronting them. If anything, it turned them on."

"What exactly did they want from you? Was it all about threatening you or was there something else?"

"They wanted me to become one of them."

"One of them?" said Brody, not understanding.

"You know, an avatar."

"They can make you into an avatar?"

"I didn't pursue the subject. I declined."

"I wish I knew how they proposed to do it."

"Not me. I don't want to find out."

"I don't understand what their game is."

"I just told you."

"There must be something we're missing."

"I don't care what we're missing. I want you to make them leave me alone."

"If you run into them again, call me. Don't go off on your own to confront them again."

"I wasn't planning to."

"Also, it would help if you could get specimens of their DNA. If they have criminal records, they would be in the FBI's CODIS DNA database."

Ivy winced in disgust. "How am I supposed to get their DNA? Give them a specimen cup?"

"Grab a cup they were drinking out of. Something like that. I could have a lab examine it for fingerprints and DNA."

"I hope I never see them again," said Ivy, but doubted she would be so lucky.

"I'll get back to you when I find out anything more about them."

Brody hung up.

Chapter 29

Brody drove his Mini to LACMA. He parked in an outdoor parking lot over the hill from the tar pits and walked to the county museum.

He found the patio where Ivy said she had met the two avatars. Standing on the concourse, he surveyed the surroundings casting around for a security camera. He spotted one.

He entered the museum and located the security office on the directory.

Brody displayed his private investigator's license to the uniformed security guard manning the office.

"I'm looking for two rapists," said Brody. "I believe they were eating at the patio café earlier today. Could I look at your video footage?"

The middle-aged guard with cropped red hair and rheumy blue eyes saw no harm in playing the video for him. Brody saw a row of CCTV screens mounted on the wall.

"Do you have any idea how boring this job is?" said the guard, yawning.

Brody said nothing.

"Look at number three," said the guard, scratching his round red nose.

Brody watched the footage on the third screen. It took a while, but at last he spotted Ivy walking into view, followed by two men in their late twenties or early thirties wearing jeans and hoodies. All three sat at a café table. Brody couldn't make out the faces of the two men because they were facing away from the camera. Their heads appeared larger than most, but other than that they looked like two guys—from the back, anyway.

When they sat down opposite Ivy, they continued to face away from the camera.

Brody wondered if they were doing it deliberately. Had they spotted the CCTV camera before they walked into view with Ivy?

He couldn't make out masks on their faces. There were no telltale strings looped over their ears fastening the masks.

"Are those two guys with the girl wearing masks?" he said.

"I don't think so. I can't tell. If they are, it wouldn't surprise me. A lot of visitors wear masks because they're scared of Covid."

"Do they look like avatars to you?"

"Avatars? Aren't they figures in videogames?"

"Yeah."

The guard concentrated on the CCTV screen. "They look like three people to me."

"Not the girl. The two guys."

"Avatars? How could they be avatars? They're people."

"Except we can't see their faces," said Brody, as if to himself.

"If it walks like a duck and talks like a duck . . ."

"Do you have another camera that can show their faces?"

"This is the only view we have of the patio café." The guard looked up at Brody from his seat. "Didn't you know?"

"What?"

"We have a discrimination policy against avatars entering the museum."

"Very funny."

Unamused, Brody left.

"You're the one that's joking, buddy," said the guard. "Avatars having lunch with a pretty woman? What kind of a fool do you take me for? Thanks for wasting my time, you two-bit peeping Tom."

Brody kept walking down the hall.

That crack about a peeping Tom got to him. Seething, he stopped in his tracks and considered returning to the guard and decking him. He didn't need a rent-a-cop telling him how idiotic it sounded to be looking for avatars talking to a woman. But he didn't want to get into it with the guard.

Brody continued walking.

When he reached the security camera mounted above the stairwell's door, he reached up and tilted the camera lens down, obscuring its view, and ducked through the door, just as the guard popped out of his office, his red face twisted with anger.

Cracking a smile Brody hustled down the stairs.

He had yet to find any proof that avatars were indeed stalking Ivy. As much as he wanted to give her the benefit of the doubt, her story was difficult to swallow. The trauma induced by the assault on her avatar in Rabbit World could be precipitating delusions in her.

The security videotape he had just watched proved nothing without clear visuals of the two faces of the guys in the hoodies sitting with Ivy.

Chapter 30

Tess was driving back to her house from a trip to her hairdresser's when she noticed in her rearview mirror a white Mercedes G-Wagen following her. Every time she turned, it turned in the same direction. What were the chances? she wondered.

Something else was bothering her about the G-Wagen. It was driverless.

What was that all about? she wondered. Another driverless car giving her problems. The last one had T-boned her Tesla. Was this one going to ram her rental from behind?

Avatars and driverless cars. They were both symbols of humans, without humans being present. Cars by themselves were stalking her? Wait a minute. What the hell? Why would someone program a driverless car to follow her? The only reason she could come up with was harassment or intimidation. Or both.

She cut her eyes to the rearview mirror again. The G-Wagen was behind her, closer, as if eager for her to see it.

She broke into a sweat. How could she shake the tail?

The G-Wagen closed in on her.

Fearing it would rear-end her, she hung a sharp left, forcing an oncoming pickup's driver to slam on his brakes to avoid hitting her. The bearded fortysomething driver wearing a red LA Angels ballcap shook his fist in rage at her.

When the G-Wagen attempted hanging a left to follow Ivy, a black Chevy Suburban broadsided it, slamming it sideways and carrying it forward the better part of twenty feet before coming to a tire-screeching halt.

Ivy glimpsed the accident in her rearview mirror and kept driving.

She pulled over to the side of the street at a parking meter, withdrew her cell phone from her purse, and called Brody.

"Another driverless car attacked me," she said.

"What do you mean 'attacked'?"

"It was following me, planning to crash into me."

"Did you get its license plate?"

"I—I didn't think to look at it. I was too worried."

"Is it still following you?"

"No."

"Did it try to ram you?"

"It would have any minute, if I hadn't gotten away."

"How did you get away?"

"A Chevy Suburban T-boned it when it tried to follow me."

She didn't hear him respond.

"Hello?" she said. "Are you there?"

"It doesn't make a whole lot of sense. Why are driverless cars trying to crash into you?"

"Somebody must be programming them to attack me."

"What's the point?"

"I bet it has something to do with those avatars."

"I'm not seeing the connection between avatars and driverless cars."

"Computers program driverless cars, and avatars are used for computer games and VR."

"Was the car carrying any passengers?"

"I couldn't see anyone in the car."

"Who's sending these cars after you?"

"The same people hiding behind the avatars that assaulted me."

"What's their motive?"

"I wish I knew."

"Did you report this to the cops?"

"What can I report? The driverless car was put out of commission before it was able to ram me."

"OK."

"I'm getting scared to set foot outside my house."

"You could hire a bodyguard."

"No bodyguards. I don't want a bodyguard following me day and night. It's an invasion of privacy."

Brody changed the subject. "I found video footage of your meeting with two people at LACMA, but it doesn't show their faces."

"There you go."

"It doesn't confirm they're avatars. They look like humans from behind."

"What are you trying to say?" she said, irritated.

"I'm just telling you what the evidence says."

"You're saying you don't believe me," she said, raising her voice. "That's what you're saying."

Enraged, she hung up on him.

He was almost as bad as her husband, she decided. Neither one of them believed her. She had a good mind to fire Brody and hire someone who believed her—if she could find such a person. She didn't have time to screen private detectives. She knew what she was saying about avatars walking around in reality was hard to believe. Even she was having trouble believing it.

Bowing her head she slammed the steering wheel with her hands three times in frustration.

She inspected her face in the rearview mirror.

She flinched when a pair of bloodshot eyes stared back at her. She had no idea she looked this bad.

She needed a pill.

She rooted through her purse, inspecting various orange plastic prescription bottles. Which pill did she need? Uppers, downers? Painkillers? She didn't know. Too bad there wasn't a pill that could solve all of your problems. But there wasn't. Not every problem could be solved with a pill.

She tossed her purse on the passenger seat in dismay.

Taking a pill wasn't going to stop the two avatars from harassing her. Since they didn't respect the law, in fact they

111

scoffed at it, what was to prevent them from gang-raping her again—this time in the real world inflicting real pain and suffering on her?

She inspected her open purse, making sure her gun was in it. The next time they tried something she wasn't going to make it easy for them. She would make them pay with their lives.

Shivering with apprehension, she glanced around her, scared she would see the avatars advancing on her.

A mother was walking with her boy and girl on the sidewalk on Ivy's right. Traffic was driving by on her left.

She fired the Volvo's engine.

Chapter 31

Orion inspected the server's office for Rabbit World. Everything looked clean. He didn't see any signs of the violence that had ended six lives. No blood anywhere. No bullet-pocked walls. The office smelled of bleach.

Brody's cleaning crew had done a good job, decided Orion.

He inspected the white walls and noticed wet paint on one of them where the crew had spackled over bullet holes and painted the spackle.

He made his way into the server's office and watched a twentysomething technician wearing wire-rim spectacles, a Dodgers T, and jeans inspecting the computer screen, a fixed expression on his face, a Dodgers blue cap turned backwards on his head.

"How is it?" asked Orion.

"It's working," answered the technician, chewing gum.

The gum smelled like cinnamon, decided Orion.

"Does that mean it's not infected?" he said.

"It looks OK, unless . . ."

"Unless what?"

"Unless they set a time bomb."

"A time bomb?" said Orion, taken aback.

"A figure of speech. The virus might be lying dormant until a certain amount of time has passed. Then it will detonate, so to speak, and the virus will be released in the server."

"Can't you tell if it's infected?"

"Everything seems to be working fine at this time."

"As I understand it, the virus was only 70 percent uploaded from a flash drive when my PI removed the drive from the server. Doesn't that mean the upload was unsuccessful?"

"Probably, but not necessarily. Enough of the virus could be inside the computer to wreak havoc on the server at a later date."

"Like next week?" said Orion in distress. *Just in time to destroy my IPO.*

"Next week or another week."

"A virus can do this if it's only 70 percent uploaded?"

"Probably not. I'm giving you the worst-case scenario. Where are Pam and Neal?"

"What?"

"Pam and Neal. Weren't they working here when it happened?"

"I don't know where they are," lied Orion.

"What happened to them?"

"I have no idea. I'm adding more security guards to this building. I don't want this to happen again."

"Who did it?"

"We're taking care of it."

"Maybe the cops can find out—"

"No cops. Don't tell anyone about this."

"They have the manpower—"

"Let me remind you, you signed an NDA when you joined this company that said you would never tell anyone what goes on here."

The technician stopped chewing his gum and shrugged. "No problem."

"We'll take care of this. We don't want anything to spoil our IPO next week." Orion prepared to leave. "Needless to say, we're tightening security here. Nobody gets in this office without my permission. I also changed the combination lock on the door."

Chapter 32

Orion drove his Porsche to Century City, parked in the underground garage, got out of his car, locked it with his key fob, and took the elevator to his office on the penthouse floor.

"A man is here to see you," said his secretary sitting behind her desk, nodding at a suit sitting on the other side of the room paging through a magazine he had selected from the coffee table.

Orion glanced at the fortyish stranger, not wanting to speak to him. He wanted to finalize preparations for Rabbit World's IPO.

"I'm busy now," said Orion under his breath. "Who is he?"

"He said he's with the FBI."

Orion wanted even less to speak to him. Could this be about the break-in? How could the feds have found out about it?

At that moment the agent glanced up from his magazine, saw Orion, and stood up.

"Orion Kingston?"

"Who wants to know?" said Orion.

"Xavier Bondurant, special agent for the Federal Bureau of Investigation," said Bondurant, withdrawing his badge from his jacket breast pocket, flashing it, and pocketing it. "I'd like to have a word with you, Mr. Kingston."

Orion couldn't help but notice Bondurant's hand was missing its pinky.

"I'm busy," said Orion.

"Your job will have to wait."

Orion didn't like the idea of messing with the feds. He decided to cooperate.

"OK, come into my office," he said.

Bondurant smiled briefly and followed Orion into his office. Bondurant had a receding hairline, a bushy black mustache, beetling eyebrows, and the shining black eyes of a zealot. His thin lips looked like razor blades.

"Have a seat," said Orion, plunking down on a leather chair behind his imposing mahogany desk, a picture window behind him. "What's this about?"

Bondurant sat on a black leather chair opposite Orion's desk, the sun in his eyes.

"Nice office, sir," he said, sitting bolt upright.

"I'm sort of pressed for time, if you don't mind."

"I like the aquarium over there. I find watching fish relaxing. What kind of fish are those?"

Orion glanced at the aquarium, which contained brightly colored fish swimming around porous salmon-colored coral.

"I don't know," he said. "My secretary might know. I thought your visit was important."

"The bureau got a report that you refused to sell land in a place called Rabbit World to the plaintive."

"What's the problem? I can sell land to anyone I want."

"Not if you're discriminating against someone."

"I'm not discriminating against anyone. Whoever told you otherwise is lying. And I resent the accusation."

"That's not what the plaintive says."

"Who is the plaintive?"

"Casino Gem Planet."

Orion shook his head in disdain. "I'm surprised you believe anything they say."

"Why is that, sir?"

"They're casino operators. It's common knowledge they're hooked up with the mob."

"Do you have proof to that effect?"

"What do I need proof for?"

"They could sue you for slander."

"Slander? Are you joking?"

"Do I look like I am?" said Bondurant, his face impassive.

"They put you up to this just because I won't sell them any land in my VR metaverse. You can't fool me. I'm not selling. Not to them, anyway."

"I suggest you change your mind."

"About what? Selling them real estate in Rabbit World?" said Orion, annoyed that the feds were pressuring him.

"If you sell, they won't charge you with discrimination."

"Nobody's discriminating against anybody. And I refuse to sell to them," said Orion, setting his jaw.

Bondurant heaved a beleaguered sigh. "That's unfortunate."

"It's my property and I can sell it to anyone I want. It's a free country."

"Except you have another problem."

"What problem?"

"The IRS has got it into their heads that you're playing fast and loose with your taxes."

Orion broke into a sweat. The feds nailed Al Capone for tax evasion, when they couldn't get him for anything else, including the scores of murders he ordered. The last thing Orion needed was a charge of tax evasion.

"I always pay my taxes," he said, hoping he sounded composed.

"Where have I heard that before?" said Bondurant, smirking.

"You're blackmailing me for Chrissake."

"That's a serious accusation, sir," said Bondurant, his black eyes flashing.

"You're forcing me to sell property to someone against my will."

"I'm stating facts to keep you informed. It's all about facts. Anyone who knows all the facts will do the right thing."

"You're extorting me."

"We're doing our job, is all."

"Your time is up," said Orion, and pointed at the door.

"That's unfortunate."

"Why? Are you gonna bust me?"

"I was hoping you would see the error of your ways so arresting you wouldn't be necessary."

"If you're not gonna bust me, beat it," said Orion, pointing at the door. "I got work to do."

Bondurant rose slowly from his seat. "It wouldn't be that difficult to get a warrant for your arrest. I'd be careful if I was you."

"If it's that easy, you would have brought it with you."

"We're giving you the benefit of the doubt. I hope you appreciate it."

"Your intimidation tactics have failed. Without them you have bupkes against me," said Orion, fiddling with a flat-bottomed spherical marble paperweight on his desktop.

"Do yourself a favor and sell virtual real estate in this Rabbit World place to Casino Gem Planet."

Back erect, Bondurant swaggered out of the office stone-faced.

Orion wondered if he had looked and sounded brave to Bondurant. With his racing heartbeat, Orion felt less than courageous. He fished a handkerchief out of his rear trouser pocket and wiped the sweat off his brow. Now he had the feds to worry about. How the hell had Riley gotten the feds on his side? Orion wondered.

Chapter 33

Ivy decided to go to the Century City mall and go shopping with Liz to calm herself down. She didn't want to go back home by herself, alone in her bathroom with her pills. The idea frightened her.

"It's not gonna surprise me if the world's about to end," said Liz, wearing her backpack and hiking boots. "Fucking avatars running around in the real world. What's that all about? Sounds like doomsday to me. And don't forget, we're in a pandemic. End-time."

"If you see those two pervs skulking around here, let me know," said Ivy, inspecting the mall with her probing gaze seeking the avatars.

"You got it."

"And that's not all."

"Huh?"

"I've got driverless cars stalking me."

Liz halted in her tracks. "Say what?"

"A driverless car was following me," said Ivy, stopping with Liz.

"Why would a driverless car follow you?"

"I know it sounds crazy."

"No, I believe you. What's going on, though? Driverless cars stalking people? It really must be the end of the world. I knew it."

"Those avatars are behind it, I bet."

"It's got Big Tech written all over it. They're the ones that invented avatars and driverless cars. Are they after you?"

"Why would they be after me?" said Ivy, rucking her brow.

"Have you been badmouthing them?"

119

"I was assaulted in virtual reality. *I'm* the one that should be mad at them. Orion told me not to tell anyone about it, though, so I haven't."

"I don't get it."

"It's getting so I'm afraid to go out alone."

It was just as scary being home alone surrounded by her pills that didn't make her feel better, Ivy decided with a shiver of anxiety. Which pill were you supposed to take to make stalkers leave you alone? she wondered.

"Did you tell the cops about the driverless car stalking you?" asked Liz.

Ivy shook her head no. "They'll never believe me."

"*I* believe you. With all this new technology come new ways to stalk and harass people."

"I hired a private detective instead of going to the cops."

"Do you think he can help?"

"He's trying to ID the owners of the two avatars, so I can at least know who's making my life a living nightmare."

"They can't get away with this."

"According to them, they can do whatever they want because there aren't any laws in the metaverse."

"I got news for them. This ain't the metaverse. We got laws here."

"Yet nobody's arresting these guys for stalking me."

"You gotta press charges against them."

"Orion doesn't want me to tell the cops about Rabbit World."

They entered the food court.

"How about lunch?" said Liz. "I haven't eaten since breakfast."

Ivy was so distraught she hadn't even eaten breakfast. She needed to eat to keep up her strength.

"Sounds good," she said.

They scoped out the half dozen restaurants that constituted the food court. Italian, Chinese, French, American, Mexican . . .

"How about Mexican?" said Liz.

Ivy agreed. She settled for a couple of hard tacos. Liz bought a burrito and Spanish rice. They found a table, sat down, and tucked into their food.

"I'm ready for them," said Ivy.

"What?"

Ivy opened her purse to expose the contents to Liz. Liz saw the gun nestled inside.

"Whoa," said Liz. "Do you know how to use that thing?"

Ivy snapped her purse shut. "More or less."

"I hope it doesn't come to that. Are you *that* worried they'll assault you in the real world?"

"They believe they can do whatever they want."

"Maybe in the metaverse, but not here. We have laws to protect people," said Liz, and took a bite of her burrito.

"They don't give a damn about laws. If you talked to them like I have, you'd know what I mean. That's why they scare the bejesus out of me."

"Here's something else to scare you."

"Huh?"

"What if bullets don't affect them?" said Liz, burrito in hand.

"What are you talking about?"

"Maybe bullets can't kill them," said Liz, arching her eyebrow conspiratorially.

Ivy felt the blood drain from her face. "I never thought of that."

"You better hope they're really people wearing masks and not avatars."

"They *are* avatars, Liz. You should see their creepy huge doll eyes and oversized pasty faces."

"I have a feeling I don't want to see them," said Liz, pulling a face. "Ever."

Feeling wired, Ivy scoped out the mall. She didn't see the avatars.

"I need to use the ladies' room," said Liz, and excused herself.

A few minutes after Liz left, Ivy picked up on the two avatars making a beeline for her.

Ivy's heartbeat accelerated.

Chapter 34

Joe Cohan grabbed a chair at Ivy's table, turned it around, straddled it, and crossed his arms on its back, facing her.

"We're gonna have to rape you again if you don't join us," he said.

"You can't threaten me," said Ivy, her nerves taut to their snapping point, wishing Liz was here. "That's illegal."

"I told you, we're from the metaverse. We have no laws in the metaverse," he said, staring at her with his glassy blue saucer eyes.

Like talking to a human-sized doll.

"You're not in the metaverse now," she said.

"Your laws don't apply to us."

"They do when you're here—like now."

Ed Vidor sat next to Cohan.

"If you don't join us, we'll kill your husband," said Vidor.

Ivy flinched.

"No, you won't," she managed to say after her initial shock.

"After we kill him, you'll be in charge of Rabbit World. And you can sell us real estate there."

"You can't buy anything. You're avatars."

"We can do whatever we want."

"I'm not going back to the metaverse, and I'm not selling you anything. You're a couple of criminals."

Ed Vidor laughed.

"Then we have no choice but to kill your husband," said Cohan.

"Leave my husband alone," she said.

"We're free to do whatever we want, and we will waste him."

"Get out of here," she said, clenching her teeth.

Her purse was on the floor, she realized. She didn't know if she would be able to reach her gun in time if they tried anything. Where was Liz? she wondered. What was taking her so long? She should be back by now.

"You can save his life if you become one of us," said Cohan.

"I don't want to become a stupid avatar," she said. "I want to be alive."

"We're alive."

"You're not human. You're things. You have no feelings. You rape and make threats and feel nothing."

"We do what we want. We're not enslaved by feelings like you. Freedom is more important than anything else."

Where the hell is Liz?

"Don't you understand?" she said. "I don't want to be like you.*"*

"Don't worry," said Vidor. "The transformation is harmless. There's nothing to be afraid of. And the end result is bliss, isn't it, Joe?"

"For sure," said Cohan, his plastic face expressionless, save for the perpetual half smile pasted on it.

They acted like they were on drugs, decided Ivy, feeling goose bumps of fear.

If she could pull out her gun, they'd leave. How fast could they move? Could they move fast enough to prevent her from withdrawing her gun from her purse? Was the speed of their reactions equivalent to that of humans?

Not only were they bigger than her, there were two of them versus one of her. Without the gun in her hand she didn't have a chance against them.

She cast around the crowded food court for a security guard.

She didn't think the avatars would try anything with so many people around. But if they really believed they could do anything they wanted, they might assault her in public.

"How about it?" said Vidor. "Do you want to become one of us?"

"No," said Ivy.

"You'll have to submit to an operation."

"I said, no. If you don't leave me alone, I'm calling security."

"All we're doing is having a discussion," said Cohan. "Even in your slave world, there's nothing illegal about having a discussion."

"Making threats is illegal," said Ivy. "You threatened me and my husband."

Vidor and Cohan stood up.

"We're leaving," said Vidor. "If you don't become one of us, I wouldn't want to be in your shoes. Why do you insist on fighting us? Why do you want it the hard way?"

"Another threat?" said Ivy.

"Why don't you tell the cops?"

She didn't answer.

She exhaled a weary sigh of relief as they strutted away.

She spotted Liz striding toward her with a flushed face.

"Did you see them?" asked Ivy, her visage earnest.

"See who?"

"The two avatars. They were sitting here with me."

"No."

"They were sitting across from me," said Ivy, frustrated.

"When I came back you were sitting alone."

"They were here, and they threatened me and Orion."

Liz shrugged. "What can I tell you? I guess they left before I returned."

"Damn," said Ivy, hangdog.

"Just because I didn't see them doesn't mean I don't believe they were here."

"Thanks, Liz. They're driving me crazy."

"Maybe that's what they want to do."

"Why? What did I do to them?"

"Dunno. Some people are just evil."

"They're avatars, not people."

"Avatars can be evil too." Liz paused, realizing how silly she sounded. "I guess," she added. "I mean, I don't know any avatars like you do. You know?"

"What took you so long?"

"My mother called," said Liz, remaining standing. "She fell and broke her hip. She came out here to visit me and was staying at a local hotel. Two of the maids found her on the floor next to her bed. She wants me to meet her at the hospital. She didn't sound good. She kept talking to me so I couldn't leave the restroom. Half the time she sounded incoherent. I had trouble understanding what she was saying. I gotta run."

"Is this the same mother that used to beat you so much when she got drunk that you left home?"

"She *is* my mother. And she came all the way out here to see me."

Liz bopped away, her retreating backpack disappearing among the crowd milling through the mall.

Sitting in the food court by herself, Ivy felt more alone than ever.

She wished she had a witness who had seen the avatars with her. It would confirm her sanity, which she was beginning to doubt.

And yet she *had* seen the two avatars sitting across from her, and they *had* threatened her and Orion.

And, damn it, they might try to kill her the next time they met.

Chapter 35

Against his better judgment, Orion had agreed to meet Riley again, who had asked for another meeting with him. Orion wanted to get to the bottom of the matter.

"What do you want?" said Orion, clad in stonewashed jeans and a red T, sitting behind his desk.

"I've been authorized to double my offer to purchase real estate in Rabbit World," said Riley, wearing a bespoke navy blue suit and a carmine tie.

"Your strongarm tactics didn't work, so you want to pay me more?"

"Strongarm tactics?" said Riley, dumbfounded. "What are you talking about?"

"Come on. You know what I'm talking about. You tried to sabotage my server."

Riley shook his head, at a loss. "You're coming at me from left field."

"You tried to infect it with a virus."

"I warn you, you're making actionable charges," said Riley, foaming at the mouth.

"Do you want me to believe you weren't behind the break-in?" said Orion, incredulous.

"I don't know anything about a break-in. I heard nothing on the news reports. You're making the whole thing up to throw me on the defensive."

"You knew I wouldn't report it to the cops because of the bad publicity it would bring on my IPO next week."

"I came here in good faith to bargain with you, and you're slinging these fantastic, unsubstantiated charges at me."

"If it wasn't you, then who was it?"

"How should I know? Maybe you have a disgruntled worker on your staff."

127

"You wanted Rabbit World to fail after I rejected your first offer to buy real estate there."

"Ridiculous. You're paranoid."

"After you failed to infect my server, you decided to raise your offer—because you know my IPO is gonna be a huge success, a fucking unicorn. And you want a piece of the action."

Riley bolted to his feet, his face twisted with rage. "I don't have to listen to these false accusations."

"The only thing false here is you."

"I demand you retract your accusations."

"I'm not retracting anything."

"If you say any of this in public, we will sue your ass off."

"Don't worry about it. What I said isn't going beyond this room."

Riley gathered himself after a fashion, adjusting his necktie, and sat down.

"Let's get back to negotiating," he said.

"There's nothing to negotiate. Your intimidation tactics didn't work, and doubling your offer won't either."

"What's wrong with you, man? You're leaving money on the table. What kind of a businessman are you?"

"Rabbit World is not gonna be a gambling mecca. Your presence will lose us money."

"On the contrary—"

"It's all about algorithms," cut in Orion.

"Algorithms?"

"My IT guys have it all figured out with algorithms. The algorithms say the presence of casinos in Rabbit World will lose us money in the long run."

"Ridiculous," said Riley, waving off Orion. "Don't pay attention to algorithms. Pay attention to your gut. People like to gamble, and they'll pay big money for the chance to do it. You'll rake in money like you wouldn't believe. How about this? We'll cut you in on our take. How many points to you want? How about two points? We'll give you two points of everything we make."

"It's not negotiable."

"How about three points?"

"No deal."

"Four points is as high as I go—and that's a steal for you."

"You're wasting your breath."

"Then why did you agree to see me?"

"To tell you not to try and sabotage my server again," said Orion, balling his fist on the desktop.

"Don't you understand? We had nothing to do with that. There's no proof it even happened. You could be making up this break-in for all I know."

Orion drank bottled water that was standing on his desktop. "You know I'm not."

"I know nothing of the sort."

Orion offered a lopsided smile. "You're not very convincing."

"Look, if you're worried about having Rabbit World linked to Casino Gem Planet—I can't imagine why you would be—but if you are, we can pay you in Bitcoin. Nobody will be able to trace it."

"It's not your name. It's what you provide. Rabbit World is not gonna be a gambling mecca. It would become like Vegas. If we let you in, all the other casinos will want in. That's not gonna happen."

"We can keep those other guys out. We know how to deal with them."

"We don't need gambling in Rabbit World."

"We'll pay you in Bitcoin with a shell company. There's no way anybody could trace the payment to us."

"You're spinning your wheels."

Riley lost his temper. "We'll accuse you of discrimination. The Justice Department will take care of you. They will destroy your reputation and put you out of business."

Orion wondered if Riley had been talking to the fed Bondurant, who had brought up the charge of discrimination. Had Riley sent Bondurant here earlier? How could Riley control a fed? Was Riley bribing the guy?

"I have the right to sell or refuse to sell to anyone I want," said Orion. "It's my property, not the government's. The government has no jurisdiction in the metaverse."

Riley thrust to his feet. "You're a stubborn little twerp. And a fucking fool. You're passing up the deal of a lifetime."

"Insulting me won't change my mind."

"You haven't heard the last of me," said Riley, and burst out of the office, ticked off.

Chapter 36

Ivy and Brody were walking down Arizona Avenue inspecting the fruits and vegetables in stands lined up in the middle of the road in the farmers' market.

Brody wasn't paying attention to the fruit. He was listening to Ivy.

"They're after me again," she said, examining a selection of avocados in a stall.

"The avatars?"

"Not only that, they sent a driverless car to stalk me."

"How do you know they were directing it?"

"I can't prove it. But who else would do it?"

"Not much we can do about it. You can't accuse a driverless car of stalking you. There has to be a human being driving it."

"They threatened me in the Century City mall, too."

"Did you get a good look at them?"

"I did."

"Do you still think they're avatars?"

"Definitely."

"Did you take a picture of them?"

She put down an avocado she had been inspecting in the stall and looked at him. "I never even thought of it."

"Try to get a picture of them next time."

"I hope there isn't gonna be a next time."

"Was anyone else with you when they threatened you?"

"Liz was with me—"

"She saw the avatars?" said Brody, all ears.

So far he had only her word that avatars were harassing her.

"You didn't let me finish," said Ivy. "Liz was eating lunch with me, but she was using the restroom when the avatars sat at my table. She said she never saw them."

131

Brody winced. "It would help to have a witness."

"You don't believe me?" said Ivy, nettled.

"I believe you. But the cops might have trouble believing you."

"I'm not going to the cops. I hired you to take their place."

"You can't press charges against these avatars without going to the cops."

"I'm not pressing charges. I just want them out of my life. That's where you come in. I want you to make them disappear."

They stood at a tomato stall.

"I'm not a hit man," he said under his breath, out of earshot of other shoppers.

"Get them to leave me alone. That's all I ask. I don't care how you do it."

"Once we know who these guys are and where they live, I can warn them off."

"They come from the metaverse."

"I don't know how to find people in the metaverse. But if they're here in the real world, they must have some place to stay while they're here."

"I can't take this much longer," said Ivy, squeezing a tomato until it burst in her hand.

"I'm sorry," she told the young, jeans-clad Hispanic saleswoman, who had large black eyes. "I'll pay for it."

Ivy gave the woman a twenty for the damaged tomato and walked to the next booth, wiping tomato juice off her hand with a handkerchief.

"Did they attempt to assault you again?" asked Brody.

"Not this time. There were a lot of people in the mall who would have witnessed it."

"Do you have the gun I gave you?"

"In my purse," she said, patting her purse. "There's one thing I don't understand."

"Yeah?"

"They keep telling me to report them to the cops."

"That makes no sense. Unless it was meant sarcastically, and they're daring you to do it."

"Why would they?"

"Another way to intimidate you and make you feel powerless."

"It didn't sound like he was being sarcastic."

"Are you sure these two aren't just a couple of guys wearing masks, instead of avatars?"

"They're not wearing masks," insisted Ivy. "They have doll faces because they're avatars. They're the same two creeps that assaulted me in Rabbit World. I'm getting fed up with nobody believing me," she said, becoming worked up.

"All right," said Brody, trying to calm her. "I'll check out the security cameras at the Century City mall to see if they recorded your meeting with the avatars."

"Don't you believe me?"

"I do. I want to see what these guys look like."

"I told you what they look like."

"I want to see for myself."

"If you don't believe me, maybe I should fire you."

"I need to see these guys in action, or at least a video of them tormenting you."

"Which is your way of saying you don't believe me," said Ivy, her hackles raised.

"I want to know what they look like so I can track them. If I had pictures of them, I could run their faces through facial recognition software."

Ivy collected herself. "It's just that I know how crazy it sounds. Sometimes I think I'm losing it."

"Don't worry. We'll get them."

She picked up a fresh mango and bought it from the fruit vendor.

Chapter 37

It didn't take long before the next attack.

Ivy was driving on PCH when she saw the black Charger in her rearview mirror.

Breaking into a sweat she hung a sharp right onto Topanga Canyon Boulevard to try to shake the tail, all bur running a red light. She checked out the rearview mirror and saw the Charger bearing down on her.

She accelerated up the winding canyon road.

She thought about calling Brody, but she was speeding and trying to negotiate the hairpin turns at the same time and unable to reach for her cell phone. She knew she was going too fast for these treacherous curves. She had no choice. The Charger was tailgating her, forcing her to increase her speed.

She drove faster, taking the next turn wide and almost careening off the road down into the pinyon-studded canyon. Eyes popping, she yanked the steering wheel in time to manage to stay on the road. The Charger closed in on her, its engine howling.

She avoided crashing into a pickup approaching from the opposite lane by swerving out of its way at the last minute. The twentysomething driver leaned on his horn, screaming obscenities at her. Her car fishtailed, burning rubber. She straightened out and accelerated up the canyon. The Charger rammed her rear bumper.

She lost control of the Volvo. It shot through the guardrail, was airborne for several seconds, then struck the ground with a thump, and, shuddering, careered down the steep coulee. She screamed, slamming on the brakes as the car skidded through chapparal and sagebrush, bumping down the rough dirt terrain.

The Volvo came to an abrupt halt as it slammed head-on into an elephantine outcropping.

Ivy heard a dull explosion. It was the airbag deploying, filling the driver's area of the car. She heard a thud like a football bouncing off a goal post and felt the airbag slam her face. The inflating airbag thrust her against her seat back, pinning her body. With the airbag smashed against her face, she could scarcely breathe, let alone move. Pinned to the seat, she couldn't exit the car, whose damaged gas tank, she feared, would leak gas and burst into flames.

She heard a noise above her in the coulee.

She wished she could see the rearview mirror to find out what was approaching her from above. The only thing she could see was the airbag jammed against her face, smothering her. She gasped for air.

After a while, she heard footsteps approaching, crunching chaparral. Paralyzed with fear, she wondered how she could escape the car. She struggled to move her hands, but the airbag was pinning them. The only things she could move were her feet in the foot well, which did her little good.

A waft of garlic brushed her nostrils.

Out of the corner of her eye, she glimpsed Joe Cohan staring at her as he tried to open her door that had been dented in the accident. When he contrived to open it, Ivy screamed in terror.

He ducked into the car and tried to yank the airbag off her and free her.

"We want your body," he said. "It's pointless to resist us. All resistance is futile."

"Get out of my car," she said, her face contorted with fear, barely able to speak with the airbag shoved in her face.

"Shut up."

Cohan wrestled with the airbag but couldn't budge it.

If she could only reach her cell phone in her purse, she decided. But she couldn't move either of her hands. The body-sized airbag had pinned both of them against her seat back, along with the rest of her body.

"Pleasure us with your body," said Cohan.

"Go to hell," said Ivy, her voice muffled by the airbag smashing her face.

With horror, she heard the passenger's-side door wheeze open.

Ed Vidor stooped in the doorway leering at her.

He crawled into the car and tried to pull her free from the airbag, but he couldn't get ahold of her body. Neither of her arms was visible thanks to the airbag that filled the driver's-side compartment.

"Let's pull a train on her," said Vidor, trying to devise a way to drag Ivy out of the car.

"We're gonna fuck your brains out," Cohan told Ivy. "You're gonna love every minute of it."

Ivy started. Sniffing the air she smelled gasoline. As if things weren't bad enough, she decided. The car could explode any second.

She struggled frantically to extricate herself from the airbag.

She wasn't the only one who was scared.

"It's gonna blow," said Vidor. "I smell gas."

He scrabbled backwards over the passenger seat out of the Volvo.

"I smell smoke," said Cohan. He backed away from the car. "Let's beat it."

"We need to get her out. Remember what the boss said. Get her and fuck her."

"No time. He didn't say anything about committing suicide by fire."

They were afraid of getting blown up, so they weren't invincible, decided Ivy. Maybe they were more vulnerable than they let on, even though they were avatars and thought they could do anything they wanted without facing the consequences.

Ivy didn't have time to think about it. She had to free herself before the Volvo turned into a fireball.

Weren't these airbags supposed to deflate at some point? she wondered, adrenaline coursing through her system. Why was it inflated? The accident was over. The Volvo couldn't move.

The airbag must be defective. It must have been one of the biggest airbags ever invented, she decided. She was having trouble breathing thanks to the airbag pressing against her face. And yet the airbag had saved her from the avatars. They couldn't pull her out from under it. But it could end up taking her life if she couldn't escape from the Volvo, which was about to explode.

The stench of gasoline was becoming stronger as more gas leaked out of the fuel tank onto the ground. One little spark would be enough to touch off the gas.

She had to pull herself together and think.

She couldn't slide out from under the airbag because her fastened seat belt prevented it. If she could reach the seat belt's buckle and release it, maybe she could slide out.

Gulping for air she slid her right hand toward the seat belt buckle, but she couldn't reach it. She got as far as the belt buckle on her jeans. An idea came to her, as she felt the buckle. What if she released the buckle and stabbed its prong into the airbag to burst it?

The smell of smoke became stronger. The fire could be spreading closer to the spilled fuel, she decided. Her heartbeat ramped up in response.

Setting her jaw with determination, she commenced attempting to unbuckle the belt holding up her jeans. There was hardly any room to maneuver her hand between the airbag and her body. She persisted in working the buckle. This was the last chance she would get, she knew. She had to make it count.

With dogged determination she managed to unbuckle her belt, which was the hardest part of her task. Grabbing the buckle she aimed the prong at the airbag and stabbed it, trying to pierce the airbag's nylon exterior.

Gritting her teeth she stabbed the airbag repeatedly until she felt it deflating.

Without the airbag suffocating her, she took a huge gulp of air, filling her lungs with oxygen.

She had no time to spare. She unbuckled her seat belt, snatched her purse, and scrabbled out of the car. Once outside, she leapt to her feet in the chapparal and bolted away from the Volvo, which could explode any second.

When the Volvo blew up, she hit the dirt, landing in underbrush, scratching her arms.

A fireball consumed the vehicle.

She looked up the canyon toward the guardrail that she had demolished with her hurtling car, expecting to see the avatars. All she saw was the breached, contorted metal guardrail.

The bastards were nowhere in sight. They must have left, figuring she would die in the blast. They were wrong, she decided with relief.

She wanted to call 911, but her cell phone's battery was dead.

Purse in hand, her face and arms smudged with dirt, she scrabbled up the canyon through the chapparal to the road.

Chapter 38

Brody didn't know if Ivy was crazy, but he suspected she might be losing her grip on sanity. He wanted to believe her about avatars stalking and threatening her, but it sounded impossible. And, he had to admit, she seemed neurotic. She acted like she was on the verge of a nervous breakdown.

Of course, if what she said was true about the avatars, he couldn't blame her.

He believed they had assaulted her in the metaverse. After that, he wasn't so sure. These so-called avatars stalking her could be guys in masks, which was more believable. Her insistence that they were indeed avatars led him to question her sanity.

To top it off, nobody else had seen the two avatars except her. None of the CCTV video recordings proved the two figures she had encountered were avatars.

He did believe two creeps were stalking her, probably guys in masks. Maybe they were trying to drive her nuts pretending to be avatars. But why? Did they hate her for some reason?

He decided to search for more security cameras that could have recorded her dealings with the alleged avatars.

Chapter 39

Brody was in the Century City mall casting around for security cameras that were aimed at the food court when he received Ivy's call.

"They tried to kill me," said Ivy, her voice charged.

"Are you all right?"

"I'm lucky to be alive. The airbag saved me."

"You were in a car accident?"

"The two avatars in their Charger drove me off the road into Topanga Canyon."

"Where are you now?"

"I'm on PCH in Malibu in a seafood restaurant's parking lot. I hitched a ride here."

"Have you called the cops?"

"I'm using a burner phone I bought in Malibu. I haven't called them yet."

"You need to tell them."

"I called Orion before you. He told me not to report to the cops that two avatars ran me off the road, because if I do I'll have to tell them about the assault in Rabbit World. He doesn't want any bad PR for Rabbit World."

"He sounds more concerned about Rabbit World than about you."

"He wants me to say a car ran me off the road, and I couldn't see the driver."

"They tried to murder you," said Brody. "Attempted murder is a lot different than an accident."

"He told me to say it was an accident, or not report it at all."

"He's telling you to lie to the cops. That could get you into trouble farther down the road."

"Look, I want Rabbit World to be as big a success as he does when it has an IPO next week. I have a lot of money invested in it."

"Are you sure it was the two avatars that drove you off the road."

"Positive. I saw their two pasty, plastic faces through their windshield."

"If you say it was an accident, you won't be able to make a case against the avatars for attempted murder with a motor vehicle."

"I know. That's why I'm calling you. What should I do?"

"Are you sure they deliberately forced you to crash?"

"Positive. We were both going fast. They rear-ended me before they rammed me through the guardrail."

"I would tell the cops they forced you off the road, if I was you."

"Orion says no. He doesn't want the avatars brought into this."

"Then how can you accuse the avatars of attempted murder?"

"I can't."

"Does Orion know what's at stake here? These avatars might try to kill you again, if you don't report them to the cops."

Ivy heaved a loud sigh of exasperation. "I know."

"Did you happen to get a picture of them while they were tailgating you?"

"I was too busy trying to escape them to do anything else. Where are you? It sounds like a lot of people are talking near you."

"I'm at the Century City mall trying to find CCTV footage that recorded your meeting with the avatars in the food court."

Brody noticed a fortyish guy staring at him twenty feet away. Clad in a charcoal grey business suit, with a military bearing, the guy sported a bushy black mustache and had intense black eyes. He approached Brody.

"I don't know how much more of this I can take," said Ivy, her voice tight. "I almost bought it today."

"Are the avatars following you?" asked Brody.

"I haven't seen them," answered Ivy, her voice quavering with fear. "Do you think they're stalking me:"

"Why would they stop?"

"They think I died when my car blew up."

"Are you sure that's what they think?"

"They were gone when I climbed up the canyon to the road. If they thought I was alive, they wouldn't have left."

"How can you be sure? Maybe they left because another car was approaching, and they didn't want to be seen in the vicinity of your accident."

"You're scaring me. Now I'm having second thoughts."

"I'm not trying to scare you. But they might have left the accident, believing you're alive."

"I didn't tell you this before, but they tried to pull me out of the wreckage and rape me."

"What?" said Brody, not sure he had heard her right.

"They only left because they smelled gas leaking from my rental."

Brody nodded. "OK. But that doesn't prove they left because they thought you died in the blast."

"I guess you're right," she said, uneasily.

"We may be able to use the accident to your advantage. Keep a low profile. If they don't see you around anymore, they might think you're dead."

"I'm taking an Uber home. I need to unwind. My blood pressure is off the charts."

She hung up.

The guy with the mustache was standing three feet away from Brody, fixing his gaze on him.

"I'm Special Agent Bondurant of the Federal Bureau of Investigation," said Bondurant, whipping his badge out of his jacket pocket and flashing it in front of Brody with a hand missing its pinky.

Chapter 40

"I'm working on an assignment," said Brody.

"So am I," said Bondurant. "Are you Scott Brody?"

"Yeah?" said Brody, his pulse quickening.

What would a fed want with him? he wondered with not a little apprehension. He had had several run-ins with the feebs while on previous assignments. Not good. Ever.

"Mind if I ask you a few questions?" said Bondurant.

"I'm a little busy."

"This won't take long."

"What do you want to know?"

Bondurant didn't beat around the bush. "Were you at the Rabbit World server's office?"

Brody started. How could the feds know he had been involved in the shootout at the server's office? Or was Bondurant taking a shot in the dark?

"No," Brody lied, knowing he was committing perjury by lying to a fed.

Bondurant searched Brody's face. "Something mysterious happened there."

Could the feds possibly know he had whacked the team of assailants that had tried to sabotage the Rabbit World server? wondered Brody. Had the assailants been working for the feds? What the hell was he getting into? Why would the feds want to infect the Rabbit World server?

"Why do you think so?" said Brody.

"A team of good men disappeared."

"Were they your men?"

"Eyes only. None of your business."

"If something happened to these guys, why wasn't it reported on the news?"

"Maybe the media don't know about it."

"If they don't know about it, how do *you* know about it?"

"I work for the federal government. We have a lot more sources than your run-of-the-mill fake news media."

"I know even less than the media."

"You're into this up to your eyeballs," said Bondurant, with an edge to his voice. "We can make your life unpleasant."

"Are you threatening me?"

"Let's put it this way. You don't want us as enemies."

"I'm trying to help you out. You're the one making threats."

"You see my hand?" said Bondurant, holding up the hand that had no pinky.

"What about it?"

"I didn't lose my finger by accident. I cut it off after I failed an assignment. I've never failed another assignment. And I won't fail this one."

"Good for you."

The guy was creepy, decided Brody. A fanatic. Fanatics meant trouble in Brody's book.

"To some people a job is just a job," said Bondurant. "To me my job is my life. More important than my life, that is."

"And my life, too."

"Your attempt at humor is feeble."

"I didn't get my eight hours last night."

"Not to put too fine a point on it, you can't win against us."

"Does the government got something to hide? Is that why you're warning me off?"

Bondurant got in Brody's face. "You're the one with something to hide. And we're gonna find out what it is."

"I'm just a PI doing my job. There's no law against that, is there?"

"I got my eyes on you," said Bondurant, pointing at his own eyes with two fingers then pointing at Brody's.

"Sounds like harassment."

"We're the law. The law doesn't harass anyone. *We* don't harass anyone. *We* do our job."

"Someone's harassing my client."

"Are you saying it's us?" said Bondurant, combative.

"You're twisting my words."

"You need to back off."

"Back off?" said Brody, puzzled.

"Back off Rabbit World. It's off limits to you."

"Actually, it isn't. It's the metaverse. And you can't tell me to back off the metaverse. It's not in your jurisdiction."

Bondurant started to walk away. "You're getting in over your head. Don't tell me I didn't warn you."

Chapter 41

Ivy confronted Orion in their living room. Orion was wearing a bone mic and had been talking to someone on the phone when she walked in.

"Am I interrupting?" said Ivy, worked up because of her hairbreadth escape from death in the canyon.

"Of course not," said Orion. "I was just finishing a call."

"I'm getting sick of you telling me what to do," she said. "Somebody ran me off the road. They tried to kill me. And all you can say is, keep your mouth shut."

"We don't want Rabbit World's reputation smeared. If you tell the cops avatars from Rabbit World are trying to kill you, people will think I'm married to a psycho. It will reflect badly on me."

"Is that what you think?" said Ivy, outraged. "That I'm a psycho?"

"What do you expect me to think? Avatars don't try to kill people in the real world."

"If that's true, why did my rental go off the road and blow up?"

"Because you had an accident. Accidents happen."

"It was no accident. They forced me off the road and tried to rape me afterward," said Ivy, fit to be tied.

"You don't know what you're saying. You're too wired. Get a grip."

"I almost died today. What do you expect?"

"Don't tell anyone, is all I'm saying."

"And let them do it all over again? Is that what you want? The attacks to continue?"

"Have a drink and take it easy. You don't want to have a nervous breakdown, do you?"

Orion poured a scotch for both of them.

"Nobody's having a breakdown," said Ivy. "I ought to pull my money out of Rabbit World. Then you're the one who's gonna have a breakdown."

"You wouldn't dare," said Orion, and tossed off his drink.

"If you keep insisting I'm nuts, why shouldn't I take back my money?"

"You're overreacting. Rabbit World is gonna be a big success. Just don't bring up these avatars you keep seeing. I can't afford to have the public think my wife's crazy. The IPO will tank next week if they do."

Ivy took a pull on her scotch and coughed thanks to her tight throat.

"I'm not overreacting," she said. "Rabbit World is dangerous. I know from personal experience."

"No harm, no foul. You weren't physically injured. Just forget about it and move on with your life. That's what everyone else does."

Ivy stared at him. "What if I told you I'm packing a gun, because I'm living in constant fear for my life?"

"What?" said Orion, taken aback.

"It's true."

"Another one of your overreactions. Avatars can't attack you in the real world."

Ivy fished out her gun from her purse. "Then why am I forced to carry this?"

Orion widened his eyes. "Put that away this minute. You're going off the deep end."

"I have the right to defend myself," she said, brandishing the gun.

"Put that away. You don't know what you're doing. You might hurt someone."

"Nobody's gonna assault me again."

"You wanna play Annie Oakley, do it somewhere else."

Ivy fired a bullet into the wall behind Orion's head. Orion flinched.

"What the fuck are you doing, Ivy?" he cried.

"I'm not afraid to use this thing."

"You put a damn hole in the wall," said Orion, eyeballing the damaged drywall. "You could've hit me. You're not *going* nuts. You already *are* nuts."

"You're the one that should be hunting down those avatars and shooting them, not me. You're my husband, and you do nothing about the assault. Time to grow a pair."

"I'm not a cop. What do you expect me to do? They'll throw me in the joint if I shoot anyone. Can you imagine what would happen to Rabbit World if its owner—*me*—shot someone? Nobody would go near it."

"Rabbit World. Rabbit World. Everything is Rabbit World with you. What about your family?"

"Our family needs Rabbit World to pay the bills."

"Sociopathic avatars are terrorizing Rabbit World. How can you *not* feel guilty about selling property there?"

"What's your suggestion? Starving to death? I'm trying to make a living for us. Failure is not an option."

Ivy drew a bead on Orion's face.

"What are you doing?" said Orion, terrified.

"Do you think I'm crazy?"

"That's not funny, Ivy. Put the gun down," said Orion, the blood draining from his sweaty face.

"Answer me. Do you think I'm crazy?"

"No. You're stressed out."

"Are you planning on committing me?"

"Whatever gave you that idea? I don't like answering questions with a gun pointed at my head."

"I'll fight it, if you try to have me committed."

"Don't worry about it. Put down that gun," said Orion, tugging at his collar, grimacing.

Ivy lowered her pistol.

"Never point a loaded gun at anyone, even in jest," said Orion, breathing easier. "You almost gave me a heart attack. You don't know the basic rules of gun safety. Where did you get that gun, anyway?"

"I got it, and it's mine. That's all you need to know."

"You point that thing at me again, and I'm not gonna commit you. I'm gonna have you thrown in the joint for attempted murder. Give me one good reason I shouldn't do that now."

"Because you know it would look bad for Rabbit World if you had your wife busted, and your IPO would fail next week. That's two reasons," said Ivy, gloating.

"If you're done throwing your tantrum, I have work to do."

She stood staring at him without saying a word.

"Or are you gonna shoot me?" he said.

"So you could have me committed? Think again."

Gun in hand, she stalked out of the living room.

Orion blew out his cheeks, dug a handkerchief out of his rear trouser pocket, and wiped sweat from his forehead.

Chapter 42

The twentysomething man with blue eyes and wavy blue hair was wearing a VR headset and haptic gloves as he balanced himself on a surfboard that was suspended from wires attached to the ceiling in his massive penthouse office in Menlo Park in Silicon Valley. He was riding the stationary surfboard while he watched himself surfing in his VR helmet.

He was also talking into a bone mic.

"Bondurant?"

"Nieman?"

"What happened at the Rabbit World server?" said Lazarus Nieman, holding his arms up at his sides, balancing himself as he rode imaginary waves.

"I'm trying to find out," said Bondurant.

"Three men don't up and disappear."

"I believe the private dick working for the Kingstons knows more than he's saying."

"What does he have to do with it?"

"I'm trying to figure it out. I know he's working for both of them. This guy is armed and dangerous. Orion Kingston might be using him as a sort of guard."

"What's his name?"

"Brody. Scott Brody. I'm convinced he knows more than he's letting on."

"Those guys I sent to the server were professionals. They know how to use artillery. Explain to me how they can just vanish like they never existed?"

"I can't find any trace of them."

"That's because they're pros. I didn't want anyone to trace them back to me, in case they were busted."

"They weren't busted. The cops have no record of it. They also don't have any record of the server office being broken into."

"Then what the hell happened to them? I paid those bums beaucoup Bitcoin to infect Rabbit World's server without getting caught."

"The cops didn't catch them, I'm sure."

"Did my team accomplish their mission?"

"I have no reason to believe so. As far as I know, Orion's going ahead with his IPO next week."

"Then we're back to square one. Where is my team of saboteurs?"

Bondurant hawked. "I'm looking for them, sir. They could be John Does lying in the morgue right now, nobody the wiser because they weren't carrying IDs."

"Check the morgue and find out."

"No problem. How do you know they didn't bug out with all the Bitcoin you gave them?"

"Because I didn't give them any yet. The deal was, I pay them *after* they do the job."

"I'll keep looking for them."

"I may need you to take their places and infect the server."

"That'll cost you."

Nieman smiled. "Do you think I can't afford you?"

"A billionaire like you can afford whatever you want."

"And don't you forget it."

"What do you want me to do with Brody?"

"Is he a problem?" said Nieman, steadying himself on his surfboard as he rode a twenty-foot wave in Waimea Bay in Oahu.

"He could be. I did a little research on him. He was charged with murder several times in his past, but never found guilty."

"Was he innocent?"

"He might be innocent of those charges, but he has definitely whacked people. He isn't the type of guy that's gonna back down."

"I'll give his name to the algorithms. They'll know how to deal with him."

"Sure," said Bondurant, not impressed.

"How do you want to handle him?"

"He thinks I'm a fed, so he should stay out of my way."

"He thinks you're a fed?" said Nieman in surprise.

"I told him I was."

"You told *me* you were ex-MI6."

"That happens to be true. I did spook work for them when I lived in the UK. I'm also ex-SAS."

"Then you're not really a fed."

"I've done work for them as an independent contractor."

"You're a mercenary."

"Aren't we all?" said Bondurant with a chuckle.

"Does Brody believe you're a fed?"

"Why not? I showed him a badge."

"If he gets in your way, remove him."

"I thought you wanted to consult your algorithms first," said Bondurant with a needling voice.

"I'm not somebody to fuck with. Fuck me, *fuck you*."

"Understood. No harm meant."

"I need *everyone* to understand that."

"I understand."

"You better."

"No problem."

"No IPO for Kingston's Rabbit World next week. He's taking his surname literally. I'm the *king* of the metaverse. He isn't. Better yet, I'm the *master* of the metaverse."

"You got it."

"If he doesn't get the message, we switch into hardball mode."

"My specialty," said Bondurant with a wheezy laugh.

"What about his wife Ivy? Has she gone to the cops about her assault at Rabbit World?"

"No."

"What's holding her back?"

"Her husband, I bet. The bad PR of an assault would tank his IPO next week."

"Let me tell you something. Success is built on piles of dead bodies. You don't get a ton of money in this world without breaking laws. I have no qualms about taking out the competition. That includes Orion Kingston."

"You want me to take him out?" said Bondurant, hanging on Nieman's response.

"Not yet. The algorithms say it's not necessary. He's got an Achilles heel. A neurotic wife. Play on that. If that doesn't work, we go to plan B."

Nieman stepped off his surfboard and stood on the penthouse's lush aquamarine carpet. He wore a thick coating of makeup on his face, affording him a pallid vampiric complexion that was perfectly smooth thanks to Botox injections. He removed his headset to reveal the bright blue contact lenses he wore that obscured his pupils and made his eyes appear unnaturally large. He stared out the picture window at the city below, an avatar eying the metaverse—*his* metaverse.

Chapter 43

Ivy was sitting at her vanity peeking over a wall of pill bottles stacked in front of her, as if the pills protected her from the world. Or as if they immured her in a prison of drugs from which there was no escape.

She studied her image in the mirror, the image of a terrified woman teetering on the edge of sanity behind rows of orange pill bottles.

Was she losing her mind, seeing avatars stalking her where there were none? she wondered. Was Orion trying to destroy her by telling her not to report the stalking avatars to the cops? Was she, in fact, paranoid? Could she trust anyone?

She studied the labels of the pill bottles stacked in front of her. The pills offered no answers. They weren't curing her problems. They couldn't protect her from the real world. They couldn't protect her from the avatars. Could they protect her from anything?

In disgust she swiped the pill bottles off the vanity. They landed on the hardwood floor and rolled helter-skelter. Some of the unsecured childproof bottlecaps flew off, allowing pills to escape onto the floor.

She had almost shot Orion, she thought, sweating. She wondered if she could bring herself to kill him. If she got angry enough at him, could she pull the trigger? She hoped she never found out. Why was she even thinking such thoughts? They were bumming her out no end.

She had to do something about those avatars. She couldn't allow them to continue to stalk her, which they were hellbent on doing.

She stared at her face in the mirror. Was this what it was like to suffer a nervous breakdown? A feeling of defenselessness suffused her. Would the avatars come to her house to attack her? She craned her head around her bedroom suspiciously, wondering if they were watching her even now.

She started when her cell phone chimed in her purse on her bed.

She got up from the vanity and checked the caller ID. She wasn't going to answer unless she recognized the caller's name. It was Liz.

"Let's get something to eat," said Liz.

"I'm not leaving my house," said Ivy.

"What? What are you talking about? Why can't you leave your house?"

"It's not safe to go out."

"Of course, it's safe. It's not a zombie apocalypse outside. What's got into you?"

"Those avatars are waiting outside to ambush me."

"Can you see them out your window?" said Liz, disconcerted.

"No. But they're out there waiting for me."

"Maybe you're suffering from PTSD. Have you seen your therapist?"

"Orion doesn't want me to discuss the rape with anyone."

"What a creep. Subjects you discuss with your therapist aren't supposed to leave the shrink's office."

"I'm just telling you what Orion said."

"Like I said, he's a creep."

Liz had never hit it off with Orion, decided Ivy.

"I shouldn't go outside with the avatars lying in wait for me," said Ivy.

"It can't be that bad."

"It is."

"Bring your gun if you feel that way."

"Every time I go outside they attack me. They ran me off the road in their Charger a little while ago and left me for dead in Topanga Canyon," said Ivy, her voice cracking.

"Jesus H. Christ. Did you report them to the cops?" cried Liz.

"Orion told me not to."

"Fuck him. He's telling you the wrong things. He's doing you more harm than good when he tells you this stuff."

"I dunno," said Ivy, rubbing her forehead, grimacing.

"He's gaslighting you. The bastard. Is he in the house with you?"

"Yeah."

"Don't stay home another minute. Get out of there, Ivy. He's gonna get you committed."

"He said he wouldn't."

"Then why's he gaslighting you?"

"You said that, not me."

"Mark my words. You could be in more danger from him than from those avatars stalking you."

"They tried to kill me. They wanted me to blow up in my car," said Ivy, shivering with anxiety at the memory.

"You need to chill. Meet me at the pier. We'll grab some seafood."

"Is it safe?"

"Of course, it is. *I'm* the one who thinks the world's gonna end any minute. If *I* think it's safe, it must be safe."

"Point taken," said Ivy with a smile flickering across her face.

That was what she liked about Liz, decided Ivy. Liz had a sense of humor—even if it was gallows humor.

"Don't let Orion gaslight you," said Liz. "Go to the pier and get some fresh air. You'll feel much better afterward."

"My rental got totaled in the accident."

"Get an Uber."

"The avatars will attack me. They tried to pull me out of my rental and rape me after it crashed."

"Stop thinking about it. You're gonna drive yourself crazy." Liz paused. "Are you sure the avatars were driving the Charger?"

"Positive."

156

"Maybe you're getting snow crashed."

"Huh?"

"*Snow crashed.* That's when you see something for real, and then start seeing it everywhere even when it's not there. You saw the avatars in Rabbit World, and now you're seeing them everywhere."

"This is serious, Liz. I escaped death by a hairbreadth today."

"I *am* serious. It's over, and you're still alive, so let's do lunch. Don't go full-bore wacko on me."

"You think I'm losing it?"

"I was joking. You're no crazier than I am. Hell, I'm the one who thinks the world is gonna end any minute, not you."

"True."

"I know, right? That's me all over. Apocalyptic Liz."

Ivy laughed despite herself. It didn't really sound like a laugh. She didn't know what it sounded like, for that matter. Maybe like she was gagging.

"I guess," said Ivy.

"Orion is bad for your health. You need to get away from him."

"He's my husband. I live with him."

"He's also gaslighting you."

"He wants to do what's best for his company."

"And that means it's OK to gaslight you? Come on, Ivy."

"Of course not. I didn't say that."

Liz paused two beats. "I'm concerned about you, Ivy. I don't want you to end up going down the rabbit hole."

"Whether you believe me or not, the avatars are trying to kill me."

"I believe you," said Liz, hastily. "But you can't hide in your house for the rest of your life because you're afraid of being attacked. What if they know where you live?"

"What?" said Ivy, her voice quavering with anxiety.

"Oh no. I didn't mean that. I was just saying," said Liz, wishing she could take back her words.

"They know where I live?" said Ivy, as if in a daze.

"I have no idea. The point is, you need to get outside. You can't lock yourself inside your house. It's not good for you. Let's do lunch."

Ivy hung up. If the avatars knew where she lived, staying home wouldn't do her any good, she decided. They could mount another attack against her any time now.

Chapter 44

Instead of driving to meet Liz at the pier, Ivy drove to her therapist's office in Beverly Hills.

"Do you have an appointment?" said the round-faced Asian American receptionist, wearing a black and yellow dress and sporting canary yellow fingernails.

"No," said Ivy. "This is an emergency."

"Your name?"

"Ivy Kingston. Please, I have to see him now," said Ivy, making for Dr. Jamal Harris's shut door behind the receptionist.

"Wait till I call him," said the receptionist, waving at Ivy to get her to stop.

The receptionist snagged her phone and called Harris.

Ivy hesitated before Harris's door, biting her lower lip with impatience.

"All right," said the receptionist. "The doctor will see you now."

Ivy opened the door and entered Harris's office.

A fortysomething African American wearing red plastic-framed glasses with round lenses sat behind his desk eying her. On the thin side, he wore a black blazer, a white T that said I Love LA, and blue jeans.

Ivy headed straight to the therapist's couch and lay down on her back.

Harris got up from behind his desk and took a seat beside her.

"What seems to be the problem, Ivy?" he said in a melodious voice.

"I want to know if I'm having a breakdown," said Ivy, her face twisted with worry.

"What makes you think you are?"

"Two avatars assaulted me in the metaverse."

"When was this?"

"At the beginning of the week."

"Why didn't you tell me sooner?"

"My husband told me not to tell anyone."

"What happened?"

"It's a long story."

Ivy debated whether she should tell Harris everything.

"Go on," said Harris, gazing at her with his mournful brown eyes.

Ivy decided she had to tell him the truth, or why had she even bothered to come here?

"After the assault, the two avatars stalked me in the real world."

At least he wasn't looking at her like she had three eyeballs dangling out of her head on their optic nerves, decided Ivy.

"How did they stalk you?" he said.

"In their car. I caught them following me as I was driving. They later confronted and threatened me."

"Hmm. Are you sure they're avatars? Couldn't they be human?"

"They have weird doll heads with blank faces and large eyes with no pupils."

"How do you know they're not wearing masks because of the pandemic?"

"They look just like the two avatars that assaulted me in Rabbit World. What are the chances?"

Harris rubbed his chin, thinking.

"Have they tried to assault you again?" he asked.

"They ran me off the road and tried to kill me."

Harris stiffened in his seat. "Have you gone to the police?"

"My husband doesn't want me to."

"Attempted murder is a serious charge. Why didn't you go to the cops?"

"My husband again. He doesn't want bad PR for his company Rabbit World."

"I see. How do you explain avatars being in the real world?"

"I can't explain it. That's why I'm wondering if I'm cracking up," said Ivy, staring at the ceiling.

"You're not 'cracking up,' as you put it, or you wouldn't be asking such a question. The very fact that you can doubt your sanity means you're sane."

"Oh."

"You could be suffering from PTSD, though, thanks to the avatars assaulting you in Rabbit World. The PTSD could lead you to imagine avatars are stalking you in the real world."

"I'm snow crashed?" said Ivy with an ironic smile.

"What? I don't know the term."

"My friend Liz said I was snow crashed. Look, I know the avatars are stalking me. I saw them and I talked to them. I'm not imaging them."

"You're under tremendous stress. When this happens, your imagination can get the better of you."

"I'm not imagining them. They tried to kill me," said Ivy, her nerves frazzled.

"Why would they do that?"

"They wanted me to become one of them. I refused. So they're gonna kill me."

"Why do they want you to become one of them?" said Harris, holding his chin with interest.

"So I can be free, they said."

"You're already free."

"They're totally free, according to them. They don't have any laws in the metaverse, so they do whatever they want, including assaulting me."

"Sounds like chaos."

"What they really want is to keep assaulting me with impunity. They can only do that in the metaverse."

Harris considered her words. "Do you feel like everyone's out to get you?"

Ivy looked up at him as he sat beside her. "Not *everyone*. Just those two avatars."

"What about humans? Do you feel like humans are out to get you?"

"No, I don't," said Ivy, staring at Harris with resentment. "Are you saying I'm paranoid?"

"I'm trying to understand. Do you feel like you imagined the avatars stalking you?"

"Not at all. I saw them, and they tried to kill me by running me off the road in the canyon."

"There's a fine line between imagination and reality. Often they blend together in a twilight area, at which time you have difficulty distinguishing them."

Ivy craned toward him. "Are you talking about me, as opposed to other people?"

"I'm talking about *you* in the general sense—not only you, Ivy."

Ivy relaxed more or less, laying her head back down on the couch.

"I can tell the difference between reality and dreams," she said. "I know what I saw."

Harris shifted in his seat. "Do you feel better now that you've talked about it?"

"Well, I don't feel worse. Better? I'm not so sure. The avatars are gonna continue to stalk me whether I came here or not," she said, sitting up.

"You shouldn't let them alter your lifestyle. Continue to live your life as you always have. Fear is never the answer."

"They don't fear anything. They think they're invincible and above the law."

"A couple of supermen?"

Ivy nodded yes.

"Am I the only one you've told about this, other than your husband?" asked Harris.

"No," she answered. "I told a friend and a private investigator."

"Probably best not to tell anyone else."

"Why?"

"People might think you're losing it."

"You said I'm OK."

"They're not professionals, like I am," said Harris with a knowing smile.

Chapter 45

After Ivy left his office Harris took a seat behind his desk and placed a call on his cell phone.

"She was just here," he said.

"And?"

"She wanted to know if she's going off the deep end. She suspects she is."

"Why?"

"Because she's seeing avatars stalking her and trying to kill her."

"Did she tell anyone else about these avatars harassing her?"

"She told one of her friends, you, and uh—a private detective."

"Yeah, I know about him. That all?"

"Those are the only ones she named."

"Did she go to the cops?"

"She said she didn't."

"Do you believe her?"

"Why would she lie to her psychiatrist? It would defeat the purpose of hiring me."

"Point taken. How about the media? Did she talk to any reporters?"

"She didn't mention anything about the media."

There was a pause on the line.

"Does she believe she's headed for a nervous breakdown?" said Orion.

Harris adjusted his spectacles on his prominent nose. "She fears she is. That's why she came to me."

"And what do you think? Is she cracking up?"

"She's headed in that direction," said Harris, shifting in his seat uncomfortably, his spectacle lenses beginning to steam up as he felt hot under the collar.

"Is she gonna cause problems?"

"What's your definition of *problems*?"

Orion hung fire. "Let me rephrase. Is she gonna be a liability to my company?"

"If she has a nervous breakdown?"

"Yeah."

"I'm a psychiatrist. I don't know anything about public relations for metaverse companies."

Didn't the guy even care about his wife's health? wondered Harris. His company, always his company.

"Anything else I should know?" said Orion.

"You know I'm breaking every medical rule in the book by telling you what she confided in me, her personal physician?"

"I need to know who she's telling about her assault because if she tells the cops or the media, my company's IPC next week will end up as a humiliating failure. My career will be destroyed forever. I don't trust her to tell me the truth."

"You don't believe your own wife?" said Harris in astonishment.

"Not on this matter. I believe she's more honest with you, her doctor."

"I could be disbarred from the medical profession because of what I just told you about what she told me in confidence."

"I'm aware of it, and I appreciate your help. I can't have her blabbing to everyone about how unsafe Rabbit World is."

"Are you paying me by direct deposit?"

"Indeed I am. Fifty grand wired into your account from a shell company, as we agreed upon to keep me informed about Ivy."

"What's the name of the shell company?"

"XBY Systems."

"When?"

"Why are you in such a hurry?"

"I have bills to pay, Orion. My main squeeze is high maintenance."

Orion chuckled. "Aren't they all?"

"Nothing like her, believe me," said Harris, brushing sweat from his broad forehead with the back of his hand. "I already owe over two hundred thousand dollars on my credit cards thanks to her."

"Fifty grand for a little intel. You don't come cheap, Jamal."

"I told you, I could lose my license if anyone found out about this."

"Don't worry. The money will be in your account this afternoon."

"I do worry, Orion. I do worry."

"One final question. Do you believe Ivy should be committed because she is mentally unbalanced?"

"In my opinion, no."

"Not yet, you mean. But she's getting there."

"That's not what I said—"

"It's what *I* said, if you take my drift."

Orion terminated the call.

A puzzled expression on his face, Harris pocketed his cell phone. It sounded like Orion wanted his wife committed.

Some days Harris wished he had never met Orion Kingston at Stanford where they had both graduated with bachelor degrees. Harris had struggled all his life to become a psychiatrist. Now he could lose his profession in the blink of an eye thanks to Orion's compromising his integrity.

Who would ever believe he had fought his way out of Compton, earned a scholarship to Stanford, and graduated to become a psychiatrist for wealthy, pampered celebrities and well-heeled Hollywood rich kids? Harris wondered. There were days he didn't believe it himself. Against all odds, including a background of poverty, he had accomplished a miracle, as far as he was concerned, by real zing his life's dream of becoming a psychiatrist. But it could all come crashing down in a nanosecond if the authorities got wind of his ethical lapses in his well-respected profession.

You have no idea how I worry, Orion.

It wasn't just Orion that was threatening his career, Harris knew. He couldn't put the blame completely on Orion. He had to shoulder some of the blame himself.

Harris had a weakness for beautiful women. He was paying the price for it and would continue to pay as long as he kept seeing Janine and ponying up for her West Hollywood penthouse rent, her Verde Mantis Lamborghini Aventador with its monster V12 engine, her pricy Beverly Hills lawyers, and whatever other luxury the woman of leisure had a yen for. The lightning speed with which she burned cash never ceased to astound him.

And there was no end to her spending in sight.

Which meant additional payoffs under the table and compromises of his professional ethics to keep her happy.

Chapter 46

Ivy met Liz for lunch at a seafood restaurant on the Santa Monica Pier. They sat at a table outside on the patio basking in the sunshine and the cool sea breeze, bawling gulls wheeling and swooping overhead. A brown pelican dove into the ocean, stunned small fish near the surface with the impetus of its crash, knocking them senseless, scooped them up in its pouch, flew off, drained the water out of its pouch, and consumed the fish.

"I'm glad you could make it," said Liz, sitting opposite Ivy. "Getting out of your house is good for you."

"I had to go to my psychiatrist," said Ivy, digging into a scrumptious halibut steak. She squirted a slice of lemon onto the halibut.

"What did he say?"

"Basically, he just listened and commiserated with me. Which is what he usually does."

"If you want advice, I'll give it to you. Stay away from your house."

"What?" said Ivy, puzzled after swallowing a morsel of tender halibut. "What are you talking about?"

Liz leaned across the tabletop toward Ivy and spoke in hushed tones. "Orion is trying to gaslight you. Stay away from him. I know the world may end before he succeeds, but I wouldn't count on it. I wouldn't go anywhere near him, if I was you."

Ivy smiled with amusement. "You watch too many movies."

Liz leaned back in her chair. "I'm telling you he is. It's so obvious. I can't understand why you can't see it. Maybe you're too close to him to realize what he's doing."

"And what *is* he doing?"

"He wants everybody to think you're nuts so he can have you committed and get his dirty hands on your money."

"That's not what he wants. He wants me to keep my mouth shut about the avatars attacking me so his IPO is a boffo certainty next week."

"That's what he wants you to think," said Liz, cocking her eyebrow archly.

Ivy thought about it. "The thing that bothers me about him is he doesn't seem to believe that I was assaulted in Rabbit World."

Liz nodded. "One of his tactics to gaslight you."

Ivy became sullen. "We had a big fight today. It was bad."

"Good. Stay away from him. He's poison to you. Can't you see that?"

"I don't know what got into me," said Ivy, becoming wan and throwing down her fork in despair. "I pulled a gun on him."

"Jesus. Really?"

"I felt like he was trying to control me, to smother me."

"He is. You're seeing the truth. You were right to pull a gun on him."

"Don't say that," said Ivy, dumbfounded. "I shouldn't have done it, but I blew my cool."

"I'm telling you, the best thing for you is to stay away from him. Don't go home. You can stay at my apartment, if you want. That is, if you don't mind sleeping on the floor next to a bunch of canned goods I have stockpiled all over my bachelor apartment for Armageddon."

"He's not as bad as you make him sound, though I resent him for not believing me and ordering me not to tell the cops."

"It's all part of his scheme to gaslight you," said Liz, and gave an emphatic nod.

Ivy stood up.

"I need to use the restroom. Could you watch my purse?" she said, leaving her purse on the tabletop.

"No problem."

Ivy needed to digest Liz's words in private. Entering the restroom she thought Liz was exaggerating about Orion. Ivy believed Orion was more concerned about the success of his IPO than about having her committed. The failure of his IPO would be a blow to his ego that would crush him. She understood that and cut him slack. But, in the end, maybe she was being too understanding and cutting him too much slack. Maybe Liz was right about Orion to some extent, but not about the gaslighting. Ivy couldn't bring herself to believe Liz about that.

Ivy studied her face's reflection in the mirror over the sinks as she washed her hands. It was unsettling. Her visage indicated she could be going crazy. Or was she reading something into it that wasn't there? Either way, she didn't look well. She wished she could relax.

How could she relax? She was terrified the avatars would assault her again—maybe even kill her next time, like they had almost accomplished by forcing her car off the road in the canyon.

Relaxation for her was out of the question as long as she knew the two avatars were at large and hunting her. But then again, if they thought she had died in the car accident, they would stop stalking her.

She needed to keep a low profile. Maybe if she hid somewhere, the avatars would go back to Rabbit World and she could resume living a normal life. But eventually she would have to return to Rabbit World because it was her job to sell real estate there.

There was no easy solution that she could see.

No wonder she looked like crap. Was this what relentless fear did to your face? she wondered, examining her hollow eyes and creased forehead.

Despite feeling miserable, she put on her best face and headed out of the restroom. It was never a good idea to look too wretched when you mingled with the public.

Chapter 47

Unable to find CCTV footage of Ivy's meet with the two avatars in the food court, Brody rode the elevator down to the parking level where he had left his Mini in the Century City mall's underground parking garage.

He had spotted two security cameras with the food court in their sights, but the owners of both private establishments—one a jewelry store, the other an optometrist's office—had refused to allow him to watch the CCTV footage. If they wanted to keep their videotapes private, so be it. Nothing Brody could do about it. He was a private detective and didn't wield the authority of a cop.

As Brody reached his Mini, his cell phone vibrated in his trouser pocket.

"Brody, help me," said Ivy, her voice fraught.

Brody started. "Where are you?"

"I'm locked in the trunk of a car."

Brody couldn't believe his ears. "What?"

Ivy repeated herself, louder this time.

"How the hell did you get locked in a trunk?" said Brody.

"Kidnapers."

"Are you sure it's locked? Try to push it open."

"Even if it's open, it won't do me any good."

"What do you mean?"

"The car is speeding down a road. If I jump out, I'll break my neck."

"What about your gun? Where is it?"

"I don't know."

"What?" said Brody in surprise. "You had it in your purse."

"It's not there anymore. I checked."

"What happened to it?"

"I wish I knew."

"All right, calm down. Who's kidnaping you?"

"The two avatars, I think."

"'Think'? Don't you know?"

"Whoever it was snuck up on me from behind and covered my mouth and nose with a handkerchief doused in some liquid. Whatever was on the handkerchief knocked me out cold. The next thing I know, I'm stuffed in this trunk suffocating on gas fumes," she said, and coughed.

"The handkerchief could've had ether or chloroform on it."

"I think it was ether. Can I die from it?"

"Are you still breathing it?"

"No."

"Then you won't die from it."

"Great. Then I can die from carbon monoxide poisoning in the trunk."

"Not necessarily. Car trunks are rarely airtight, and the exhaust isn't being pumped directly into the trunk."

"I need your help, Brody," she pleaded.

"At least you have your cell," said Brody, clambering into his Mini's driver's seat. "I can track your signal. Don't hang up."

"I think I'm gonna puke. The noxious gas fumes are suffocating me."

"Do you have any idea where you are?"

"None. All I know is, the car's in motion. I can't see anything in this trunk."

"Can you hold on till I find you?"

"Unless the avatars kill me first."

"They would have killed you by now, if they planned on killing you."

"Thanks for the cheery news." She coughed. "If they don't plan on killing me, what are they gonna do with me?"

"I can't read their minds."

"Don't give me that. You know the answer, just like I do. They're gonna assault me again."

"You can't be sure of that."

"Give me another reason they would kidnap me."

Brody chewed it over. "To hold you for ransom?"

"And cut off my fingers to prove it's me? I saw that movie. No thanks."

"I'll call the cops—"

"No. No cops," she cut in.

"They can reach you faster than I can."

"The bad publicity of my kidnaping," said Ivy, sobbing. "Orion would be furious."

"The hell with him. Your life's at stake."

"No cops. Help me."

"Keep calm. I'm on my way," said Brody, firing his Mini's engine and backing out of his parking space.

He couldn't make out what she said next. The transmission was garbled. Maybe the kidnaper's car was going under a tunnel, which was interfering with her cell phone's signal.

"You're breaking up," he said.

Chapter 48

With his cell phone mounted on his dash, Brody could follow Ivy's cell signal on Google maps.

He had no idea where they were taking her. As of right now they were headed for the beach. He turned onto Wilshire Boulevard.

He put on speed. He had to reach Ivy before her kidnapers had their way with her.

Adrenaline coursing through him, he drove aggressively, switching lanes often. He almost rear-ended the SUV in front of him. He hit his brakes and skidded within inches of the SUV.

An accident would cost him precious time, he knew, fetching a sigh of relief at having avoided a collision.

He was tempted to call the cops. They had enough manpower that they could reach her in minutes. He had no idea how long it would take him to locate her, especially with the heavy traffic on Wilshire.

He couldn't go against Ivy's wishes, even though he thought she was wrong about not contacting the cops. She was too deferential to Orion. She could end up dead because of it.

It was Brody's job to protect her. He couldn't foist the responsibility onto the cops. He had to get moving.

Wilshire was too jammed.

Cursing, Brody drove off Wilshire and got onto Santa Monica Boulevard, where the traffic wasn't quite as congested.

He consulted his cell phone. The kidnapers were on the Coast Highway, making for Malibu.

Traffic was slowing to a crawl.

He could see the reason.

The cops had closed off the road thanks to an accident at an approaching intersection.

Brody detoured left, hung a right onto Olympic Boulevard, and headed west for the ocean. He pounded his steering wheel with the bottom of his fist in frustration. The kidnapers were putting distance between them and him.

Brody accelerated.

He talked at his cell phone. "Can you hear me, Ivy?"

No answer.

He didn't know if Ivy's connection was still open. He didn't even know if his phone would work if he was logged onto Google maps.

"Can you hear me, Ivy?"

Nothing.

He hung a right onto Ocean Avenue, then a left onto the California Incline, and a right onto the Coast Highway.

Ivy had reached Zuma Beach.

Brody floored his gas pedal. When traffic became congested, he veered onto the dirt shoulder on his right, and illegally passed the vehicles in front of him.

He noticed Ivy had stopped at Zuma Beach.

Bad news, he decided. Whatever her kidnapers were going to do to her, they were doing it now.

He sped across the dirt shoulder. His Mini's tires kicked up clouds of dirt behind him. Drivers stuck in snarled traffic glared at him. The shoulder would end soon.

Vehicles on the Coast Highway were stopped for a red light at an upcoming intersection.

Brody blew through the light from the shoulder. A pickup almost T-boned him as his Mini crossed the intersection. The pickup's driver slammed on his brakes, burning rubber, screeching to a halt, fishtailing. He leaned on his horn and flipped Brody the bird.

Brody made it through the intersection onto the Coast Highway, which was clear after he passed the traffic light. He mashed the gas.

He glanced in the rearview mirror. No cops. Luck was on his side for a change. But would he have enough luck to reach Ivy in time to save her? He couldn't count on luck.

He drove only five miles over the posted speed limit, hoping the highway patrol cops wouldn't pull him over. There were few cars up ahead. He was making good time.

He eyeballed his cell phone. Ivy remained at Zuma Beach. She wasn't stopped at a light. The kidnapers must have parked there.

Brody drove past Point Dume State Beach. He would reach Zuma soon.

"Ivy, can you hear me?" he said, leaning toward his mounted cell phone.

No reply.

Brody turned into the Zuma Beach parking lot and found a place to park. He scanned the vast beach, casting around for Ivy.

She was here somewhere, according to the signal he was receiving on his cell phone.

Chapter 49

Brody removed the cell phone from its mount, clambered out of the driver's seat, and wondered which direction to try. Why would her kidnapers take her to the beach? he wondered. There were other beachgoers here. If the kidnapers tried to rape her on the beach, there would be witnesses.

He punched her number on his cell and called her again.

Nothing.

Scattered pockets of visitors mottled the beach that fanned out in front of Brody. The sun blazed down on the glittering sand and on the ocean that rippled like turquoise muscles.

She had to be here, decided Brody, passing a shop that was selling cheap sunglasses hanging on a pegboard.

The ocean breeze blowing into his face, he sat down on a cement bench that bordered the asphalt parking lot and removed his shoes and socks. Clutching them in one hand, he rose from the bench and plodded through the hot sand toward the nearest knot of visitors.

He searched for groups of three people because Ivy had said the two avatars had kidnaped her.

Traipsing around, he had no luck finding her.

He kept combing the beach.

He checked Google maps on his cell phone. The screen continued to indicate Ivy was here at the beach. At least, her phone was.

Had the avatars found Ivy's phone, discarded it here on the beach, and taken her elsewhere to rape her? he wondered. The thought chilled his blood. If true, he had no way of finding her. He hoped he was wrong.

He wasn't going to give up his search. He checked out everybody he saw at the beach, making sure he got close enough to see their faces.

There were several loners either sitting or lying on the beach soaking up the sun. Brody approached them and inspected their faces.

He didn't see anybody who looked like Ivy.

He kept slogging through the sand. He approached a woman lying on her side in the sand. She was facing away from him. She was wearing jeans and a baggy T-shirt. He heard a transistor radio playing tinny music next to her purse. Listening to the surf crashing on the shoreline, he heard "I Get Around" by the Beach Boys playing on the radio.

He walked around her to get a good look at her face.

It was Ivy.

Her eyes shut, she was lying motionless.

"Ivy?" he said.

She didn't respond.

He saw a crumpled handkerchief lying two feet from her face.

Crouching beside her he shook her shoulder to wake her up, hoping she was asleep and not dead.

"Ivy," he said, shaking her.

He couldn't tell if she was sleeping.

She moaned and opened her eyes.

"Are you OK?" said Brody.

She blinked several times, not recognizing him at first.

She jackknifed up and scoped out her surroundings, trying to comprehend where she was.

"What happened?" she said.

"Don't you remember?"

She frowned, searching her mind for memories.

"I was locked in the trunk of a moving car," she said. "The car stopped and the trunk opened. I saw the blinding blue sky above me. Then the avatar called Joe pressed a smelly handkerchief to my face . . . and that's the last I remember. The next thing I remember is seeing you crouching near me."

Brody glanced at the rumpled handkerchief lying near her.

"Is that the handkerchief?" he said.

"Looks like it."

Brody got down on his hands and knees, bowed his face closer to the handkerchief, and sniffed it. He didn't smell anything. Which proved nothing. Maybe most of the chemical odor had dissipated.

He didn't pick up the handkerchief with his hand, figuring there might be fingerprints on it. Fingerprints that could be lifted off fabric were rare, he knew, but possible. If not fingerprints, there might be DNA on the handkerchief or residue from the drug the kidnapers had used.

He fished out a pencil from his trouser pocket, used the pencil to lift the handkerchief, and deposited the handkerchief in his breast pocket. He had a connection in the LAPD's Forensic Department who would examine it.

"How long have you been lying here?" asked Brody.

Ivy glanced at her wristwatch. "I have no idea."

"What did they do to you?"

She shook her head, her expression blank.

"Did they assault you?" asked Brody.

"I don't remember," answered Ivy in frustration.

"Let's go back to my car."

Ivy nodded and got to her feet, continuing to look confused and disheveled.

Chapter 50

"I have a lot of questions," said Brody, as he and Ivy trudged through the sand.

"So do I."

"Why didn't they take your cell phone? They must have known you would call for help."

"Maybe they're not as smart as they think they are."

"Why did they kidnap you in the first place?"

"No idea. They said nothing to me."

"But they didn't demand a ransom. They just dumped you on the beach for no reason."

"Maybe they assaulted me when I was unconscious," she said, shivering with dread at the thought.

"I don't see any bruises on your body."

"I didn't have a chance to put up a fight. They doped me before I had a chance to resist."

Brody nodded. "Maybe it's part of their campaign to terrorize you. But I don't know what their motivation is."

"They told me earlier that they wanted me to become one of them. This time they didn't tell me anything."

"I wonder who's pulling their strings."

"You think someone's controlling them?"

"If they're avatars, humans are controlling them."

"They *are* avatars, I'm telling you. But nobody's controlling them."

"Without a ransom note, this kidnaping doesn't track."

"Why did they even assault me in Rabbit World in the first place?"

"You said they want you to become one of them."

She looked askance at him. "Assaulting someone isn't a good way to recruit them."

They climbed into Brody's Mini.

Despite himself, Brody was starting to doubt her story. She could have made the whole thing up, for all he knew.

She could have faked her kidnaping and come to Zuma Beach to wait for him to find her. But what would be the point of faking a kidnaping? To elicit sympathy because her husband wasn't giving her any?

Brody couldn't get his head around it.

Maybe she was going nuts, he decided. In her mind she believed she had been kidnaped. Maybe in reality, it never happened.

Brody wanted to believe her. She sounded earnest. She also acted terrified of being assaulted by the avatars. Yet he had no proof her two stalkers *were* avatars. No witnesses had corroborated her meetings with the avatars, nor did any security camera footage he had viewed.

Brody didn't know what to believe. He tended to give people the benefit of the doubt. Her story about the avatars stalking her sounded too fantastic to be made up. And why would she want people to believe avatars were stalking her, unless it was true?

On the other hand, she could be a paranoid schizophrenic who didn't even know she was making up her assaults. In which case, it would be impossible to tell she was lying because she believed her own lies.

"What happened to your gun?" asked Brody, as they sat in his car.

Ivy snapped open her purse and rooted through it. "I can't find it. The avatars must have taken it."

It made sense to disarm her, decided Brody, since they wouldn't want her to shoot them.

"What did you say their names are?" he asked.

"Joe and Ed," she answered. "I heard them talking to each other at the mall when they confronted me in the food court."

Brody watched a family of four dressed in bathing suits leaving their parked SUV. They lugged beach chairs, a striped particolored umbrella, and a red cooler carried by the two teenage sons across the parking lot to the beach.

They headed toward the nearest weathered powder blue lifeguard tower hard by the breaking surf.

"Where do you want to go?" said Brody.

Ivy twisted her mouth. "Liz told me not to go home because she's convinced Orion is gaslighting me."

"Liz?"

"She's my friend. She's worried about me."

"Then where do you want to go?"

"I have nowhere else to go. I want to go home."

Breathing the brackish ocean air gusting over the beach, Brody fired the Mini's engine and backed out of his parking space, his tires crunching the sand on the asphalt.

"Why does she think he's gaslighting you?" he said.

"Because he won't let me report the assault to the cops."

"There's nothing the cops can do about a virtual assault. Our laws don't apply to the metaverse."

"Believe me, I know. The avatars keep telling me that over and over. I'm sick of hearing it. What kind of a sick world allows people to assault each other with impunity?"

"I don't understand why Liz thinks Orion's gaslighting you."

"According to her, he wants my money. If he gets me committed, he gets it all for himself."

Brody nodded. "I see. Do you think she's wrong about him?"

"She *is* wrong. Orion loves me. He's just concerned about his IPO next week."

"You sound sure of yourself."

"One thing's for sure. He's putting a lot of pressure on me to make his IPO look squeaky clean. No assaults, no stalking, nothing the papers will report. He doesn't want me to talk to anyone. He'd lock me in my bedroom if he thought he could get away with it. But he knows I wouldn't stand for it."

"Do you think he's doing the right thing?"

"He's doing what he thinks is best for his company. I have problems with his decision. The metaverse is the wild, wild west, as far as I'm concerned. It's a dangerous place. I have reservations about selling real estate in a place where all crimes are permitted. It's scary like that movie *Purge*. But in that movie, crime is allowed only on certain days. In the metaverse, crime never takes a holiday."

"Did you tell him your reservations?"

"About not wanting to sell real estate in Rabbit World?"

"Yeah."

"Of course. But he doesn't agree. He thinks that the assault on me was an isolated incident, and that I didn't get physically hurt. No harm, no foul," she said, flinging up her hands.

"Did you object?"

"I did." She paused in thought. "He talks too much to Nieman, is the problem."

"Nieman? Who's Nieman?"

"Lazarus Nieman. He's a hotshot in Silicon Valley. He sells real estate in his metaverse, where Orion got the idea. Did you notice the bone mic Orion is always wearing? He uses it to talk to Nieman."

"Is Orion consulting with Nieman?" said Brody, puzzled about their relationship.

"I couldn't say what they talk about. Orion doesn't confide in me. Sometimes I get the impression Orion is competing with Nieman and he wants Rabbit World to do better than Nieman's metaverse."

"Where's Nieman's office?"

"In Menlo Park."

"Maybe he knows something about avatar rapists in the metaverse who stalk their victims in the real world."

Ivy shrugged. "He might. Nobody knows the metaverse better than Nieman."

Brody was driving along PCH when a bullet pierced his Mini's rear window and embedded itself in the dashboard a few inches to the right of his right hand that gripped the steering wheel.

Chapter 51

Brody cursed.

Ivy's eyes bugged out.

"What happened?" she said, eyeballing the fresh hole in the dashboard.

"Somebody's shooting at us," said Brody, his fingers locked around the steering wheel, glancing at the rearview mirror to see if he could spot the shooter.

Brody made out a gun pointed out the driver's-side window of the black sedan driving behind him. It looked like Bondurant at the wheel.

Brody hung a right at the upcoming beach parking lot's entrance, figuring Bondurant wouldn't risk a shootout at a crowded public beach.

On the other hand, maybe Bondurant had shot at Brody to get him to pull over so he could bust Brody. Bust him for what? wondered Brody. If so, Bondurant would follow him into the parking lot and arrest him.

Brody doubted Bondurant wanted to bust him.

What was an FBI agent doing shooting at him? Brody wondered in disbelief. He felt his blood boiling. Feds didn't go around shooting out of their cars at people without identifying themselves, the last he heard. Did Bondurant have something to do with Ivy's kidnaping? What was he doing driving in the area where Ivy had been abandoned?

Brody pulled into a parking space and killed the Mini's engine. He was packing his SIG P365 in his ankle holster. He didn't want to pull a gun on a fed. He decided he wasn't going to reach for it.

He waited for Bondurant to pull into the parking lot.

"Why is that guy shooting at us?" said Ivy.

"Search me."

"Are you gonna just wait for him to come here and kill us?" said Ivy, her eyes bright with apprehension.

"He's FBI."

Ivy did a double take. "FBI? You're kidding. Why would the FBI shoot at us?"

"Shooting at us without ID'ing himself is against every rule in their book. Something's hinky. I doubt he'll try to blow us away with all these people around," said Body, taking in the beachgoers milling around the sand-dappled parking lot.

"How do you know he's FBI?"

"I met him at the Century City mall. He showed me his badge."

"What did he want?"

"He wanted me to back off your case."

His heartbeat racing, Brody watched Bondurant's car approach the entrance to the parking lot. He didn't think he could bring himself to shoot a fed. He would have to allow himself to be arrested, if that was Bondurant's intention.

Brody's only other option was to flee. But he didn't want the feds chasing him for an inexplicable reason. Better to find out what this was about.

Bondurant's car passed the entrance and kept barreling down the Coast Highway toward Venice.

Brody breathed easier.

He turned to Ivy. "Why are the feds interested in you and Orion?"

"It's news to me. We're not doing anything illegal."

"It must be me he wants."

"Why you?"

"I have no idea."

"What are we supposed to do?"

"This isn't how the feds operate," said Brody, baffled. "The hell with it."

He produced his cell phone.

"What are you doing?" said Ivy.

"I'm calling FBI headquarters in Westwood."

"They'll trace your call and arrest us."

"For what? What law did we break?"

Ivy shook her head. "I don't want any trouble with the government."

"Neither do I, but Bondurant's abusing his authority."

"Leave me out of your conversation."

Chapter 52

Brody found the Westwood FBI branch contact number on the Internet and punched it on his cell phone. He put the call on speaker.

"This is the office of the Federal Bureau of Investigation," said the receptionist.

"Hello. I want to report one of your agents for abuse of power," said Brody.

"What abuse of power?"

"He shot at me from his car and just missed me."

"Were you resisting arrest?"

"He made no attempt to arrest me. He opened fire on me without warning."

"What's his name?" she said in an even tone.

"Xavier Bondurant."

"I'll check the directory for his name. Please hold."

"OK."

Five minutes later, the receptionist returned to her phone.

"No such agent is employed at the FBI," she said.

"What?" said Brody, incredulous. "That's impossible. I saw his badge. His name is Xavier Bondurant. Check your records again."

"I already double-checked them. There are no Bondurants working for the bureau."

"Then he's illegally impersonating one of your officers."

"That's a serious charge," said the receptionist, taking umbrage. "Are you making an official complaint? What is your name?"

Brody terminated the call.

He didn't want to get mixed up with the feebs.

If Bondurant really wasn't a special agent at the FBI, who was he? And who was he working for? wondered Brody.

"I don't understand," said Ivy, looking at him.

"Bondurant impersonated a fed to try to scare me off your case."

"Why? I never even heard of the guy."

"When that didn't work, he tried to whack me."

Ivy shook her head in confusion. "What the hell is going on?"

"This must have something to do with Rabbit World. Maybe Riley hired Bondurant."

"Who's Riley?"

"According to Orion, Riley's the guy representing the Mafia syndicate that wants to buy real estate in Rabbit World to build casinos."

"Orion doesn't want anything to do with casinos. He thinks the Mafia runs them. His algorithms say it's a bad idea. He'll never sell to the Mafia."

"Then why would Bondurant shoot at me?"

"I dunno."

"Unless—"

"Unless what?"

Brody didn't want to upset her. She had enough on her mind. However, he decided to go ahead and tell her. Leaving her dangling would upset her even more.

"Unless he was shooting at you, not me," he said.

After all, the bullet had landed smack dab between them in the dash. Bondurant could have been aiming at either one of them.

Ivy widened her eyes. "Do you think he's working with the kidnapers?"

"Could be. But why would the kidnapers send an FBI impostor after you?"

"True. They're harassing me enough without the fed's help. Then who is he working for?"

"Someone who wants to isolate you."

"I want to go back home."

Brody drove to her house in Brentwood.

He was becoming curious about the Big Tech poohbah Lazarus Nieman in Menlo Park. Was Nieman helping Orion with his IPO next week or was he hindering him?

"Have you ever met Nieman?" said Brody.

"No," said Ivy. "As I understand it, he rarely leaves his office."

A few minutes later, Brody drove up Ivy's driveway, parked, and let her out. She took the path to her front door and let herself in.

As he was getting ready to pull out of her driveway, he heard her ear-piercing scream.

Chapter 53

Brody bolted out of his Mini, whipped out his SIG from his ankle holster, and pelted to Ivy's front door, which hung ajar.

Gun in hand, jacked up with adrenaline, he expected trouble as he entered the manse's lobby. He cut his eyes around the house, casting around for signs of danger.

A mirror with a filigreed gold frame was hanging on the wall in the foyer. From his angle he saw no one's reflection in it. A Matisse still life, genuine or not, hung on the wall opposite the mirror. He stole toward the living room, ears alert to any sound, eyes cutting back and forth. He didn't pick up on anything untoward.

Where was Ivy? he wondered, making his way forward with caution. Could Bondurant have gotten here before them and lain in wait for her? How did he get into the house? Even worse, had he killed her?

Keeping his eyes peeled, Brody stepped into the living room and froze in surprise at the sight before him.

Her face contorted with anguish, Ivy was standing over Orion's inanimate body, which lay sprawled on its back on the living room carpet.

Brody heard a siren approaching outside.

"What happened?" he said.

"I came in and saw him like this," she said.

Brody scrutinized the body. Orion had a bullet hole in his forehead and two in his chest. There wasn't much blood. The bullet to the head had finished him without any help from the other two.

After a cursory glance around the room, Brody didn't pick up on the murder weapon.

"This is the LAPD," said a voice from the lobby behind him. "Drop your weapon."

Brody turned slowly to see a uniform training a pistol on him, using the Weaver stance.

Brody dropped his SIG.

Ivy gazed at the cop in surprise. "How did you get here so fast?"

"A neighbor heard a gunshot and alerted us," said the cop.

Lieutenant George Macready from the Robbery-Homicide Division entered the premises, clad in a brown blazer, a maroon necktie, and black slacks. Wearing a surly visage the middle-aged Macready had a port-wine stain on his cropped head which added to the ominous aspect of his face.

"Our old pal Brody," he said. "I can't say I'm surprised to see a trigger-happy keyhole peeper standing over another stiff."

Brody had a history with the guy.

Brody was about to speak when Macready said, "I know what you're gonna say—"

Brody said it anyway. "He was dead when I got here, Lieutenant."

Looking bored, Macready mouthed the words as Brody spoke them.

"It's true," said Brody. "Ask Ivy."

"Who is the deceased?" said Macready, eyeballing the corpse.

"Her husband Orion Kingston."

"Is that your piece on the rug?"

"They told me to drop it. Check it. It hasn't been fired."

"Call forensics," Macready told the uniform who was holding his gun trained on Brody. "You can holster your gun."

Macready scoped out the living room. Something caught his eye. He walked behind a leather recliner and spotted a pistol lying on the carpet.

"What have we here?" he said, removing a purple latex surgical glove from his trouser pocket and slipping it onto his right hand.

"Lieutenant, can I pick up my piece?" said Brody.

"We've got two pieces here," said Macready, stooping and collecting the newfound handgun from the carpet with his gloved hand.

"Lieutenant?" said Brody, watching Macready.

"Everybody stay put," said Macready. "I don't want anybody contaminating the crime scene before forensics get here."

Brody hunkered down to retrieve his piece.

"Don't," said Macready. "You're not cleared yet. Leave it."

Brody stood up without his SIG, looking displeased.

"What are you doing here anyway?" asked Macready.

"I brought Ivy home from the beach."

Brody decided not to go into the kidnaping, since he knew Ivy didn't want to report it to the cops. On the other hand, the only reason she didn't want to report it was because of Orion—who now lay dead at his feet. Did that mean Ivy would allow him to tell the cops about the avatars stalking and kidnaping her?

Brody would save his questions for her for later—when the cops were gone.

"What were you two doing at the beach?" said Macready.

"Soaking up rays," said Ivy, avoiding the issue of the kidnaping.

"While Orion was here at home?"

"That's right," said Ivy, wiping tears from her eyes with a handkerchief.

"I know this is a difficult time for you," said Macready, "but I need to find out who murdered him."

"It's OK."

Two EMTs in navy blue uniforms burst into the lobby pushing a gurney.

"Don't contaminate the crime scene," said Macready.

Chapter 54

Wearing paper booties the EMT team left the gurney in the lobby and made for Orion.

Grim-faced, Macready shook his head at them.

They did their job anyway. Chewing gum the thirtysomething rangy EMT with long, unruly black hair and a long neck got down on his haunches and felt Orion's carotid with his forefinger to see if the victim was alive. To the surprise of no one, the EMT stopped chewing his gum and shook his head, face impassive.

Macready gave him an I-told-you-so look.

The EMTs retreated into the lobby.

"Do you know if anyone was supposed to visit Orion while he was here alone?" Macready asked Ivy.

"I can't help you," answered Ivy. "He doesn't tell me everything he does."

"Was he involved in a dispute with anyone?"

"Not to my knowledge."

"You don't sound sure of yourself," said Macready, curling his lips just short of a sneer.

"I don't know everything he does at his business."

"Do you have any idea who killed him?"

Ivy sobbed. "No. He never hurt anyone. I don't understand who would do such a thing."

Macready changed tack. "Were you two getting along OK?"

Ivy bridled. "We had arguments now and then. Nothing serious. What are you implying?"

Macready chose not to answer.

When a spouse was murdered, the other spouse was always the first suspect, Brody knew. He remembered he had the handkerchief the kidnapers had used on Ivy in his breast pocket. He wanted forensics to inspect it for fingerprints, DNA, and ether, but he didn't want to tell

Macready about the kidnaping—unless Ivy brought up the matter. So far she hadn't mentioned it. Still, Orion was dead. She didn't have to keep mum about it to please him anymore.

Maybe she wanted to salvage Orion's IPO next week by not tainting it with bad PR, even with Orion dead. Yet Orion's murder couldn't help make the IPO a success next week. Or could it? For sure, the IPO would get publicity from his murder, but Rabbit World had nothing to do with the murder. Maybe Rabbit World would stay untarnished by Orion's demise. There was no way Ivy could cover up his murder now that the cops knew about it. The media would be the next to know.

"I don't understand how you fit into this," Macready told Brody.

"I told you, I drove Ivy home from the beach," said Brody.

"You two are beach pals? Maybe you were seeing each other on the sly and Orion caught wind of it. So you decided he had to go."

"Lieutenant, there's nothing between me and Ivy. I was helping her out."

"After your little fling at the beach," said Macready, jacking up his eyebrows and leering.

Brody knew his beach tryst with Ivy sounded strange, but he didn't want to change his story without Ivy's permission—and she didn't look eager to spill the beans about the avatars kidnaping her.

Macready turned to Ivy. "Is he on the level about your beach jaunt?"

"He did give me a ride home from the beach, if that's what you're asking me."

"I'm getting the strong feeling I'm missing something here."

At that moment, the forensics team arrived. Wearing their white Tyvek uniforms and paper booties, they fell to investigating the living room combing it for evidence.

Macready ushered Brody and Ivy out of the way of the team into the lobby, which was becoming crowded what with the presence of the EMTs, their gurney, and two of Macready's uniforms watching over the proceedings. Macready remained in the lobby and sniffed the SIG P365 in his gloved hand, as he watched his forensic techs do their job.

Brody realized with a start that the SIG in Macready's hand was the one he had given Ivy to protect herself from the avatars.

"This one's been fired recently," he said. "I bet it's the murder weapon."

Brody felt the blood drain from his face.

"You OK, Brody?" said Macready. "You don't look so good."

"Fine," said Brody.

Chapter 55

Brody wondered if he should tell Macready right off the bat that the SIG was his. Then he remembered he had sanded off the serial numbers on that particular gun. Macready wouldn't be able to trace it back to him.

How had the gun ended up being here? wondered Brody. Ivy had had it in her possession, but said it had vanished from her purse while she had been kidnaped. Or, rather, she had said that was the first time she had noticed it wasn't in her purse anymore. Did the kidnapers blow away Orion? What was the motive?

"Whose prints do you think are on the piece?" Macready asked Brody with the trace of a malicious smile on his lips.

"Beats me," answered Brody.

Macready snorted with derision.

He noticed Brody's gun, which remained on the carpet where Brody had dropped it in compliance with the first responder's request.

"I'll be damned," said Macready. "They're both SIG P365s. What are the chances you'd have a piece just like the murderer?"

"Pretty good, I guess."

"Hard to believe."

"Coincidences happen."

"I don't believe in coincidences."

Macready retrieved Brody's SIG from the living room carpet and sniffed it.

"You see, it hasn't been fired," said Brody.

"And yet it's the same model the perp used."

"Can I have it back?"

"Not till I'm done with you."

Ivy was eying the murder weapon apprehensively.

She must have recognized it as the one he had given her, decided Brody. He doubted she would volunteer the information to Macready. It didn't take a genius to figure out she would be suspected of Orion's murder if she said Brody had given her the murder weapon.

Brody wondered if Ivy's fingerprints were on the weapon. Maybe Ivy was wondering the same thing. The forensic techs would come up with the answer after they examined the gun at their downtown lab.

Watching Ivy, Macready must have come close to reading her thoughts. "Why did you murder your husband, Mrs. Kingston?"

"What?" said Ivy in astonishment.

"You went white as a sheet as you eyed the murder weapon in my hand."

"I didn't kill him."

"Then why did you react in such a way to the sight of the murder weapon?"

"I'm feeling under the weather," she said, making a face and rubbing her stomach. "My husband was murdered, for Chrissake."

"He was, indeed."

"You can't imagine how upset I feel," she said, sobbing.

"Don't get that gun mixed up with mine," said Brody.

"I can't very well, can I?" said Macready, looking smug.

"What do you mean?"

"Yours has a serial number on it. The murder weapon doesn't. Somebody removed it."

"Maybe a professional did Orion. They like using cold guns that can't be traced."

"Or maybe Mrs. Kingston did it," said Macready, searching Ivy's face.

"I want a lawyer here, if you're gonna accuse me of something," said Ivy.

"I'm asking questions, not making accusations."

"No, actually. You suggested I killed Orion," said Ivy, her voice cracking with emotion.

"I asked if you did it. That's what cops do. They ask questions to ascertain the truth."

"You're trying to freak me out to get me to confess to something I didn't do."

"Absolutely not. You misunderstand." Macready paused a beat. "Now if my excellent forensic techs find your fingerprints on the murder weapon, then I would suggest you lawyer up."

"That wouldn't necessarily prove she killed Orion," said Brody.

"Are you a lawyer now? I thought you were a keyhole peeper. I ought to give both of you a paraffin test."

Brody shook his head. "Trying to intimidate us again, Lieutenant? You know as well as I that paraffin tests are grossly inaccurate."

"Is that right?" said Macready, jutting his jaw at Brody.

"They only determine if nitrates or nitrites are on the hand. Not what they're from."

"And by the same token, if they aren't on the hand, it doesn't prove you're innocent. You could have washed them off with soap and water."

Brody held out his hands, palms up. "Go ahead and give me a paraffin test. I have nothing to hide."

"I just got through telling you, you could have washed your hands after you shot him."

"You're going around in circles. Either bust us, or let us go."

Macready's eyes twinkled. "That's a thought. Maybe the *two* of you murdered him."

"You got jack."

Brody began to wonder if Ivy had shot Orion. It was possible. The gun he had given her had been used in the murder. But the kidnapers had drugged her. How could she have killed anyone if she was unconscious? Maybe one of the kidnapers had taken her gun and shot Orion.

On the other hand, he had to take Ivy's word for it that she had been kidnaped. He had not seen any kidnapers. He glanced at the handkerchief she had given him that protruded from his breast pocket. He needed to find out if the handkerchief had ether on it. The presence of ether would go a long way in verifying her story.

He had as yet no proof the kidnaping had actually occurred.

"Beat it," said Macready. "The next time I see you, I'll have a warrant for your arrest for murder."

"But this is my house," said Ivy. "I have nowhere else to go."

"I wasn't talking to you. I was talking to the lawyer in his own mind. As for you, I'd rather have you stay here so I know where to find you after we get prints off the murder weapon. As long as you don't mind having guests in your house for the next hour or so."

Ivy knew enough not to argue with police investigating a crime scene.

"Fine," she said.

Chapter 56

Nieman was standing in his penthouse office ogling his reflection in the cheval glass that stood along the wall that ran perpendicular to the picture window beyond his desk. He wasn't paying attention to the panoramic view of Menlo Park.

Pleased with his getup of turquoise board shorts, a navy blue wife beater, and espadrilles, he was even more pleased with his chalk white geisha complexion, wavy blue hair, and blue saucer eyes that dominated his face. He looked like a character out of Japanese anime or manga come to life. Or, more to the point, he looked like an avatar that had just stepped out of the metaverse.

After all, he was the master of the metaverse. Who would want to be a master of the universe when you could be the master of the metaverse? He had no equals in the metaverse and was determined to keep it that way.

His cell phone vibrated in the cargo pocket of his board shorts. He took the call.

"I'm keeping an eye on Brody," said Bondurant. "He's seeing a lot of Ivy Kingston. How do you want me to handle this?"

"He's working for her. Correct?"

"Correct."

"The algorithms say he's too dangerous. He must be taken out."

"No problem. What about Ivy? Do you want me to deal with her?"

"Leave her alone."

"She could be a problem."

"She's *not* a problem."

"She will be. I'm pretty sure."

"I'm calling the shots. Not you. The algorithms don't lie. They say she's not a problem."

"You put too much stock in your algorithms, if you ask me."

"I'm not asking you. The algorithms have everything factored in and figured out. They are never wrong. You don't know half of anything."

"I'm a pro. My instincts tell me Ivy is gonna be trouble farther down the line. I lived all my life by my instincts. They're rarely wrong. The proof is, I'm still alive."

"Whether you're alive or not doesn't impress me."

Bondurant let the insult slide. "I'm giving you the advice of a professional man of action."

"Are you refusing to follow orders?" said Nieman, his voice steely.

"Not at all. I'll take out Brody—"

"Then why are you continuing to run off at the mouth?"

"I'm giving you my professional opinion as a world-renowned problem solver with a gun."

"And I'm giving you your orders."

"There's something strange going on between Brody and Ivy."

"Strange?"

"He picked her up at Zuma Beach and drove her home."

Studying his face in the cheval glass, Nieman fixed his hair. "He's working for her. That's all."

"She looked out of it."

"So she has psychological issues. They don't concern you."

"Maybe not now, but they will."

"The algorithms disagree with your assessment."

"Garbage in, garbage out, is what I say about algorithms."

"They made me rich beyond your wildest dreams."

Bondurant harrumphed. "They're gonna make you broke beyond your wildest dreams if you don't take off your VR headset once in a while, open your eyes, and see what's going on."

Nieman adjusted his bone mic alongside his jaw. "I'm not wearing my headset. Your job is to follow orders. If you can't handle it, you're fired."

Silence on the line.

"Am I getting through to you?" said Nieman.

"No problem."

Nieman consulted his wristwatch.

"This call took five minutes longer than it should have," he said between his teeth, his jaw clenched.

He terminated the call and forgot about Bondurant.

Nieman admired himself in the cheval glass, prinking his blue hair. He was perfect. What everyone aspired to be. He had transcended his manhood and become an avatar. He wanted more people to join him as his servants and disciples.

Chapter 57

When Ivy entered her kitchen, she picked up on a note tacked to the corkboard on the wall next to the mounted beige landline phone and froze in her tracks. She recognized the phone number scrawled on the note in Orion's handwriting. The number belonged to her psychiatrist Dr. Jamal Harris.

Why had Orion written Harris's number on the notepad? she wondered. Harris was her own personal psychiatrist, not Orion's. Orion had no business writing down Harris's number.

She relaxed more or less when she realized Harris would never reveal to anyone what she had told him in confidence as his patient. Their conversations were protected by doctor-client privilege. Harris would never break his oath of confidentiality, knowing he would lose his medical license.

Then why did Orion have Harris's number? wondered Ivy, as she heard the forensics team working in her living room. Could what Liz had said about Orion's gaslighting her be true? Was Orion trying to get Harris to help him gaslight her? Was that why Orion had Harris's phone number?

Ivy had to get to the bottom of this.

She withdrew her cell phone from her purse and called Harris.

"Dr. Harris speaking."

"This is Ivy Kingston. I found your phone number written on a note in my husband's handwriting. Do you know anything about that?"

"I—uh—I don't know."

"Did he talk to you?"

"Why—uh—no. Of course not. Why would he?"

"Why would he have your number then?"

Could Harris and Orion be conspiring against her to drive her insane? wondered Ivy.

"Maybe he was seeking help for himself and found my number while searching the Internet," said Harris.

"You said he didn't call you."

"Well, he didn't. Not yet anyway. Maybe he will in the future. I will, of course, tell him I can't accept him as a client. After all, I'm not a marriage counselor. If you two are seeking a marriage counselor, I can recommend—"

"We aren't."

"If he calls to hire me, I'll tell him to find a different psychiatrist."

"He isn't gonna call you," said Ivy, her voice breaking.

"Why not? Are you OK, Ivy?"

"I'm not OK. Someone murdered Orion."

"What?" said Harris, dumbfounded. "How awful. I'm so sorry for you."

Detective Macready entered the kitchen

"Who are you talking to?" he demanded.

"It's personal," said Ivy.

"Your boyfriend, maybe?"

"No."

"Telling him it's done?"

"What's done? The pot roast?"

"You know what I mean," said Macready, his expression stony.

"What are you trying to insinuate?" said Ivy, feeling her hackles rise.

"I know the way things work," said Macready with a wink.

Ivy shook her head in befuddlement. "Whatever that means. If you don't mind, I'm busy."

"I just came to tell you my men will be busy for a while in your living room." Macready paused. "Then the ME's assistant will remove the corpse."

Ivy didn't want to think about it. "I get the idea."

"I'm sorry for the inconvenience, but we have to do our job. I'm sure you understand."

Macready moseyed away from her toward the kitchen exit, snatching a Granny Smith apple from the fruit dish on the island. Pausing in the doorway, he rubbed the apple clean on his shirt, inspected the shiny green skin, and took a loud, crisp bite. He nodded with approval and walked into the living room.

Ivy's cell phone chimed. She realized Harris must have hung up, while she was talking to Macready.

She took the call.

"Are you OK?" said Brody.

"Macready is acting a bit indelicate with me."

"Indelicate? He's an asshole."

Ivy emitted a short laugh, despite herself. "I wish he'd leave."

"He's trying to rattle you to get you to confess."

"Confess to what? I didn't do anything."

"The spouse is always the prime suspect in these types of homicides."

"We had our differences, but I would never think of shooting—" she said, cutting herself off, remembering she had pulled a gun on him earlier that day.

"Of course not. Do you want me to come back to your house after he's gone?"

"No. I'm fine. I just need some rest. And some peace and quiet," she added, hearing Macready's men mauling her living room as they did their job.

She realized she had an incoming call.

"Gotta run," she said, and hung up.

She answered the incoming.

"Hi, Ivy," said Liz. "I just wanted to check in to see if you're OK. You seemed disturbed at lunch today."

"Hi, Liz. Bad news." Ivy sobbed. "Somebody murdered Orion. The police are here investigating."

"What?" gasped Liz.

"I know. It's incredible. I still can't believe it happened. I'm trying to come to grips with it," said Ivy, grief-stricken, her voice frail.

"How awful. Do you want me to come over?"

"No, that's OK. The cops are here, anyway."

"I'm sorry for your loss."

"Thanks, Liz. Oh, you know what?"

"What?"

"I'm beginning to think you were right about Orion gaslighting me. He had my psychiatrist's phone number. They must have talked. Dr. Harris isn't supposed to tell anyone what I said to him as a patient."

"No way. That's illegal. I told you I was right about Orion gaslighting you. It was plain to see he was driving you off the deep end."

"Maybe. But I can't believe it."

"You can't believe it, because it's too close to you. But to anyone else, it was obvious. And he had the shrink working with him to gaslight you. What a piece of work."

"I don't want to jump to conclusions. I wish he was alive so I could ask him why he had my psychiatrist's phone number."

"He would have lied."

"Harris said Orion never called him."

Liz clucked. "He's lying, too. He'd lose his medical license if anyone found out he was giving out patients' confidential statements made to him during therapy."

"I can't get my head around it," said Ivy, at a loss. "It's too mindboggling to even consider."

"Do the cops have any suspects in the murder? Who would do such a horrible thing?"

"No suspects. They recovered what they believe is the murder weapon, though."

"Wow. Avatars try to kill you. Now this."

"Not my day, I guess."

Ivy realized how lame that sounded after all she'd been through.

"I'll let you go," said Liz. "If you need help, don't hesitate to call me. I'm telling you, it sounds more and more like the end of the world. It's coming, and it's coming soon. Get your go-bag ready. You're gonna need it any minute. We all are. Wars, pandemics, global warming, you name it. What's gonna happen next? A comet could collide with the world next, the way things are going, and wipe us all out."

Liz hung up.

Ivy rubbed her forehead. Maybe Liz was right, she decided, downcast. She certainly felt like her world was collapsing around her.

Chapter 58

The cops left Ivy's house an hour and a half later.

She wandered into the living room. It had a medicinal odor to it. Maybe it was from the different chemicals the cops had used to obtain latent fingerprints, she decided.

She felt played out. She didn't know how she could keep her eyes open much longer.

She scoped out the living room. The corpse was gone. The cops had rearranged the furniture, but at least they hadn't left a mess. They had cleaned up their trash when they left. On the other hand, the chemical odors they had left behind would linger for a while.

She opened a few windows to air out the place.

The forensics team had tried to get Orion's blood out of the carpet, but Ivy could make out remaining bloodstains. Memento mori. She would need to have the carpet replaced.

She doubted she would sleep well tonight. Not just tonight. The image of Orion's bullet-riddled stiff sprawled on the carpet would haunt her for years to come.

She climbed the staircase to the second floor and entered her bathroom. She opened her medicine cabinet and wondered which pills she should take tonight. She thought about calling Harris and asking him. Then she remembered Orion had Harris's phone number and the whole gaslighting thing came to her mind.

If Orion and Harris had been plotting to gaslight her, how could she trust Harris on which pills to take tonight? Then again, Orion was dead. Why would Harris continue the scheme to gaslight her with Orion out of the picture? Harris had nothing to gain from it anymore.

She couldn't trust Harris. From now on, she would suspect he didn't have her best interests in mind. She would have to decide on her own hook which pill to take—even though she wasn't a psychiatrist. Maybe she should hire another psychiatrist.

The idea of rehashing her ordeal with yet another psychiatrist daunted her. Well, she wasn't going to be able to make an appointment with a new psychiatrist tonight. It was too late. Unless she could find one on the Internet that worked at night. Did hospital emergency rooms have psychiatrists on duty?

She yawned. Maybe she didn't need any pills to help her sleep. She was too tired to find another psychiatrist. Maybe another day.

She sat on her bed and was about to lie down when her cell phone chimed in her purse.

She got up and took the call.

"We're coming to get you tonight," said the avatar.

She recoiled in horror as she recognized the voice. She didn't know whether it was Joe's or Ed's but she knew it was one of them.

The caller hung up.

Grimacing, Ivy threw her cell onto the bed like it had three-inch-long spikes protruding from it.

Jacked up with adrenaline, she belted down the stairs and ran around the house making sure all the doors were locked. Nudging aside the curtain a smidgin, she peeked out the living room picture window, wondering if the avatars were lurking outside in the dark.

She dashed around the house shutting and locking all the windows on the first floor. She wondered if she should lock the windows on the second floor as well. But how could the avatars reach the second floor unless they had a ladder? Maybe they did have a ladder.

She darted up the stairs and, sprinting from room to room, locked all the windows.

Where was her gun? she wondered. If the one used to kill Orion was hers, the police had confiscated it. It had looked like hers, but she wasn't an expert on guns and couldn't be certain. In any case, the gun Brody had given her was gone. Either the kidnapers had taken it, or the cops had.

How was she supposed to defend herself? she wondered, her heartbeat accelerating like mad.

She wished she had installed an alarm in the house, but she and Orion didn't believe in them. After all, they had neighborhood watch. The thought of neighborhood watch settled her down after a fashion. They would protect her from the avatars.

She had doubts. Could she trust neighborhood watch to keep her safe? Why not? That was their job.

Maybe the avatars were just trying to freak her out when they called. Maybe they had no intention of invading her house and attacking her. If they really were planning on invading tonight, why would they warn her in advance, giving her a chance to lock all her doors and windows?

They were trying to panic her, she decided. And they were succeeding.

She froze, petrified with terror, when she heard a knock on her front door. She ran to the head of the stairs and looked down at the first floor, wondering what to do. She had no idea who would be knocking on her door at this time of night.

If it was an avatar and she asked who it was, they would know she was here. She decided to pretend she wasn't home.

The knocking resumed.

She strained her ears to hear if the stranger outside was saying anything that would identify them. She didn't hear anyone's voice.

Another set of knocks. More urgent this time.

Ivy wished the stranger would leave. Didn't they get the message? She wasn't here.

For sure, she wasn't going to answer the door.

Curiosity getting the better of her, she crept downstairs, trying not to make the treads and risers squeak under her footsteps. Halfway down the staircase, she thought she saw someone outside run past the picture window, their shadow cast by the porch light fluttering across the closed curtain.

Gripping the banister handrail, she halted on the stairs, heart in her mouth.

The stranger was running around the house trying to find an opening, since the front door was locked.

She had to call Brody. He was the only one who could help her. The cops would never believe her if she told them avatars were invading her home.

Where was her cell phone? she wondered.

She couldn't remember what she had done with it.

She could always use the landline in the kitchen, but she couldn't remember Brody's number. His number was on her list of contacts on her cell phone.

She didn't know if she wanted to enter the kitchen, anyway. The avatar might be able to see her, if he was circling the house and peeking through the windows in search of her. She couldn't recall if she had drawn all of the curtains shut in the kitchen. If they were open, the stranger would see her walking in the kitchen. She couldn't allow that to happen.

Her best defense was to stay out of sight and make it look like the house was vacant. She wondered how long the stranger would prowl around outside.

Unwilling to risk being seen at the landline phone in the kitchen, she had to locate her cell phone in order to summon help from Brody.

She tapped her head. She couldn't recall where she had left the cell phone. She had been talking to Liz on it in the kitchen. Had she left the cell in the kitchen? she wondered with dread.

She didn't think so.

Where had she been when the avatar had phoned her? Wasn't she in her bedroom?

She decided to check it out.

She was about to head up the rest of the stairs to her bedroom, when she stood rooted to the spot. She could have sworn she heard someone trying to open the kitchen door.

Hadn't she locked it? She was sure she had locked all the doors.

What if the intruder had a lock pick? she wondered.

She had to find something she could use as a club to defend herself.

Chapter 59

Ivy remembered Orion kept a set of TaylorMade golf clubs stored in his closet in the bedroom.

She ascended the steps, entered their bedroom, opened his closet, and withdrew a five iron from Orion's golf bag. Getting hit in the back of the head with this thing couldn't feel good, she decided. Like having a divot gouged out of your skull.

This was the room where she had received the avatar's call, she remembered. Her cell phone must be here.

She cast around the room. She didn't see her cell. What had she done with it?

If it would only ring, she could locate it by homing in on its chime. Or was it set on Mute? She couldn't recall.

She didn't have a landline in the bedroom. The only one in the house was in the kitchen.

She tensed when she heard knocking on one of the windows on the first floor. Fifteen seconds later she heard knocking on another window.

What were they doing outside? she wondered.

They seemed to be running around the house looking for an opening. But why knock on the locked windows? Another intimidation tactic? She had to admit it was unnerving. But at least she didn't hear the sound of breaking glass, which would indicate they were entering through the windows.

The avatars wanted to carry on with their campaign of terror before launching into attack mode, she decided. Would they enter through the windows? Which one? She couldn't guard all of them.

The avatars continued running around the house rapping on all the windows on the first floor.

With a start she heard her cell phone buzzing and wondered where it was. It had to be in this room, or she wouldn't have been able to hear it. Indeed, the buzzing sounded near her bed. She strode to the other side of the bed and checked it out.

The cell phone lay on the floor, where the phone must have fallen when she had tossed it on the bed.

Leaning over she picked up the vibrating cell phone and answered it.

"Why don't you answer your door?" said the avatar.

"Get out of here or I'll call the cops," said Ivy.

"Good idea. And tell them about the first time we raped you."

"You poor excuse for a human," said Ivy, furious.

"Human?" the avatar said with a laugh. "What makes you think we're human? We met in the metaverse in Rabbit World. Don't you remember?"

How could she forget? decided Ivy.

"Tell it to the cops," said Ivy.

"You're not gonna call them. You didn't the first time. And you won't now."

"My friend will be here any minute. He has a gun."

The avatar yawned noisily. "Good try. But you haven't called anyone. You're afraid people will think you're nuts if you tell anyone avatars are attacking you."

"Sorry to disabuse you. He'll be here soon."

"Remember the first time we had fun together, Ivy. This time it will be much worse. You'll feel all the pain and suffering in your body when we take turns with you."

"Shut up, perv."

"This is the real world we're talking about now. Your body's gonna be black and blue all over after we get through with you. You had it easy when we gang-raped you in the metaverse."

"I didn't have a weapon in Rabbit World. I have one here. You're the ones that will be black and blue when I'm done cracking your bones with 9 millimeter slugs."

The avatar guffawed. "You couldn't hurt us if you tried. You forget, we're avatars."

217

"You're a couple of freaks, is what you are. You can't tell the difference between sex and violence."

"Every inch of your body will be throbbing in pain when we're done with you—"

Ivy terminated the call.

Her face and palms sweaty, she called Brody.

"Brody here."

"I need your help. The avatars are trying to break into my house."

"Aren't the cops there investigating Orion's murder?"

"They left."

"Have you called them?"

"They'll never believe me." Ivy thought she heard breaking glass downstairs. "They're breaking a window."

"Hold on. I'll be right there."

"Hurry," she said, her eyes bugging out in fear.

"Do you have a gun?"

"We don't own any guns."

"Keep everything locked. I'm coming."

Chapter 60

Brody had fallen asleep in his disintegrating leatherette recliner in his apartment in West LA while watching Romero's *Night of the Living Dead* on TV, when Ivy had woken him up with her call.

In the movie the zombies were trying to break into the house where the humans had boarded up the windows and doors and taken refuge.

Brody bolted out of his recliner and sprang into action.

He sprinted out of his apartment to his Mini, which he had parked on the street. He flung the driver's-side door open, clambered into the driver's seat, keyed the ignition, and fired the engine. He peeled off in the direction of Brentwood.

Were the home invaders really avatars? Brody wondered. He wanted to believe Ivy, but, as far as he knew, avatars didn't exist outside of the metaverse. He had as yet been unable to find any proof that avatars had stalked her or tried to kill her by running her vehicle off the road in Topanga Canyon.

Ivy could be cracking up, he decided, what with her assault in Rabbit World, her husband murdered, and her life unraveling. He couldn't blame her if she was. A person could take only so much suffering before they cracked. She could be imagining avatars attacking her house.

However, she sounded genuinely terrified on the phone.

He stepped on the Mini's gas then braked for a traffic light as it turned red. Blowing a light could get him broadsided in the intersection or pulled over by a cop.

Which was when a car rear-ended him from behind and shoved him halfway into the intersection.

What the hell? thought Brody, his head jerking back against his headrest, as he kept his foot on the brake.

The maniac behind him continued to accelerate, forcing Brody farther into the intersection in the path of onrushing cars. The guy was driving a black Mercedes AMG that had twice as much horse power as Brody's Mini.

Brody was fighting a losing battle trying to halt the Mini with the Mercedes continuing to bear down on him. Grinding his teeth he saw a gap in the oncoming traffic, released the brake, and floored the Mini's accelerator. Tires squealing, the Mini shot through the intersection. Its driver blasting his horn and cursing, an SUV careered out of Brody's way to avoid a collision in the nick of time.

His face sweaty, Brody checked his rearview mirror.

The Mercedes with the maniac at the wheel was speeding after him. Brody couldn't make out the driver's face in the dark.

Whoever it was must have been watching Brody's apartment, which meant the guy was lying in wait. This wasn't a spur-of-the-moment thing. The guy was a coldblooded assassin who planned to target Brody from the get-go.

Brody kept driving, but unable to outstrip the guy, he had to outmaneuver him by hanging frequent, sharp rights and lefts without signaling. Which could lead to an accident, Brody was well aware. He had to take that risk, because the guy behind him had it in for him.

The maniac took it to the next level by sticking his hand out the driver's-side window. In his hand he clutched a pistol. He fired at Brody's Mini.

Brody hung a right, jamming the cement curb with his right rear tire. The Mini jerked to the left as the tire caromed off the curb.

He had no idea who had him in their sights. He didn't think the bullet had hit his car, but he couldn't be sure. A car was a big target and difficult to miss.

He had to lose this guy.

Brody saw a squad car driving toward him. He slowed down and pulled over to the side of the road at a parking meter. The maniac behind the wheel of the Mercedes must have seen the squad car, too. Instead of shooting at Brody, or crashing into him, the guy kept going, obeying the speed limit to avoid drawing the cop's attention.

Brody watched the Mercedes drive through the next intersection, then pulled away from the curb in his Mini, and hung a right at that same intersection.

He had lost track of which direction he was headed with his constant turning to escape the pursuing Mercedes. Getting his bearings, he made for Ivy's house in Brentwood. He had wasted a lot of time shaking the Mercedes, but it couldn't be helped. Wasting time was better than ending up dead. He was of no use to Ivy dead.

Now that he knew where he was, he put on speed. He could only hope the intruders hadn't broken into Ivy's house yet.

He was tempted to call the cops and report the home invasion to them, but Ivy had said no cops. He could leave out the part about the home invaders being avatars so the cops would believe him. But Ivy had said no cops. He would take her at her word. He should be at her place soon anyhow.

Had the avatars murdered Orion? Brody wondered. Maybe they were returning to finish the job by taking out his wife.

This was turning into a full-blown shitshow.

Chapter 61

Brody drove onto Ivy's street and made out her pink Mission Revival mansion bathed in moonlight. The red pantiles on the roof rippled like gentle russet ocean waves.

He debated whether to pull into her driveway. Doing so would alert the home invaders to his presence. It might be enough to scare them away. On the other hand, they might blow him away as soon as he exited his car.

He figured it was best to park on the side of the street to avoid alerting the avatars, or whoever they were, to his presence.

He parked the Mini, climbed out of the driver's seat, withdrew his SIG P365 from his ankle holster, and stole toward the front door of Ivy's house. He withdrew a sound suppressor from his cargo pocket and screwed it onto the SIG's muzzle. Gun in hand, he scoped out the front yard for any sign of movement. He didn't see anyone.

He racked the SIG's slide, chambered a round, and released the safety, ready to do battle. No sign of the avatars near the house. They could be in the backyard. Or maybe they had already entered the house, though he didn't see any evidence of forced entry.

If the avatars were already inside the house, it would make things tricky, decided Brody, striding across the stoop and reaching the front door. His rapping on the door would alert the avatars that he was here—if they were within earshot. Brody had to figure they were.

Instead of knocking, he decided to call Ivy on his cell to let her know he was here. He produced his cell phone and speed-dialed Ivy's number.

Ivy accepted the call.

"I'm here," Brody said into his cell, keeping his voice low. "Where are the avatars?"

"I saw one of them sneaking around downstairs."

"They're in your house?" said Brody in surprise.

"I can't be sure. I didn't see anyone enter, but it sounded like one of them was running around in the living room."

"Running around?"

"Spooking around, like they were looking all over the house for me."

"I'm at the front door. I don't see anyone prowling around the front yard. Can you let me in?"

"I'm upstairs. I'll have to go downstairs to let you in."

"OK."

"But what if they're downstairs waiting to ambush me?"

Brody scanned the front yard and saw no one hiding in the stand of bottlebrush trees limned in the moonlight. "I could go around the house and see if they're anywhere in your yard."

"OK. Hurry though. I think at least one of them is inside my house."

Brody stole past a riot of burgundy bougainvillea flowers that were climbing the house's façade. A bed of sweet-scented jasmine grew beneath the bougainvillea.

His pulse picking up speed, Brody rounded the corner of the house, sweeping his SIG back and forth, expecting to confront the home invaders. He saw no one running across the grass lawn. He strained his ears to hear footsteps. Silence.

All of the windows on the side of the house looked intact.

He made for the backyard.

He reached the back of the house and peeked around the corner. He didn't see anyone.

The water in a kidney-shaped swimming pool twenty-odd feet behind the terra-cotta patio wimpled in the soft breeze.

Gun at the ready, Brody crossed the backyard, cutting his eyes to and fro seeking the intruders. They weren't in the backyard. The back door looked secure. To make sure, he approached it and tried the doorknob. It wouldn't turn. He didn't see any scratches on the door that would suggest forced entry.

If Ivy had left the door open, the avatars could have entered the house and locked the door behind them, decided Brody. But he had told her over the phone to lock all her doors and windows. He figured she had taken his advice.

He rounded the backyard to the other side of the house, poised to fire his SIG.

A couple of rhododendrons and a bird of paradise stood before him.

None of the windows were broken. He didn't see how anyone could have entered the house here.

Unless the avatars had returned to the front of the house, he didn't believe they were on Ivy's property. He completed his circuit of the house and returned to the front. He didn't see the avatars.

He didn't see how they could have gotten inside unless Ivy had left one of the doors open. He climbed the stoop, approached the front door, and tried the doorknob. It was the same as the back door. Locked.

He swept his eyes across the front lawn and saw no intruders. He produced his cell phone and called Ivy.

"I don't see anyone out here," he said. "Maybe they saw me coming and bugged out."

"I heard someone running around downstairs searching for me."

Brody saw a sedan's headlights probing the road that skirted Ivy's front yard. The sedan was tooling past Ivy's house.

Brody lowered his SIG out of sight, knowing he could be seen in the wash of the stoop's light. He didn't want the neighbors to report him as a prowler.

The driver of the sedan pulled over to the side of the road, killed his engine, and parked.

Brody broke into a sweat. The driver must have spotted him and his gun.

Brody descended the stoop's steps to get out of the lamplight.

Chapter 62

The driver got out of his car, strode up Ivy's driveway, and fired a laser-sighted silenced pistol at Brody.

Brody dove to the ground behind a bush and returned fire at the figure's silhouette. Despite the darkness, Brody had a feeling the car that had just parked near the curb was the Mercedes AMG that had hung a tail on him earlier. The driver had found him and was out to whack him.

The guy ducked behind Ivy's rented Volvo in the driveway when Brody fired at him.

He was a pro, decided Brody. Only pros went around whacking people with silenced pistols with laser sights.

Brody had to move. The bush he was lying behind wasn't going to stop any bullets.

He launched himself to his feet and dashed behind Orion's silver metallic Porsche 911 Turbo S cabriolet parked in front of Ivy's rental.

The shooter fired at him. The bullet nicked Brody's shoulder. Stationed behind the Porsche, Brody let loose two shots at the gunman, who, firing back, ducked behind the Volvo.

Brody felt his cell phone vibrate in his trouser pocket. He took the call.

"Where are you?" said Ivy. "I thought I saw one of them downstairs. Help me."

"Somebody's shooting at me in your driveway. Your door's locked. How am I supposed to get in?"

"I can't open the door. If I go downstairs, they'll attack me."

"I'll have to break down your door. Are you OK with that?"

"Do whatever you have to," she said, her voice tense. "What am I gonna do when they come upstairs?"

"Hide in a room and lock the door. Push furniture behind the door so they can't break through."

"Hurry. I can't stand this much longer. I feel lightheaded."

"Maybe it's time for you to call the cops."

"I told you before, they'll never believe me."

The shooter fired at Brody. It sounded like the guy had changed position, while Brody was preoccupied on the phone.

"Don't tell the cops about the avatars," said Brody. "Just say people are trying to break into your home."

"Can't you protect me? I paid you a lot of money to protect me."

"As soon as I take care of this shooter, I'll break down your door."

"The cops'll never get here in time. It's up to you," said Ivy, on the verge of screaming.

"All right. Hold your voice down. If they don't hear you, maybe they'll think you're not home and leave."

Brody looked up in time to see the shooter dart across the front lawn to the side of the house, where he peeked around the corner and opened fire on Brody, who, from the shooter's new vantage point, was crouching in the line of fire.

Brody was springing away from the front of the Porsche even as the shooter began squeezing off rounds. Brody could continue to use the Porsche as a shield by circling around to the passenger side and taking cover.

Brody wondered if the shooter had anything to do with the avatars? Were they all in cahoots? Was the shooter planning on breaking into Ivy's house to help the avatars assault her? Or was the shooter's mission to whack Brody?

Brody had to take the guy out ASAP. He didn't want the guy entering Ivy's house. The shooter was in position to do just that. He could circle around back, kick down the back door, and enter the premises.

If the shooter was in league with the avatars, wouldn't they be coming out of the house to help him take out Brody any time now? wondered Brody. Or was the shooter out of contact with the avatars?

The shooter opened fire on Brody. Two bullets tore holes in the Porsche's windshield and blasted through the passenger's-side window. Brody stayed hunkered down behind the passenger's-side door.

Squatting, remaining behind the Porsche, he maneuvered behind the car's rear, where he had a better angle to blow away the shooter. Brody drew a bead on the shooter's exposed body and let loose two shots.

The shooter jerked backward. Brody couldn't tell if it was because his bullets had found their mark, or the shooter had ducked out of the way of incoming fire.

Brody's cell phone vibrated in his trouser pocket. He withdrew the phone.

"I think they're coming up the stairs," said Ivy, at her wit's end.

Brody wanted to find out the identity of the shooter.

But he couldn't put off Ivy any longer. He forgot about the shooter and tore across the lawn to the front door. He commenced kicking the wood panel near the doorknob. It took several well-placed kicks, but at last the doorjamb splintered and the door burst open.

Gun in hand, Brody stole into the lobby and made for the living room, seeking the avatars. He whipped into each room, primed to whack out both avatars. He didn't see them. Maybe he was too late. Maybe they had already gone upstairs and assaulted Ivy, he decided with dismay.

He flew up the stairs two steps at a time and charged into the hallway.

He didn't see Ivy or the avatars in the corridor. He would have to inspect each room.

He shoved his SIG in front of him as he went from room to room. All of the rooms' doors were open, except one. Brody figured Ivy must be hiding in that room. He tried the doorknob. The door was locked.

"Ivy, it's me," he said through the door, his face a half inch away from the wood.

"Who?" she said. "Your voice is muffled."

"Me. Brody. Let me in."

"Are the avatars out there?"

"I don't see any," said Brody, taking in the empty corridor. "You can open the door."

"Where are they?"

"I haven't seen them."

"I heard shooting outside."

"Somebody shot at me."

"Was it one of the avatars?"

"The shooter followed me here. You said the avatars were here before I got here."

"I don't understand why you didn't see them in the house."

"Maybe they left after I kicked in your door."

"Are you sure they're not in the hall?"

Brody checked the corridor a second time. "Positive."

He heard movement behind the door that sounded like furniture scraping the floor.

Ivy unlocked the door and cracked it, peeking out, her face drawn.

"I didn't see any place where the avatars broke in," said Brody.

"I heard them running around downstairs."

Ivy craned into the corridor to inspect it. Satisfied no one else was present, she stepped into the corridor.

"I know they're gonna kill me the next time they see me," she said. "They're mad I survived their running me off the road in the canyon. They wanted me to be blown to pieces in my exploding rental."

"I better check on that guy I shot outside," said Brody, making a beeline for the stairs.

"Is it safe downstairs?"

"I checked it out. Nobody's there."

Ivy followed him to the stairs, but didn't look eager to descend.

Chapter 63

Brody strode through the broken front door, down the stoop steps, and toward the body near the side of the house.

Brody stood rooted to the spot.

The body wasn't there.

He withdrew his SIG P365 from his ankle holster and proceeded to the spot where the body should have been lying. Coagulating blood mottled the grass in place of the corpse. Maybe the shooter had crawled elsewhere to die, decided Brody.

Brody cast around for the corpse. He didn't see it.

He inspected the stand of bottlebrush trees. No corpse there.

He decided to check out the sedan the shooter had parked on the side of the street in front of Ivy's house.

The car was gone.

The shooter was alive, decided Brody. It was the only explanation, even though Brody was convinced he had hit him with at least one bullet.

Ivy appeared, framed in the front doorway, her face pale, the foyer light shining behind her.

"Is he an avatar?" she asked.

"He's gone," answered Brody, approaching her.

"Gone? You said you shot him."

"I did. I'm convinced I hit him. I saw his body hit the ground and lie still. There's blood on the grass where he fell. I didn't have time to examine the body, because you were in need of help when I shot him."

"Was he an avatar or a human?"

"I couldn't tell. I didn't get close enough to see him clearly."

"What should we do?"

"Did you call the cops?"

"No."

Brody eyeballed her busted front door. "You need to call someone to repair your door."

Ivy followed his gaze. "I can't stay here tonight. The avatars might return to kill me. I'll have to check in at a motel."

"Good idea."

"I bet the avatars murdered Orion."

"How did they get the gun I gave you?"

"When they kidnaped me. It wasn't in my purse when you found me on the beach."

"Why did they kill Orion?"

Ivy gazed at him with hopeless eyes. "I don't know why they're doing anything. Why did they assault me? Why did they come here to kill me? Why did they force my car off the road into the canyon?"

"You said they told you they could do anything and get away with it. Maybe that's what they're trying to prove to you."

"If they're gonna kill me, why do they feel like they have to prove anything to me?"

Brody nodded yes. He mulled it over. "Maybe it has something to do with the IPO of Rabbit World next week."

"They said they wanted me to join them as avatars. What does that have to do with the IPO?"

Brody shrugged. "This whole thing's bizarre." He paused, wondering if he should tell her. It would break client confidentiality. On the other hand, Orion, his onetime client, was dead, which invalidated confidentiality, as far as Brody was concerned. After all, Orion was in no position to complain or sue him for breach of contract. "I think I should tell you, a team of professionals tried to sabotage Rabbit World's server."

"Orion told me about the break-in."

Brody raised his eyebrows. "He did? He told me he wanted it covered up. He didn't even want the cops to know about it."

"What does it mean?"

"It means, someone doesn't want Rabbit World's IPO to take place next week."

Ivy's cell phone chimed in her purse. Ivy took the call.

"Ivy, are you OK?" said Liz. "I wanted to check on you after all that's happening to you."

"Hi, Liz. I'm OK. The avatars tried to kill me, but they're gone now."

"What?" cried Liz. "What are you talking about?"

"I'm OK. Brody's here."

"Ohmigod. I'm telling you, it's the end of the world. Pack your go-bag. Avatars taking over the world and trying to kill us. What the fuck? I'm on my way over."

"No, I'm going to a motel. The front door's broken."

"They broke down your door?"

Ivy heaved a sigh of exasperation and exhaustion. "It's a long story."

"Are you sure you're all right? You can stay at my place, if you want. It's cluttered and it's not very big, but you—"

"Don't put yourself out, Liz. I'm fine."

"I don't know about you, but I'm stockpiling supplies."

"It *does* feel like the end of the world."

"They killed Orion. Now they're coming for you. This is insane."

"The cops haven't told me who they think killed Orion. Maybe tomorrow."

"The bastard tried to gaslight you."

"I think you're right about that, but I never wanted anyone to murder him. I'm worn out from all of today's excitement. I need to find a place to stay before I pass out. I'll call you tomorrow. Bye."

Ivy noticed blood on Brody's shoulder and screwed up her face. "You're bleeding."

"Just a nick," said Brody, forgetting he had been shot. "I'll get a butterfly at the hospital emergency room."

"You don't want that to get infected," said Ivy, heading for her new rental.

"I'll leave first so you can pull out," said Brody, returning to his Mini, which was parked behind her Volvo. "I'll drive behind you until you find a motel, in case the home invaders are out there waiting to hang a tail on you."

Ivy halted.

"You don't think . . . ," she said, her quavering voice trailing off.

"I think they're gone." *If they were here in the first place.* "I'll check to see if anyone follows you, though, to make sure."

Face glum, she kept walking to her car. "This feels like the longest day of my life."

Chapter 64

"I took a bullet," Bondurant told Nieman over his cell phone, hunched in his rented Mercedes, gritting his teeth, sweat beading above his lips.

"I don't understand," said Nieman.

"I did what the algorithms said and tried to take out Brody. He was packing. I told you the guy's dangerous."

"Are you saying you failed the mission?"

"I'm saying the mission isn't complete."

"You're not getting the rest of your Bitcoin till you complete your mission."

"Not a problem. There was some kind of a ruckus at the Kingston house tonight."

"I need more information," demanded Nieman.

"Brody kicked down the door to get into the house."

Nieman laughed.

Bondurant did a double take. "I don't get the joke."

"I believe Ivy is cracking up," said Nieman, amused. He became serious. "Did she call the cops?"

Bondurant thought about it. "I didn't see any cops near her house. She must have called Brody instead."

Nieman harrumphed. "Why isn't she calling the cops?"

"Beats me. I don't know why Brody kicked down her door either."

"If you remove Brody, do you think she'll go to the cops and report the avatars attacking her?"

"Where else would she go? I guess, she could hire another private dick," said Bondurant, wincing at the pain in his wounded thigh.

He was fortunate Brody's slug hadn't hit the femoral artery. However, he needed to have the wound treated. The bullet was lodged in his leg. Infection was imminent.

"She's not doing what the algorithms say she should do," said Nieman, voicing his frustration.

Nieman and his algorithms, decided Bondurant with disdain. Everything was algorithms to him.

"I guess they're wrong," said Bondurant.

"They're never wrong. She *will* go to the cops. It's only a matter of time. We need to force her hand. She should be terrified and desperate to talk to the cops to get them to help her."

"I don't see what I can do."

"I'm not sure what's holding her back."

"She's off her rocker, if you ask me."

"Do your mission and take Brody out," snapped Nieman. "I'm not paying you to think."

"I couldn't do much worse than your algorithms."

"You're not in the same league. They're light years ahead of your limited mental faculties."

"Then let the algorithms take out Brody."

"Don't be a fucking idiot. If you can't do the job, I'll hire someone who can."

"I'm on it. Don't have a cow."

Bondurant hated taking marching orders from a blue-haired whack job who spent most of his life with his head buried in a VR headset and thought he knew everything.

"Convince me you can handle the job," said Nieman.

"I made my bones with the SAS. That's the Special Air Service, the finest fighting force in the UK—make that the finest fighting force in the world. I've spooked for MI6 and I've freelanced for the FBI. What more do you want?"

"I want results. Don't call me again till you've finished the job."

Nieman terminated the call.

Moron, thought Bondurant, and flung his cell onto the passenger seat. The snot-nosed punk had no concept of reality, locked away in his penthouse, his swollen blue-haired head stuffed up his ass.

Bondurant fired his Mercedes engine and put the transmission in Drive. He was glad he wasn't driving a stick. Working the clutch with his bum left leg would have been a bitch. He found a ramshackle dive on Wilshire Boulevard and rented a room for the night from a manager who bore an uncanny resemblance to Norman Bates.

Bondurant limped into his room, dug a first-aid kit out of his leather valise, and entered the bathroom. He removed his trousers, sat on the toilet seat, and doused his open wound with alcohol. He winced at the stinging sensation. He stanched the wound with his handkerchief, which he kept pressed against it.

The bullet was buried in his leg, he decided, since he didn't see an exit wound. He would have to go to a hospital, or buy a forceps at a drugstore and remove the lead himself. Otherwise, the wound would get infected. If he checked in at a hospital, he would have to stay overnight. He didn't have the time. Also, the doctors would follow protocol and report the gunshot wound to the cops.

Bondurant put his pants back on, googled the nearest drugstore on his smartphone, found a CVS three blocks away, and limped to it. He bought gauze, bandages, a pair of tweezers, and another plastic bottle of alcohol.

He returned to his motel room, entered the bathroom, and went to work.

He removed his trousers, poured alcohol on the tweezers and on his wound to disinfect them, and stuck a washcloth form the towel rack into his mouth for something to bite down on when the pain became overwhelming.

With the tweezers he picked open the wound so he could dig out the bullet. Blood resumed streaming out of the wound. Grinding the washcloth between his teeth, he fished around inside the wound for the bullet. Pain exploded in his head as he scraped the tweezers against his femur. Where was the damn thing?

He probed deeper with the tweezers. His face drenched with sweat, he thought he would pass out any second. He told himself he had to stay conscious or he would black out and bleed to death. He held onto consciousness by the skin of his teeth, probing deeper into his wound.

The tips of the tweezers found something hard. Bondurant hoped it was the bullet. He opened the tweezers and tried to pinch the bullet. Every time he opened the tweezers he felt waves of pain course up his leg as the tweezers pressed against raw tissue in his leg.

Face red and dripping with sweat, he pressed the tweezers around the bullet, secured it, and withdrew it gingerly from his leg so the tweezers wouldn't lose their grip. He gasped with relief as he plucked the blood-smeared bullet from his leg and tossed it into the sink along with the bloody pair of tweezers.

He stanched the wound with a bathroom towel, wiped the blood off his thigh, and tossed the towel into the bathtub.

Instead of stitches, he used superglue to seal the wound. Lightheaded, he stood up, halted out of the bathroom, found the bed, fell on it, and was asleep before his head hit the pillow.

Chapter 65

After Ivy checked into a hotel room in Brentwood, she called Liz.

"Sorry I was so abrupt with you before," said Ivy.

"No problem. You're probably worn out from everything that's happening to you."

"I checked into a motel and feel better already."

"I've been thinking. I bet those avatars that attacked you were hired by Orion."

"What do you mean?" said Ivy, perplexed.

"I bet he hired them to attack you. It was all part of his scheme to gaslight you so he could have you committed and gain control of your money."

"I can't believe he would hire thugs to assault me," said Ivy, resisting the idea.

"I've given it a lot of thought. It makes sense to me."

"It makes no sense to me. He wanted me to sell real estate in Rabbit World. Why would he hire two thugs to assault me? Why would I want to sell real estate in a place I'm afraid to set foot in?"

Ivy shook her head in confusion.

"To trigger your nervous breakdown," said Liz.

"Why would he tell me not to report the assault to the cops?"

"Because he didn't want anybody to know about it other than you and him. He didn't want anyone to figure out he was gaslighting you."

Ivy thought about it. Maybe Liz was onto something. But Ivy found it hard to believe. The most important thing in Orion's life was his company Rabbit World. Its success was what he lived and breathed for. Why risk its IPO's success by hiring goons to assault her? The resulting bad PR would sink the IPO. Which was why he didn't want her to go to the cops. How could he be sure she wouldn't report it to the cops? What Liz didn't know, but Ivy knew, was that Orion would never risk doing anything that resulted in bad PR for Rabbit World.

"He wouldn't gaslight me if it meant losing Rabbit World," said Ivy.

"I know you desperately want to believe he wouldn't, *but he wanted your money more than Rabbit World's success.*"

"I don't agree. Rabbit World was everything to him. It was his pride and joy."

"You're blinded by your love for him. Can't you see that?"

"You watch too many Lifetime movies."

"Lifetime movies? *Puh-lease.* I watch horror movies. I have a subscription to Shudder. The end of the world is right around the corner. I own a Louisville Slugger to kill zombies. I never leave home without my go-bag."

Sometimes Ivy couldn't tell if Liz was kidding. Ivy laughed despite herself.

"If the avatars are working for Orion, why are they harassing me after he's dead?" said Ivy. "They have no reason to anymore."

"Maybe they don't know he's dead."

That was possible, decided Ivy. After all, the murder hadn't been reported in the news yet, as far as she knew. *Wait a minute . . .*

"How could they *not* know?" she said. "They're the ones that killed him."

"You can't be certain of that."

"I'm certain the avatars do whatever they want. They don't take orders from anyone, because in the metaverse there are no laws. That's what they told me. They don't sound like they're working for anyone but themselves."

"Orion told them to say that as part of his scheme to gaslight you."

"You have an overactive imagination."

"And you're blinded by love. Misplaced love, if you ask me. I'm telling you, Orion had it in for you."

Ivy rubbed her eyes. "I'm getting a headache. I don't want to talk about this anymore."

"I'm good with that. I just want you to relax, Ivy. Your ordeal is over. Your tormentor is gone."

"My ordeal's never gonna be over till the two avatar rapists are gone."

"Don't worry about them anymore. Chill out. You're free. No more gaslighting. Have a good night—what's left of it, anyway."

Liz hung up.

Ivy wanted to believe Liz that her troubles were over, but Ivy continued to believe the avatars were going to keep coming for her until she was dead. They were a law unto themselves and believed nothing could stop them.

Ivy jumped when her cell phone vibrated in her hand.

"Are you OK?" she asked, thinking it was Brody.

"You got lucky tonight," said Ed Vidor. "Next time will be your last."

"You bastards," she said, venting her wrath. "Come after me again, and you'll regret it."

Vidor laughed. "We never regret anything. We're avatars. We do whatever we want, so why should we feel regret? Join us or die."

"You're in the real world now. You have to play by the rules and obey the law, or else."

"Rules are for losers. We live in the total freedom of the metaverse. If you're not for us, you're against us. If you're against us, you die."

Vidor terminated his call.

White-faced, Ivy stared at her cell phone.

She consoled herself with the realization they had no idea where she was staying. She felt safe—for now.

Chapter 66

The next morning, Ivy had a Belgian waffle smothered with maple syrup for breakfast, a glass of orange juice, and a bowl of blueberries at a nearby waffle joint. She finished her meal with a cup of cappuccino.

She checked out of her motel and drove back to her house.

When she arrived home, she was surprised to see squad cars parked in her driveway and police officers standing on her front stoop.

As she pulled into her driveway, Lieutenant Macready climbed out of an unmarked black Dodge Charger parked in front of her and swaggered toward her rental.

She killed her rental's engine.

"What happened to your front door?" he said, approaching her and glancing back at her house. "The doorjamb's busted all to hell."

Ivy didn't know if she wanted to tell the cops about the avatars yet. Her bringing up the avatars' assault on her in Rabbit World would sink the IPO next week, and Rabbit World belonged to her now that Orion was dead. She no more wanted the IPO to fail than had Orion.

"Somebody tried to break into my house last night," said Ivy, sitting in her Volvo driver's seat and speaking through the powered-down window.

"It looks like they succeeded."

"It was Brody."

"Brody?"

"My private detective."

"Brody broke down your door?" said Macready, frowning.

"He was trying to help me."

"He helps you by breaking down your door?" said Macready, incredulous.

242

"Maybe I should come back another time," said Ivy, fired her rental's ignition, and prepared to back out of the driveway.

"Please step out of your car, Mrs. Kingston," said Macready, signaling to one of his uniforms who was standing in the driveway.

A five-eight clean-cut uniform pushing thirty took up position behind Ivy's rental and stood at attention.

"I don't want to get in the way of your investigation," she said. "I can come back later. You should have let me know you were coming."

"Cut your engine and hand me your keys."

"I'll come back later. It's no problem."

"Give me your keys, Mrs. Kingston," said Macready, holding out his hand. "You're under arrest for the murder of your husband Orion."

Ivy did a double take. She couldn't believe her ears.

"This is insane," she said. "*I* didn't do it."

"We have a warrant for your arrest. Please step out of your car. We're taking you to the station."

He Mirandized her.

For a split second Ivy considered backing out of the driveway and fleeing. She decided against it. She would cooperate with the police. Her lawyer would get her out of jail in no time.

"On what grounds?" she said.

"We found your fingerprints on the murder weapon's muzzle."

Ivy decided to come clean about the gun. "I had that gun in my purse. Someone stole the gun from me."

"Did you report the gun as stolen to the police?"

"I didn't have time. When I found Orion dead on the carpet, I went into a state of shock. All I could think of was him lying there."

"You can tell it to the jury. For now, please step out of your car. We're booking you for your husband's murder."

"I want my lawyer."

"Of course. You have that right. When we're at the station, you can call him."

"You don't understand. I didn't shoot Orion. He was already dead when I entered the living room and found his body."

"He was already dead because you had shot him two hours earlier."

"What?" said Ivy, bewildered. "That's not true."

"The ME says Orion had been dead for two hours at the time you found the corpse."

"I—I have no idea how long he'd been dead."

"Where were you two hours before you say you found your husband's corpse?"

"I—I—uh—don't remember."

She didn't know whether she should tell him about avatars kidnaping her—and yet her innocence might depend on it. She would consult with her lawyer first.

"How convenient," said Macready, a cynical smile slashing his face.

"I have a witness. Brody was with me when I returned home and found Orion dead in the living room."

"And were you with Brody two hours before you found Orion's stiff?"

"Uh—no."

Macready cleared his throat. "I don't have all day. Please step out of your car, ma'am."

Her body riddled with apprehension, she opened the rental door and climbed out of the driver's seat.

"I'll take your keys," said Macready, holding out his hand.

Ivy handed her keys to him.

He summoned the uniform who was standing at the foot of the drive. When the uniform approached, Macready gave him Ivy's keys.

"Back her car out so we can pull out of here and book her downtown." Macready turned to a stocky Hispanic

244

uniform who was standing near the front stoop. "Cuff her, Rincon."

As the reality of her situation sank in, Ivy's heartbeat skyrocketed. She struggled not to pass out.

"Avatars," she blurted.

"What?" said Macready.

"Avatars kidnaped me two hours before I found Orion dead."

Macready stared at her in disbelief.

"It's true," said Ivy.

"I see where you're going," said Macready, his expression jaundiced. "You're gonna plead not guilty by reason of insanity. The judge should find it amusing." Macready brushed his finger against his nose. "But it doesn't pass the smell test."

"Could I call my lawyer first?" said Ivy, pushing away Rincon's attempt at cuffing her. "I'm gonna pass out if I don't."

She felt the walls closing in on her. She struggled to breathe.

Macready heaved a sigh of impatience. "Go ahead. For all the good it'll do you." To Rincon: "Let her use her cell phone. Then cuff her," he added with a gleeful snarl. "Even your pricy mouthpiece won't be able to get you off."

Chapter 67

Brody was sitting at his laptop in his apartment that doubled as his office. He was searching for images of avatars that resembled the two Ivy had described as her attackers in Rabbit World.

He saw images that resembled the attacking avatars, but how could he find out whose avatar belonged to who? Was there a directory of avatars that listed who owned which avatar? If there was, he didn't know about it.

The whole metaverse thing was frustrating to him. It seemed like anyone could hide in the metaverse without ever being found. And they could commit whatever crime they felt like without fear of punishment in the lawless metaverse.

His cell phone chimed.

"Brody here."

"The cops arrested me for Orion's murder," said Ivy, at the end of her rope.

"Wait a minute," said Brody, taken aback. "Do they have some kind of proof?"

"They said my fingerprints are on the murder weapon."

Possible, decided Brody, since she had handled the SIG he had given her to protect herself.

"Where are you?" he said.

"The cops are booking me downtown."

"Did you call your lawyer?"

"He's on his way. I want you to find evidence to clear me."

"Got any suggestions?"

"Can you find the kidnapers that stuffed me in their trunk?" she said, struggling to breathe on account of stress.

"The two avatars?"

"My lawyer told me over the phone we need proof they kidnaped me. It would prove I wasn't home at the time of the murder. Please help me."

Ivy hung up.

Brody had yet to see either of the two avatars in the flesh. He had only seen video recordings of the backs of their heads on CCTV security tapes. When he had found Ivy alone on the beach asleep, he hadn't seen the avatars anywhere near her. Nor had he seen them when he had gone to her house last night to protect her from them. The only one he had seen at her house was the guy who had hung a tail on him in a black sedan and had exchanged gunfire with him. Brody couldn't make out the guy's face. He had no reason to believe the guy was an avatar.

Brody wanted to believe Ivy about the avatars trying to kill her, but he had no evidence bearing out her story. Avatars roaming around the real world with murder on their minds was hard to believe. He had seen the alleged avatars talking to her on videotapes, but he couldn't be sure they were avatars. They could have been guys wearing masks.

Maybe they were pretending to be avatars to make Ivy go nuts, Brody decided. But why would they want her to go nuts? Had Orion hired them as part of a scheme to gaslight her? But Orion was dead. Who had murdered him?

If Orion had indeed been gaslighting Ivy, she had to be considered the prime suspect in his murder.

If Ivy didn't do it, who did? wondered Brody.

The two avatars, or whoever they were, had to be placed on the short list of suspects, because they had it in for Ivy and could have framed her for Orion's murder by using Brody's gun to commit the murder and incriminate her.

What about Dr. Jamal Harris? wondered Brody. Orion had bribed the guy to violate doctor-patient privilege to get dirt on Ivy. Maybe Harris was mad at Orion for compromising him and jeopardizing his career as a psychiatrist. Mad enough to murder Orion?

What about the shady FBI agent with the missing pinky Xavier Bondurant? Brody didn't know how that guy fit into this. What attracted the FBI's interest in the avatars that had assaulted Ivy? Then again, the guy was a fake FBI agent. What kind of a racket was he running?

No matter how Brody looked at it, Ivy had to be considered the main suspect in Orion's murder, especially since the murder weapon had her prints on it. Which didn't mean she necessarily committed the murder, but he could see why the cops had busted her.

Chapter 68

Bondurant had just woken up. He was lying in his motel-room bed watching the news on the flat-panel HDTV mounted on the wall. He had slept longer than he had planned. His bullet wound and do-it-yourself surgery must have exhausted him. His leg throbbed, but he felt refreshed from sleep.

He couldn't believe the TV news.

He produced his cell phone and called Nieman.

"Did you hear the news?" said Bondurant.

"What news?" said Nieman.

Bondurant pictured Nieman with his VR headset strapped to his head, ignorant of the world around him.

"Do you ever watch the news?" said Bondurant.

"The billionaire owners of the media only let you see what they want you to see."

"I ask you a simple question, and you give me a philosophy lecture."

"Does this call have a point to it? I'm surfing monster waves in Waimea Bay."

Nieman's head was stuck in his VR headset, decided Bondurant. The klutz couldn't ride a two-foot wave, let alone a monster wave, if his life depended on it.

"Somebody murdered Orion Kingston," said Bondurant.

Silence.

"Say again," said Nieman.

"You heard me. The cops busted Ivy Kingston for the murder."

Nieman snorted. "Interesting." He paused, waiting. "And?"

"And what?" said Bondurant, puzzled.

"The reason you should be calling me. To tell me you took out Brody."

Bondurant sniffed. "He got lucky. He's still alive."

"The algorithms say he has to go," said Nieman, raising his voice.

*Fuck your algorithm*s, thought Bondurant.

"He's as good as gone," he said. "I need a little more time, is all."

"The algorithms say he's a threat to our system. You need to take him off the table."

"Consider it done."

"According to the algorithms, you should have completed the job by now."

"They're wrong. I'm in the field. They aren't. They don't know what's what."

"Don't be an ass. You're a foot soldier. They're the brains. Do as they say."

Bondurant pulled a face. "As long as you deposit the seven hundred grand you owe me into my offshore account in the Caymans."

"I thought you wanted Bitcoin."

"Bitcoin's value is plummeting."

"I'll need proof of Brody's removal."

"How about I Fed Ex his dick to you?"

"This isn't a joking matter," said Nieman, put out.

"I'll include his balls."

"You fucking ass," screamed Nieman.

"Take it easy. I know what I'm doing. I'm a pro."

"Then act like one."

Bondurant would be glad when this assignment was over. He hated working for spoiled Big Tech know-it-all punks. Especially ones with blue hair and wacko avatar eyes.

"What kind of proof do you want?" said Bondurant.

"Are you sure your line is encrypted?"

"You're talking to a pro. How many times do I have to tell you? And I'm using a burner. Don't worry about eavesdroppers."

"OK. Let's see. a photo of Brody's face with a bullet hole in the forehead would be sufficient."

"No problem."

"What are you waiting for?"

Nieman terminated the call.

Bondurant sneered at his cell phone. *The things I do for money.*

Chapter 69

Ivy was sitting alone at a rectangular table in a windowless interrogation room in the downtown LAPD station when she saw the door open. A five-ten, black-haired, blue-eyed man entered, gripping a briefcase in his right hand. His hair neatly coiffed, in his midforties with a smooth-shaven tanned face, he was wearing an all-white tennis outfit, including white sneakers.

"I came over as soon as I got your call on the tennis court," said Anderson Glass, Ivy's lawyer. "I didn't even have time to change, as you can see."

"Fine," said Ivy, her nerves frayed from enduring the humiliating procedure of being booked as a murder suspect.

"My game needs work. I'm not in Roger Federer's class yet," he said with a toothy grin worthy of a matinee idol.

Ivy flashed a tense, polite smile.

Glass sat down across from her, snapped open his briefcase, and whipped out a pen and a yellow legal pad.

"Let's get down to business. Why do the police think you murdered your husband?" he said, leveling his gaze at her eyes.

"They found my fingerprints on the murder weapon," said Ivy, reaching for the cup of water on the tabletop in front of her.

"Did you two have fights?"

"Once in a while."

Knowing it would hurt her cause, she wasn't about to tell Glass she had pulled a gun on Orion.

"Forgive me for asking, but it's my job," said Glass. "Did you murder him?"

Ivy took a gulp of water and cleared her throat. "No."

"I need you to be honest with me. I'm your lawyer. I can't give you the best legal advice unless you tell me the truth."

"I didn't murder him."

"Can you explain why your fingerprints are on the murder weapon?"

"A PI gave me that gun for self-protection. Someone stole the gun from my purse," she said, setting down the half-full cup.

Glass wrote on his legal pad.

He searched her face. "Self-protection from whom? From Orion?"

"Not him."

"Then who?"

Ivy wasn't sure how to answer. Did she want to bring up the avatars? She decided she better. After all, Glass was her lawyer and needed to know. Anyhow, she had already told the cops about the avatars.

"The two avatars that assaulted me in Rabbit World," she said.

Glass leaned back in his chair in astonishment. "Wait a minute. Fill me in about these avatars."

"They assaulted me in the Rabbit World metaverse then stalked me in the real world and tried to kill me."

"Avatars tried to kill you?" said Glass, bemused.

"They drove a black Dodge Charger that rammed me off the road into the gulch at Topanga Canyon."

"Whoa," said Glass, waving his hands. "Slow down a minute."

"You wanted to know, so I'm telling you."

"Did you report the vehicular assault with the Charger to the police?"

"No. I didn't think they'd believe me."

Glass drummed a tattoo on the tabletop with his tanned fingers. "Who do you think stole the gun from you?"

"It could have been the avatars."

"How could they have gotten it?"

Ivy rubbed her forehead. "Maybe when they kidnaped me."

Glass widened his eyes. "They tried to kill you *and* kidnaped you? When did the kidnaping occur?"

"Before I returned to my house and found Orion's corpse in the living room."

"How did you escape from the kidnapers?"

Frowning, Ivy shook her head. "I dunno. I blacked out."

"Let me get this straight. When you woke up, the kidnapers were gone?"

"I found myself lying alone on the sand at Zuma Beach."

"Why did they let you go? Did somebody pay a ransom for you?"

"Not that I know of."

"Then why did they let you go?"

"They knocked me out with some drug. I don't know what happened when they had me. Once, when I awoke, I found myself stuffed in the trunk of a moving car."

Glass scribbled on his legal pad.

"I don't understand why they let you go," he said.

"I don't either."

"Did you see the avatars steal your gun?"

"No."

"Then how do you know they stole it?"

"I looked in my purse when I was in the car trunk and I saw that the gun was missing. That was the first time I noticed it wasn't there."

"But it could have been missing before then. Is that possible?"

"Yes. But I don't know who would have taken it. Few people knew I had it. The PI Brody knew because he gave it to me. Orion knew."

"How did he know?"

Ivy didn't want to tell him she had threatened to shoot Orion with it. She knew it would make her look guilty in the lawyer's eyes.

"He saw me with it," she said.

Glass paused in thought, chewing on the end of his ballpoint. "I don't want to appear nosy or skeptical, but I need to know certain things. Are you seeing a psychiatrist?"

Ivy took offense. "Why do you think that?"

"Not everybody sees avatars walking around in the real world."

"Are you suggesting I'm making it up?"

"Not at all. I'm your lawyer. I need to know as much as possible about you in order to mount the best possible defense."

Satisfied with his answer, Ivy said, "Yes, I'm seeing a psychiatrist."

"What for?"

"I went to him after I was assaulted by avatars in Rabbit World. The attack traumatized me."

"I'm sorry. I didn't know. Are these the same avatars that rammed you off the road?"

"They are."

"I can see how you would have nightmares about them."

"It wasn't a nightmare," said Ivy, vexed over Glass's skepticism. "It happened in the real world. They tried to kill me by ramming my car off the road into Topanga Canyon."

Glass studied his notes then looked up. "Who do you think killed your husband?"

"Maybe the avatars."

"The ones that assaulted you?"

"Yes."

"Why would they want him dead?"

Ivy chewed it over. "Maybe they wanted to frame me for his murder."

"They must hate you."

255

Ivy's eyes bugged out. "They tried to kill me for Chrissake."

"Why did they try to kill you?"

"They wanted me to be one of them and I refused."

Glass searched her face. "Why did they kidnap you?"

"I can't figure that out."

"How did you escape from them?"

"You already asked me that. I can't recall." She paused two beats. "Maybe the PI Brody scared them away."

"He helped you?"

"He picked me up at the beach and took me home."

"Did he tell you he scared away the kidnapers?"

"No. I said *maybe* he scared them away."

Glass nodded and wrote something on his legal pad.

"Then he didn't see the kidnapers?" he said.

"I don't think so."

"You're the only one that saw them?"

"As far as I know."

"Did you describe the kidnapers to the police?"

Ivy took a sip of water. "I did. Ed is tall, in his late twenties, and wears his hair in a mullet. Joe is shorter and looks older by a couple of years. He has a shaved head and blue eyes."

Glass wrote everything down. "Are you sure they're avatars?"

"Positive. They assaulted me in Rabbit World."

Glass narrowed his eyes. "Why didn't you report this assault to the police?"

"There aren't any laws in the metaverse. You, a lawyer, should know that. The cops can't do anything about the assault, so why tell them? Also, my husband told me not to go to the cops."

Glass nodded. "The ME has determined that Orion was shot about two hours before you found him dead." He leaned toward her. "This is very important: where were you at that time?"

Concentrating, Ivy bit her lower lip. "I was in the hands of the kidnapers, I think."

"Did anyone see you with them? Think hard. Any witness would corroborate your alibi."

Ivy shook her head. "I can't remember. I might have been in the car trunk at the time of the murder. Nobody could have seen me there."

Glass tapped his pen against his legal pad. "We need to find a witness for your alibi."

"Find the avatars that kidnaped me."

Glass trained a cynical gaze on her. "How do I do that?"

"That's why I'm paying you the megabucks."

"Not to put too fine a point on it, it's gonna be hard to convince a jury two avatars are out to get you in the real world."

"What do you want me to do? Lie?" said Ivy, frustrated.

"No."

"The avatars must have killed Orion."

"How could they if, like you say, they were in the process of kidnaping you at the time of his murder?"

"Oh, yeah," said Ivy, slouching her shoulders. "I didn't think of that."

"We need another suspect," said Glass, as if to himself, fiddling with his pen.

"I can't stand being locked up. I'll have a breakdown. I need you to get me out of here." Ivy trembled at the memory of her booking. "The strip search they subjected me to was unbearable."

"Don't worry. We'll post bail. It'll be expensive, but you can afford it," said Glass, standing up.

"When can I get out?"

"They have to charge you within seventy-two hours of your arrest."

The color drained from Ivy's face. "I don't know if I can last that long in here."

"You can post bail right now, since they're done booking you—if you can get the cash."

"No problem," said Ivy, brightening.

Glass inserted his legal pad and ballpoint into his briefcase. Snapping the briefcase shut, he stood up.

"They'll arraign you quickly, because your fingerprints are on the murder weapon. At that point, the judge may raise or lower your bail."

"I'd rather they never arraign me."

"I can't promise that. Your fingerprints on the murder weapon incriminate you."

"Let's post bail and get out of this dungeon," said Ivy, expressing disgust and standing up. "I need to save Rabbit World."

"You need to prove you're innocent."

Ivy rounded on him. "I thought I was innocent until proven guilty."

"Ordinarily, that is so. The problem is, your fingerprints on the murder weapon are damning evidence. And you had a history of fighting with Orion."

"What couple doesn't fight now and then? Are you a bachelor, or something?" said Ivy, eying him with perplexity.

"No. I have a husband."

"Oh. Well, don't you two ever fight?"

"We do."

"You see."

"I'm not arguing with you. It's just that your fingerprints on the gun . . . This will be a difficult case to win."

Ivy's spirits sank. She knew she was in trouble when her own lawyer was pessimistic.

Chapter 70

In his apartment Brody phoned the LAPD forensic tech who helped him with investigations on and off in his spare time. Of Indian descent he went by the name of Ari Khan. Wiry, pushing forty, he wore black plastic-framed spectacles on his narrow nose and had an antsy demeanor, blurting out his sentences in a high-pitched rapid-fire staccato.

"Ari, have you had a chance to look at that handkerchief I gave you?"

"What's it to you?"

"How about a ticket to a game starring the world-champion Los Angeles Rams?"

"That's what you promised me last time and didn't deliver."

Brody couldn't remember if what Ari was telling him was on the level.

"OK," said Brody. "How about two tickets to two different Rams games?"

"That's more like it. As long as you keep your promise this time."

"You know I'm good for it."

"Actually, I don't, Brody."

"If I forget, remind me."

"What about the Playboy Mansion? Are you still getting tickets to the Playboy Mansion?"

"Ari, where have you been, my man? You're putting in too much overtime. Don't you keep up with the times? Hef is dead. The Playboy Mansion is being rebuilt. The sex-party grotto was filled in with cement."

"Oh, hell. You mean, I missed out? I was looking forward to a hot date with a pneumatic bimbo playmate of the month with bedroom eyes and bee-stung lips."

"Not gonna happen, Ari."

Ari fetched a forlorn sigh. "Oh well. I guess I'll have to settle for two Rams tickets."

"What did you find out? Did you find traces of ether on the handkerchief?"

"Nope. Which doesn't mean there was never any on it. Ether evaporates quickly. It could easily have evaporated before you gave me the handkerchief."

"Or maybe ether was never on it in the first place."

"Correct."

"What about DNA or fingerprints?"

"Negative to both."

"OK, Ari, I owe you."

"You do, indeed. Two tickets. And I expect you to deliver this time. Or you can quit asking me favors."

Ari cradled his handset with a loud bang.

Wincing at the noise, Brody pulled his cell phone away from his ear.

The intel didn't verify Ivy's story about the kidnapers knocking her out with ether, decided Brody. On the other hand, it didn't disprove it. Like Ari had said, any ether on the handkerchief could have evaporated before Brody gave the handkerchief to him for analysis.

But why would Ivy concoct such a bizarre and unbelievable story about avatars kidnaping her? wondered Brody. Sure, she needed an alibi for Orion's murder, but who was going to believe *avatars* had kidnaped her while Orion was murdered? If she left out the part about avatars, her alibi would be more believable. Then it must be true that she believed avatars had kidnaped her. She also believed they had run her off the road in an attempt to kill her. And she believed they had tried to kill her at home last night.

Yet the fact remained that nobody had witnessed any of these attacks, decided Brody. Believing her was difficult because her claims were so fantastic. Even though he knew she had psychiatric issues, he wanted to believe her.

But if she didn't kill Orion, who did? The only way to get her off the hook was to find the identity of the real killer.

Chapter 71

Ivy entered Orion's office. She wanted to save Rabbit World, to make sure its IPO next week would be a huge success. With Orion gone, she would have to take the reins of the company.

It was good to get out of the house. It reminded her of the murder and of the home invasion by the avatars. It was even better to get out of jail, which reminded her of hell.

A large picture of a silver Porsche 911 hung on the wall near the door. Orion had a thing about Porsches, she knew. Their engines were a work of art, he had once told her.

She walked over to his aquarium, which bubbled soothingly. The brightly colored fish swam inside the glass tank, calming her nerves. The aquarium looked so serene. She swiped her fingers across the glass. Not a trace of dust on it. The office cleaners were worth their salt.

Even though the fish looked tranquil as they swam around, Orion had told her they didn't get along and frequently got into fights, biting and chasing each other. She didn't want to think about it. She wanted to picture them forever as they were now—peaceful and content.

She crossed the carpet to the leather chair behind the mahogany desk and sat down. She felt the leather armrests under her arms and squeezed them with her hands.

Now that she was the only one with skin in the game—hell, she was the boss—she wanted Rabbit World to succeed more than ever. And yet . . . was the Rabbit World metaverse safe? she wondered, remembering the vicious assault the two avatars had mounted against her. She shuddered at the memory.

She had to shut it out of her mind and proceed as if it hadn't happened.

This was Orion's baby. She owed it to him to make it succeed. It wasn't his fault the avatars had attacked her. Or was the assault part of his scheme to gaslight her, as Liz believed?

It made Ivy's head spin trying to figure out what was really going on. She was seeing conspiracies and plots all around her. She would think about it later.

How could she make Rabbit World safer than it was? By kicking those two avatar thugs out of it. And how could she do that? The metaverse had no laws or rules. Its total freedom was what attracted people to it.

She wouldn't tell the media about her assault. She had to keep it out of the news—at least until after Rabbit World's IPO next week. Her testimony to her lawyer Glass about the assault was confidential, protected by attorney-client privilege. No one would hear it.

She opened Orion's laptop that lay on the desktop.

She had no idea how to run a metaverse. She would have to learn from the ground up. A daunting task. Where to begin? she wondered.

"There's a Mr. Riley here to see you, Mrs. Kingston," said the receptionist over the speakerphone next to the laptop. "He says he has urgent business with Orion. I told him you're in charge now."

Ivy didn't know what Riley wanted. Orion hadn't told her about him. Or had he told her and she forgot? She wasn't thinking straight lately. She decided to see Riley. After all, she was the boss now.

"Fine," she said. "Let him in."

Riley entered, wearing a white seersucker suit with navy blue stripes and a turquoise moiré tie.

"The name's Jeff Riley and I'm interested in buying property in Rabbit World," he said, taking long strides toward her, smiling.

"Have a seat, Mr. Riley," said Ivy, gesturing to the chair in front of her desk.

Riley placed his business card on her desktop with a fillip.

"I'm prepared to offer you one million dollars for real estate on the main street in Rabbit World," he said.

"What do you plan to build there?"

"Why does that matter?"

"It matters to us. We're the owners."

"Fine. No problem. We plan on building a casino."

Ivy knew Orion didn't want gambling in Rabbit World. He wanted it to be family-friendly.

"I will have to turn down your offer," she said, politely.

"What?" said Riley, flabbergasted. "Why in this day and age won't you allow a casino in Rabbit World? It will make tons of money and attract millions of people. Rabbit World will be the most popular metaverse in the world, and you'll be able to raise the price of your real estate."

"We don't want Mafia types in Rabbit World."

"Mafia types?" said Riley, outraged. "I object. I represent the totally legit corporation Casino Gem Planet LLC."

"We're very firm about our vision of Rabbit World. No gambling will be allowed."

Riley bolted to his feet. "I can't believe this. What kind of outdated, half-assed operation are you running here? Are you getting into business to lose money? Is that your ludicrous business model?"

"We will not stand for intimidation in Rabbit World," said Ivy, jabbing her finger down on the desktop several times.

"I can't believe this. What business school did you graduate from? DeLorean University?"

"Are you suggesting we're gonna sell cocaine in Rabbit World?" said Ivy, livid with rage.

"I'm suggesting you're gonna go bankrupt like the carmaker DeLorean."

"It's time for you to leave, Mr. Riley," said Ivy, grinding her teeth.

"How can you pass up a once-in-a-lifetime deal like this? We're doing you a favor by offering to buy property from you."

"We will not tarnish the image of Rabbit World by accepting your offer. That is final."

"Doesn't anybody have a brain in this out-of-step outfit?" said Riley, exasperated. "You're living in the Middle Ages. Gambling is everywhere. Look at Powerball and Mega Millions."

"If you don't like my business, you know where the door is."

"Can't you listen to reason?"

"Rabbit World is gonna be the Disneyland of metaverses."

"You're worse than your husband. And look what happened to him."

"Is that a threat?" said Ivy, thrusting to her feet.

"We're gonna sue you for discrimination. You'll regret fucking with us."

Ivy screamed. It wasn't a scream of terror. It was a scream of anger and frustration.

"You nutcase," said Riley, widening his eyes.

He stormed out of the office.

Ivy realized her hands were shaking with rage. She had already been strung out from her ordeal in jail. Then she had to put up with this creep. Maybe it hadn't been a good idea to come here, but it did get her mind off her own difficulties. She was becoming too self-absorbed. She had to get out of herself, even if it meant dealing with a bully-boy louse like Riley. Otherwise, she'd end up back on her shrink's couch.

Chapter 72

Ivy produced her cell phone and called Brody.
"I'm out of jail on bail," she said.
"Good."
"My lawyer said you need to find out who killed
Orion. It's the only thing that will get me off because of my
fingerprints on the murder weapon."
"I agree. Who do you think killed him?"
"The avatars."
"As I understand it, they kidnaped you while Orion
was shot. How could the avatars kidnap you and shoot
Orion at the same time?"
Ivy scratched her jaw. "I've been thinking about that.
Maybe only one of them kidnaped me, while the other shot
Orion."
"Didn't you say they both kidnaped you?"
Ivy closed her eyes and shook her head. "My
memory's fuzzy on this because of the ether they gave me
to knock me out. It could be that only one of them kidnaped
me, while the other was at my house shooting Orion."
"By the way, my connection at the LAPD Forensics
Department found no ether on that handkerchief you gave
me at the beach."
"I don't know what to tell you. It smelled like ether
when he pressed it against my face, and it knocked me out
cold. Wait a minute. Are you saying you don't believe
me?" said Ivy, becoming touchy.
"I believe you. But I'm not the one who counts. The
jurors are the ones who count. It would help if we had
evidence proving you'd been kidnaped."
"The handkerchief is the only evidence I have."
"I can't find either of these guys. I have no idea where
to look for them."
"Maybe they went back to Rabbit World."

"If they're back there, the cops aren't gonna touch them. The cops can't bust anyone in the metaverse."

"We have to find them," said Ivy, terrified of being convicted for murder.

"What if . . . ?"

"What if what?"

"I can understand if you don't want to do this, but it's the only way I can think of to get to them."

"It doesn't sound like something I want to do," said Ivy, warily.

Brody demurred, reluctant to tell her. "What if we use you as bait to attract them? Then I can catch them."

"The less I see of them, the better."

"It's just a suggestion. I couldn't trace their license plate. The CCTV video that had a picture of it didn't show enough of it to do me any good. The first part of it isn't enough to make an ID."

"Bait, huh? A sacrificial lamb? Is that what you're suggesting?"

"We're not sacrificing you. You're acting as a lure. I won't let them harm you."

"You're asking a lot of me."

"I know. And I don't blame you if you refuse. But if one of them killed Orion, I need to grill them. It's the only way to get you off the hook for his murder with your prints on the murder weapon."

Her nerves tense, Ivy thought about it with apprehension. "I don't know if I can go through with it."

"If you have a better idea, let me hear it. I'm not gonna kid you. This is gonna be risky if you go through with it."

Ivy didn't have a better idea. "I can't face going back to jail." She chewed on the inside of her cheek. "I guess, I'll have to agree."

"Of course, if these guys aren't the killers, this trap won't exonerate you from the murder. After all, what was their motive? What did they have to gain by killing him?"

"They did it to terrorize me. Who else could have done it?"

"Do you know of anyone who hated Orion?"

"Now that you mention it, that Riley guy I just saw hates Rabbit World because I refused to sell him real estate. And I know Orion rejected his offer, too."

"Orion mentioned Riley to me."

"He's a slick sleazeball who works for a casino company. I forgot that Orion told me he thought the Mafia owns it. He didn't want anything to do with them."

"I need to have a talk with Mr. Riley. If the mob's backing him, I wouldn't put murder past him."

"He blew his stack today in my office, trying to bullyrag me."

"Did he know you were carrying my gun in your purse before Orion's murder?"

"Hmm. I don't see how he could have known. This is the first time I met him." She scratched her cheek. "Unless Orion told him. Orion knew I had it."

"Would Orion tell him you were carrying a gun?"

"If he thought Riley might attack me, I could see Orion telling him to scare him off."

"Did anyone else know you had my gun in your purse?"

Ivy furrowed her brow in concentration. "I can't think of anyone. Somebody else might have seen it. I can't be sure."

"What about your psychiatrist?"

"I never thought of him. I guess he could have seen it at one of our sessions. I didn't deliberately show it to him."

"You said he told Orion what you said during therapy."

"Orion had Jamal Harris's phone number tacked near the kitchen phone. I know that much. Harris must have told him everything I was saying."

"Why would Orion want to know the details of your illness?"

268

"Because he was gaslighting me, according to Liz."

"Which would give you a motive for killing him."

"I thought you were working for me," said Ivy, taking offense.

"Don't take it personally. I'm just telling you what the DA will say during your trial. Who is Liz?"

"Didn't I tell you about Liz?"

"I don't remember."

"She's my friend. She's a survivalist. She thinks the world will end any day now. She carries a go-bag with her day and night."

"Why did she think he was gaslighting you?"

"To have me committed for insanity so he could get his hands on my money. I have a large inheritance, you see."

"How was he driving you insane, according to her?"

"She thought Orion hired the avatars to assault me in Rabbit World in order to drive me nuts."

"Do you believe that?"

"I didn't until I found out he knew Harris's phone number. Now I'm not so sure. Liz might have been right about Orion."

"Which would give you a motive to kill him."

"There you go again, accusing me. Are you a mole working for the DA?" said Ivy, resentful.

"I'm letting you know what they're gonna say at the trial. It doesn't mean I believe any of it."

"Liz can't understand why I keep defending Orion. She's certain he was gaslighting me."

"And you? What do you believe?"

"I have my doubts. I can't believe he would hire those two avatars to assault me and then have them run me off the road in Topanga Canyon to kill me. Jesus. I can't believe he would ever do that," said Ivy, shaking her head.

"Then why was he getting information about you from your psychiatrist, if not to use it to gaslight you?"

"I don't know. I believe he loved me till the end."

"Do you have Riley's address?"

Ivy picked up Riley's business card, which he had dropped on her desktop, and gave Brody the requested information.

"Do you think Harris might have killed Orion?" said Brody.

"Harris? He's my psychiatrist. Why would he want to kill Orion?"

"If he was giving information about your therapy to Orion, it would be unethical. Harris could lose his medical license if anyone found out. Maybe he thought Orion would tell someone, so he killed Orion to save his license."

"I guess that's possible. According to you, everyone wanted him dead."

"It's my job. I see motives in everyone."

"I'm glad I'm not as cynical as you," said Ivy, and gazed at the fish swimming in the aquarium, wishing she was at home swimming in her pool without a care in the world.

But she had to make sure Rabbit World's IPO was a resounding success—even if she didn't know the first thing about running a metaverse company.

Chapter 73

Wincing at the pain in his wounded leg in his motel room, Bondurant phoned Nieman.

"Good news?" said Nieman, expectantly.

"I doubt it. Ivy Kingston posted bail."

"Brody, damn it. What about Brody? Did you take care of him?"

"I'm working on it."

"Work harder. You said you were a pro."

Get your head out of your ass, blue boy, thought Bondurant.

"I thought you should know about Ivy," he said. "Do you want me to take her out with Brody?"

"No way. How did she post bail for a murder charge?"

"Simple. She's got the best justice money can buy."

"How strong is the case against her? Do you know?"

"I got a mole working for me in the downtown LAPD station. He says they found her fingerprints on the piece used to waste Orion."

"Sounds open and shut. How can she beat the rap?"

"I don't know the details of the case. All I know is, she plans to plead not guilty."

"Does she admit she shot him? Is she pleading self-defense?"

"She says she didn't whack him."

"Do you believe her?"

"Frankly, I don't see how she can explain away her prints on the murder weapon."

"Did she say she knows who wasted him?"

"I don't have intel on that. My mole said something like she's claiming she was kidnaped at the time of the murder so she couldn't have offed Orion."

"Do the cops believe her?"

"My mole says the DA is gonna arraign her. How do you want me to proceed?"

"I need to consult the algorithms."

"Do you consult the algorithms to figure out whether to pick your nose?"

"No wonder the SAS fired you, you idiot."

"I can think for myself." *Unlike guys with blue hair*, thought Bondurant, tired of hearing about algorithms.

"That's the problem. When you do the thinking."

Bondurant smoldered. He had a good mind to bust Nieman's jaw. Maybe he would do it after he completed the job. *Fly up to Menlo Park and ram my fist down the blue-haired punk's throat.*

"I can't believe the cops let her out on a murder charge," said Nieman. "It saves me the trouble of bailing her out."

"You grease the right palms, anything's possible."

"Like the Bible says, money is the answer to all your problems."

"I thought it says, money is the root of all evil."

"It says a lot of things that contradict each other. Which is why I don't have much use for it, since it's a tissue of lies."

"Wait a minute. Did you say you were gonna bail Ivy out of jail?" said Bondurant, confused.

"Your hearing aid must work. Congrats."

Bondurant ignored the dig. "I don't get it. I thought you wanted her out of the way."

"Your microscopic brain can't conceive of what I want."

Bondurant shook his head, fed up with talking to Nieman. "What do you want me to do?"

"What you keep failing to do. Take out Brody."

"No problem. I thought you should know about Ivy, though—"

Nieman hung up before Bondurant finished his sentence.

"Your blue hairdo sucks," said Bondurant into his cell.

Chapter 74

Ivy wanted something to eat. She arranged to meet Liz at a burger joint on the Third Street Promenade.

Wearing khaki Bermudas with cargo pockets and hiking boots, her ever-present backpack on the ground at her feet, Liz sat across from Ivy, as they dug into their burgers at their table on the patio under the bright afternoon sun, a gentle breeze wafting over them.

"The sun burned through the fog finally," said Liz, glancing at the sky.

"I thought it might not make it today," said Ivy.

"Does the DA agree that you had every right to resort to self-defense to protect yourself from Orion?" said Liz, finishing chewing a bite of her cheeseburger and pulling a face. "We should have gone to Johnny Rockets. I like their onion rings and vegan shakes."

"Maybe next time," said Ivy, and munched a French fry. "Do you ever go anywhere without that backpack, Liz?"

"That's me. Apocalyptic Liz at your service. And don't forget it. When the world ends, I'll be ready, my go-bag packed. And it's gonna end soon. Mark my words."

A short, thirtyish bearded guy clad in faded jeans and a yellow T paraded down the promenade speaking into a megaphone, carrying a poster that said Repent in large red block letters. His long, grizzled, disheveled hair fell to his narrow shoulders.

"The end of the world is near, sinners," he said. "The hair on your head is numbered. Repent before it is too late. There is always time to repent. God will forgive any sinner who repents, no matter how much you have sinned. God is good. Man is evil. Every human that walks this planet is corrupt. Repent now, sinners. Repent and save your

tortured souls. Ask God for forgiveness. Or you will burn
in hell for eternity."

"Get a job," a bum cried at him.

"Repent, sinner. Give up the demon rum. Your time is
near. Forsake prostitutes and booze, sinner, before God
levels this world to ashes. Flush your drugs down the toilet.
Remember what happened to Sodom and Gomorrah? Do
you want God to rain down sulfur and fire on your head?
Your fate is sealed, sinner."

"Lighten up, wacko," said the bum. "Let's get a drink."

"The end of the world is nigh. He who has eyes, let
him see the truth," said the street preacher, his eyes burning
with zeal. "Woe unto him who sees and worships evil. I say
unto you, brother, if thine eye offends thee, pluck it out."

"See," Liz told Ivy with a chuckle. "The world is
gonna end any day now."

"He's probably been saying that his entire life, and
we're all still here," said Ivy, regarding the street preacher.

"Well?"

"Well what?"

"Does the DA agree that you had the right to defend
yourself against Orion? Jesus, Ivy, he was gaslighting you."

"I didn't do it, Liz."

"Oh, I'm sorry," said Liz, taken aback. "I thought . . .
I—uh . . ."

"That's OK."

"I knew the guy was gaslighting you. I thought you
finally realized it and retaliated. Isn't that why they let you
out on bail? Because you pleaded self-defense."

"I pleaded not guilty because I didn't do it."

"You could get off if you pleaded self-defense. No jury
in the world would convict you after what Orion put you
through."

"I'm not gonna plead guilty to something I didn't do."

"I don't want to see you go to jail. I don't want the jury
to think you're lying when you say you didn't do it but
your fingerprints are on the murder weapon."

"I'm not gonna lie on the stand."

Liz sipped her shake through a straw. "How are you gonna explain the fingerprints on the gun?"

"It was my gun. Uh, I mean, I didn't own it. Someone gave it to me for protection."

"From Orion?"

"From the avatars."

Chapter 75

Brody paid a visit to Dr. Jamal Harris in his psychiatric office in Century City. He wanted to know more about Harris, since Ivy had discovered Orion possessed Harris's phone number.

Harris had reproductions of still lifes and pastoral landscapes in expensive frames with ornate scrollwork hung on his walls to convey a feeling of serenity for his patients, decided Brody. Harris also had his diploma from Stanford hung on the wall near his desk, making sure everyone would see it.

Brody saw the black leather couch in one corner of the room, where Harris listened to his patients confess their hang-ups.

"What is the nature of your business, Mr. Brody?" said Harris, a thin man in his early forties, dressed in a bespoke turquoise suit, sitting behind his neat, uncluttered desk. "Are you interested in making use of my services?"

"I'm not gonna beat around the bush. I'm a private detective. I'm investigating Orion Kingston's murder."

"I'd like to see a badge," said Harris, pointing to his red plastic-framed glasses perched on his nose.

"Private detectives don't carry badges. At least, I don't."

"Then why should I answer any of your questions?" said Harris, adjusting his pink necktie.

"I can show you my PI license."

"Fine."

Brody fished his wallet out of his trouser pocket, withdrew his PI license from the wallet, and showed it to Harris.

Harris nodded with satisfaction. "OK. Shoot."

"I know you knew Orion Kingston, the murder victim."

277

Harris adjusted his necktie again. Brody figured Harris was overdoing it, acting out of nervousness the second time.

"I didn't know Orion Kingston," said Harris. "He wasn't one of my patients."

"Then why did he have your phone number?"

"A lot of people have my phone number. What does that prove?"

"Are you saying he never contacted you?"

"That's right."

"But Ivy Kingston is one of your patients."

A shiny film of sweat appeared on Harris's mug. His eyes, which seemed too big for his face, became even bigger. The lenses of his red glasses misted.

The man looked uncomfortable, decided Brody.

"She is, indeed," said Harris. "But I'm not giving you any information about her. Her case is private, as are all of my patients' cases."

"It would be illegal for you to discuss your patients' maladies with anyone. Wouldn't it violate psychiatrist-client privilege?"

"It would. I never discuss my patients' illnesses with anyone."

"You could lose your license to practice psychiatry."

"Why are you pestering me with these questions?" said Harris, becoming combative. "You're telling me the obvious. Why bother bringing this up?"

"I'm doing my job."

"Why do I have to put up with this nonsense? You come here acting like you have some kind of authority. In reality you have the authority of a besotted wino. You're—uh—a PI," said Harris, pulling a face as he said "PI." "You should hang your head in shame."

"I should think you'd want to clear the air," said Brody, enjoying Harris's discomfort.

"Want to? Why would I want to? There's no air to clear."

278

"To cast suspicion away from yourself."

"There's no suspicion on me. Why should there be?" said Harris, removing his spectacles and, with a handkerchief he retrieved from his jacket's breast pocket, wiping off the sweaty mist that filmed the lenses.

"There is speculation you were reporting Ivy's psychiatric problems to her husband—which, if true, would get your license suspended."

Harris bolted to his feet. "That's outrageous. I'll sue you for slander."

"It's just speculation going around. Nobody knows who's spreading it."

"I have to deal with temperamental, narcissistic, drugged-out Hollywood celebrities day in, day out, and now I have to deal with a two-bit PI making slanderous accusations against me. Are you kidding? I may have to put up with the rich celebrities because they pay me well. But you, I don't have to put up with *you* at all. Get out of here," said Harris, placing his arms akimbo, frowning.

Brody stood up slowly. "You never talked to Orion Kingston?"

"That's right. I never talked to him. And it's none of your business. Good-bye."

"Then why did he have your phone number?"

"I have no idea."

"Did Ivy voice her concern to you that Orion was gaslighting her?"

"Good-bye," said Harris, steaming.

Brody retreated to the door and paused.

"If you were telling Orion what Ivy was telling you in confidence, it would give him leverage over you," he said. "He could testify against your unethical behavior and torpedo your career."

"I'm not gonna say this again," cried Harris. "*Good-bye.*"

Brody departed.

Having rattled Harris's cage, Brody hoped Harris might do something rash, something that would reveal Harris had taken out Orion. Of course, if Harris hadn't blown away Orion, Brody didn't care what the guy did next. This was all about finding Orion's murderer.

Chapter 76

Ivy and Liz were polishing off their burgers when Ivy's cell phone chimed in her purse. Ivy wiped grease off her fingers and took the call.

"We want you to join us," said Vidor.

Ivy widened her eyes, recognizing his voice. "How many times do I have to tell you I don't want to join you? Why would I join a pack of rapists?"

"We don't want to have to kill you."

"I don't have to listen to your threats. I'm gonna hang up."

"Don't you want to know why we want you to become one of us?"

"I want you to leave me alone."

Vidor said nothing.

Ivy was about to hang up.

"I want you to have my baby," he said.

Appalled, Ivy gasped. "Never."

"We can't reproduce without you. You were chosen to bear our young."

"You're insane. Stay away from me," said Ivy, raising her voice.

"Leave your doors open for us tonight."

"Fat chance. Get out of my life."

"Do you want to die?" said Vidor, his voice edged.

Trembling with rage and fear, Ivy terminated the call.

"Who was that?" said Liz, on edge.

"It was them. One of the avatars," said Ivy, stuffing her cell phone into her purse.

"I had a feeling it was. What a bunch of creeps."

"Did you hear what he said?"

Liz shook her head. "I couldn't hear. There's too much background noise in this restaurant."

"He said he wants me to have his baby," said Ivy, all but choking on the words.

"Holy shit."

"They can't reproduce without me."

"I guess that's why they killed Orion. So they could marry you. How sick can you get?"

"The perv didn't say anything about marriage. The metaverse doesn't have any rules or mores. I'm sure they could care less about marriage. It's all about doing whatever you want."

"And they want a baby."

"It's revolting to even think about it," said Ivy, pushing away her remaining French fries in front of her. "I can't eat anymore."

"This must prove it's the end of the world. Don't you see? Why else would avatars want to have babies? The avatars must be dying out."

"How can they die if they're not alive in the first place?"

"Why else would they want to reproduce?"

Ivy clutched her head. "I don't know. None of this makes sense."

"Can you imagine having one of their babies?"

"No, I can't. Thinking about it makes me sick."

"Wouldn't it be impossible?"

"Avatars walking around in the real world is supposed to be impossible, too. But they're doing it."

Liz nodded grimly. "It's the end of the world."

"We can't let it happen."

"Do we have a choice?"

"I'm not gonna join them. That's for sure."

Liz paused in thought. "Do you think this avatar loves you?"

"Nobody loves anyone in the metaverse. That's what they told me when they demanded I join them. They told me they have no feelings for anybody. They do whatever they want, no matter what anyone thinks."

"What are you gonna do?"

"I can't let them find me," said Ivy, cutting her eyes around the promenade in search of the avatars. "Do you think they're here?"

Twisting in her seat Liz surveyed the crowd milling around the promenade. "I don't see them."

"How did I get myself into this?" said Ivy, feeling like kicking herself, even though she couldn't understand what she had done to deserve this.

"Maybe you should call the cops for protection."

"They're trying me for murder. Put yourself in their shoes. They're not gonna help me. They'll throw me in jail."

"Jail could be the safest place for you. The avatars can't get to you there."

"I can't stand that place. You have no idea how awful it is. There's no way I'm going back to jail. I'd hang myself in my cell."

"Or maybe an avatar would sneak in and 'Epstein' you."

"You're doing a great job of terrifying me," said Ivy, rearing up.

"I'm trying to help you, Ivy," said Liz, her eyes earnest.

"I know," said Ivy, pulling herself together. "I'm not blaming you. I got myself into this mess somehow. It's up me to get myself out."

"Don't blame yourself. *Orion* did this to you. He gaslighted you and scrambled your brains, undermining your self-esteem and filling you with guilt."

Ivy didn't know what to think.

"OK," she said. "Maybe that's true to some extent. But it doesn't solve my problem. Orion's dead. He can't do anything to me now."

"I hate to say this, but the damage is done."

Ivy stared at Liz. "You're freaking me out, Liz."

"Ah, don't listen to me," said Liz, waving her hand. "I exaggerate. Remember it's me, Apocalyptic Liz. If there's a silver lining to every cloud, I sure can't see it. Forget what I'm blathering about. Like you said, Orion is gone. He can't mess up your head any longer."

"I got the avatars to do that for me."

"Do they know where you're staying?"

"Hopefully, they think I'm in jail."

"Can they track your cell phone?"

"Good question," said Ivy, becoming alert. "We better get out of here. These Big Tech geeks can track anything that sends out a signal."

They scrambled to their feet.

"First let's get some ice cream and pickles," said Ivy.

"Ice cream and pickles?" said Liz, pulling a face. "I'll pass on the pickles and opt for the ice cream."

Ivy looked bewildered. "That's funny. I have this crazy urge for pistachio ice cream and pickles."

"Pardon me while I puke."

Chapter 77

Brody sat in Riley's office. It was massive and had a balcony outside, where Riley could watch the pedestrians fifteen stories below. Riley had paintings of thoroughbred racehorses hung on his office walls. A dartboard hung on the closed door.

"Like the bangtails, huh?" said Brody, sitting in front of Riley's desk.

"I play the ponies, and I'm good at it. I win when I bet, not like most gamblers, who are losers," said Riley, sitting behind his desk, tilting back in his chair, and leering at the thoroughbreds in the paintings with approval, almost as if they were beautiful women.

"I came to ask your advice. I'm thinking about buying real estate in Rabbit World. What do you think? Is it a good deal?"

Riley gawked at Brody. "Are you kidding?"

"I want to build a casino in Rabbit World. I'm told you're an expert on casino development. I would like your opinion."

"What's your name again?"

"Sam Quester. Rumor has it you've had dealings with Orion Kingston."

"The guy's an asshole. A dead asshole, I heard on the news."

"You sound like you didn't care for him."

Riley snickered. "You could say that."

"Why didn't you two get along?"

"He told me he didn't allow casinos in Rabbit World. Can you believe that? In this day and age, prudes like Kingston still exist. Well, he doesn't exist anymore. He found out the hard way his kind are extinct. Good riddance, is what I say."

"You hated the guy's guts."

285

"His kind annoy the hell out of me. They think gambling is the root of all evil or all casinos are owned by the Mafia. Not anymore, I tell you. Not anymore. Those days are long gone. Casinos are owned by legitimate businesses nowadays."

Brody figured Riley had a good reason to blow away Orion.

"How do you deal with a guy like that?" asked Brody.

"In the old days, why the mob would give a motherfucker like that cement overshoes and dump him at the bottom of Lake Mead. *Luca Brasi sleeps with the fishes.*" Riley laughed. "Remember that line from *The Godfather*? Say what you will, those guys knew how to treat assholes back then. And it got results, I shit you not."

"You sound like you know a lot about the Mafia."

"I saw the movie, like everybody else."

"I believe there's a lot of money to be made in the gaming racket."

Riley narrowed his eyes. "What'd you say your name is?"

Brody tried to remember the name he had given Riley. It began with a *Q*. Didn't it?

"Quester," said Brody.

"I never heard of you."

"Well, I've heard of *you*. You're a rock star among gaming investors, a big-timer in Vegas."

"Which is weird, because I mostly fly under the radar."

"Don't sell yourself short. You're a damn legend in the business."

"I wouldn't go that far. What do you want anyway?"

"I want to know if I should buy real estate in Rabbit World for a casino."

"Don't waste your time. Kingston's wife is as bad as he was." Riley adopted a feminine voice. "Rabbit World is family-friendly, and we don't want casinos there," he said, flicking his wrist like a woman. He resumed his normal voice. "That's what she told me."

Riley withdrew a dart from his desk drawer and flung it at the dartboard.

The dart landed near the bull's-eye, Brody noticed.

Riley withdrew another dart from his drawer. "I got a twenty that says I hit the inner bull's-eye this time."

"No bet."

"Whaddaya mean, 'No bet'? Do you know how hard it is to hit the inner bull's-eye?"

"You throw like a pro," said Brody, eyeballing the dart stuck an inch away from the bull's-eye.

"I missed the outer bull's-eye by an inch. That's not close. I'm talking about the inner bull's-eye, which is much harder to hit. What kind of gambler are you?" said Riley, scowling.

"I don't gamble. I want to build casinos in the metaverse. That's where the money is nowadays. The metaverse."

"What was the last casino you built?"

Brody got up to leave. "I'm new to this game."

He retreated to the door.

As he reached for the doorknob, he felt something whizz by his left ear and thud into the closed wooden door. A dart. The thing had missed him by less than an inch, he realized, furious.

He wheeled around and glowered at Riley.

"Are you a cop?" said Riley with a grin that looked like a sneer.

"No."

"You smell like a cop."

"What if I was a cop? Do you have something to hide?"

"Nothing at all."

"Did you whack Orion?"

"I wouldn't waste good lead on that loser," said Riley, face smug.

Brody glanced at the green dart jutting from the door. "You almost hit me with that."

"My aim was off."

Brody shot a dirty look at him. "I suggest you be more careful."

"I suggest you get the hell out of here and never come back."

Brody managed to resist the impulse to yank the dart from the door and fling it back at Riley.

Chapter 78

Ivy returned home and promptly vomited in the toilet.

Flushing the toilet and leaving the bathroom she heard knocking on the front door. Her pulse accelerated. Could it be the avatars? she wondered. At least, repairmen had fixed her front door so she could lock it.

She stole toward the door and peeked out the peephole. Brody.

She let him inside.

"Do you think it's safe for me to stay here?" she said.

"The front door is fixed. If the kidnapers think you're in jail, they won't bother you here. Are you OK? You look pale."

"Something didn't agree with me at lunch," she said, rubbing her stomach. "I don't usually eat pistachio ice cream and pickles."

Brody looked sick. "Yummy. I paid a visit to Riley. He doesn't care for you."

"That's because I won't let him build his casino in Rabbit World."

"He hated Orion for the same reason."

"Do you think Riley killed Orion?"

"If he didn't know about your gun, I doubt he shot Orion—even though he had motive. I also paid a visit to your psychiatrist Jamal Harris. He denied knowing Orion."

"He's lying. Orion had his phone number."

"I agree. Harris was nervous when I questioned him. He could have killed Orion to prevent him from telling the authorities he was unethically telling Orion about your therapy sessions with him."

"Do you think he would go to that extreme?"

"To protect his career? Yeah. The question is, did he know you had a gun in your purse?"

"I never told him about it, if that's what you're asking."

"He might have seen it when you opened your purse at one of your therapy sessions."

"Yep," she said, nodding.

"Which means he could have murdered Orion."

Ivy narrowed her eyes into slits. "I haven't changed my mind. I believe one of the avatars did it, while the other kidnaped me."

"I wish I could find them. Are you open to the plan I suggested before about setting a trap for them?"

"Do you mind if I sit down?" said Ivy, her face wan.

"Not at all. Are you sure you're OK?"

She sat down on the grey cashmere sofa. "Fine. Just something I ate. Where were we? Oh, you want me to act as bait to capture the avatars."

"Only if you're up to it."

"Did I tell you the latest?"

"About what?"

"One of the avatars called me up and said he wanted me to have his baby."

"What?" said Brody, incredulous.

"I know it sounds crazy, but that's what he said. Of course, I said no."

"What did he say?"

"He said he'd kill me if I didn't agree."

"Did he say anything about killing Orion?"

"No."

"Regardless, he's already committed a crime by threatening you on the phone."

"And don't forget their kidnaping me."

"Do you have a witness for the threat to your life he made on the phone?"

Ivy leaned back on the sofa, feeling lightheaded.

"Liz was there," she said. "But she couldn't hear what the avatar was saying because of the noisy restaurant we ate at."

"Liz?"

"She's my friend. She believes the world is ending soon. Avatars running around in the real world have convinced her the apocalypse is at hand. Didn't I tell you about Liz?"

"Oh, yeah, I remember you mentioned her. What about her?"

"She's my bestie."

"Has she seen the avatars?" said Brody, eyes lighting up.

"I told her about them. She hasn't seen them. She just missed seeing them at the café at the Century City mall, but they left before she got back from the restroom."

"Too bad," said Brody, slumping.

He had trouble believing avatars were running amok in the real world, which left doubts in his mind about the veracity of Ivy's story about their kidnaping her. He couldn't figure out why she would lie about it, so she must be telling the truth. Or she was imagining them. Or she was the one who had wasted Orion and needed the alibi provided by the avatar kidnapers.

"I can think of one other person who could have wanted Orion dead," said Ivy.

"Who?"

"Have you ever heard of Lazarus Nieman? He lives in Menlo Park."

"The name sounds familiar, but I can't place it."

"He's a big shot in the metaverse. He owns the biggest metaverse in the world. He didn't like the idea of Orion's start-up competing with him, and he gave Orion an earful about it over his bone mic. But Orion didn't back down. He was going through with his IPO to the very end."

"Are you saying this Nieman character could've blown away Orion?"

"He wouldn't do it himself."

"A hit man?"

Ivy raised her eyebrows. "Who knows?" She shook her head no. "I still think the avatars did it. And framed me for it."

"I need to add Nieman to my list of murder suspects. Is there anyone else I should know about?"

"Anyone that hated Orion?"

"Right."

"I guess I should add Liz. She was convinced Orion was gaslighting me."

"I'll talk to her."

"Do you feel that's necessary?"

"I'm covering all the bases."

"You're wasting your time. Liz is my BFF. Why would she frame me for Orion's murder? That makes no kind of sense. The avatars killed Orion and framed me. They hate me."

"Which leads us back to setting a trap for them with you as bait."

Chapter 79

Jamal Harris was sitting in his office thinking about his high-maintenance ex-model girlfriend Janine who was bankrupting him, even though he made out well in his profession. Janine wanted the best of everything, cost be damned. She couldn't stand Wrangler jeans. She had to have Christian Dior jeans. Why should she could care about the cost? She paid none of her own bills. He had to pay all of them.

Love was like quicksand, he decided. The more you struggled to get out of it, the deeper you sank. He felt helpless to fight it. He needed to get more money for her. If you wanted a thoroughbred girlfriend, you had to keep shelling out the big bucks.

His cell phone chimed.

It was her.

"Baby, I just bought the most marvelous Balenciaga dress," said Janine. "It's only ten thousand dollars. Send the money to me via Venmo."

"Could you at least have asked me before buying the dress?"

"I knew you wouldn't refuse. I love you so much."

Another ten grand out the window, decided Harris, distraught.

"Do you really have to have this dress?" he said.

"Don't you want me to look good, baby, when we party with Leonardo DiCaprio and his girlfriend?"

She didn't give him a chance to answer. She hung up.

Harris rolled his eyes in despair. She burned through a million bucks a year without giving it a thought. He needed more money.

His receptionist interrupted his thoughts via the speakerphone on his desk.

"There's a Mr. Bondurant to see you, sir," she said. "He says a Mr. Nieman sent him."

"OK," said Harris, not anxious to see him. "Send him in."

Gripping a briefcase, Bondurant limped into Harris's office, clad in jeans, a white T, a black blazer, and sneakers.

"Nieman sent me," said Bondurant, taking a seat in front of Harris's desk, his jacket opening and exposing his shoulder rig.

"What does he want?" said Harris, unnerved by the sight of the pistol.

One of Nieman's thugs, decided Harris with distaste.

Bondurant placed the briefcase on Harris's neat desktop and snapped it open so the lid blocked Harris's view of the contents. Bondurant removed a brown glass vial from the briefcase and set it on the desk.

"Nieman wants you to give this vial to Ivy Kingston to drink," he said.

"Why do I want to do that? What's in it, anyway?" said Harris, eying the vial with suspicion, noting it lacked a label.

"You don't need to know."

"You expect me to give one of my patients a vial of God knows what?" said Harris, outraged.

"It will benefit her health, he says."

"And he's a doctor?"

"He doesn't need to be. He's one of the ten richest men in the world."

"Meaning what?"

"Meaning he can do whatever he wants. He's a Big Tech boy wonder. He can access anyone's information. He knows everything about you."

Harris shivered with trepidation. He knew it was true. Nieman *could* find out anything. He had found out Harris was Ivy's psychiatrist. Harris had been telling Nieman about Ivy's therapy sessions. Not that Harris wanted to. *He*

294

had to. To pay Janine's bills. Nieman was paying him a stack of money in exchange for the info. Every dime of it was going to Janine. The same was true for the money Orion had been paying him for the same info. Janine got it all. Even so, Harris didn't have enough dough to pay Janine. The woman was insatiable when it came to cash.

"How do I know that vial doesn't contain poison?" said Harris.

"It doesn't contain poison," said Bondurant. "It's for Ivy's health. Give it to her to drink."

"What kind of psychiatrist does Nieman think I am?"

"This kind," said Bondurant, and spun the briefcase around, revealing its contents, scores of rubber band–bound bundles of hundred-dollar bills. "That's two hundred grand for you, tax free."

Harris's eyes widened, as he took in the sight of the cash.

"Are you sure that vial doesn't contain poison?" he said, glancing at the vial.

"Nieman promises it's for Ivy's health. Why are you hesitating? You've done work for Nieman before."

True, decided Harris with regret. He had hoped he would never have to do anything for Nieman again. Nieman had never asked him to give a patient a vial of an unknown substance, however. Usually Nieman wanted info on some of Harris's rich celebrity patients.

The temptation of two hundred grand in front of him was too much for Harris to resist, even though he knew he was breaking every rule in the book as far as medical ethics were concerned. Hell, his medical license was already on the line with his telling Orion what his wife was blabbing about during her therapy sessions. But Orion was dead. And nobody would ever be the wiser about that indiscretion.

Then there was Janine.

"I'm taking a huge risk doing this," said Harris. "You're taking ten years off my life with the pressure you're putting on me."

"You know what Ben Franklin said. No pain, no gain."

"OK," said Harris, pulling the briefcase toward him.

"Of course," said Bondurant, with a wide grin. "Nieman knew you would accept. He understands people. He has algorithms. Algorithms never lie."

Bondurant got to his feet and hobbled to the door. Before he reached it he turned around and eyeballed Harris.

"Don't try to pull a fast one," said Bondurant.

"What do you mean?"

"There will be retribution if you do."

Harris shook his head in puzzlement, looking lost.

"Don't lie to Nieman about giving Ivy the medicine," said Bondurant. "He'll know one way or the other. There are electrolytes in the medicine that he can trace with his equipment. If he can't trace them to her body . . ."

Harris widened his eyes with fear.

"Then I'll have to come back," said Bondurant, patting his shoulder rig with a wink and a smile at Harris. "You don't want that."

Bondurant opened the door and halted out of the office.

Harris wiped sweat from his forehead with a handkerchief.

The things he did for Janine could get him killed, he decided. Yet he kept doing them—even though he knew she was a gold digger.

Chapter 80

An hour later, Ivy walked into Harris's office.
"What's so urgent that it couldn't wait another day?"
she said, approaching Harris's desk.
"I've been going over your records," said Harris,
shuffling papers on his desktop. "I've discovered you're
heading for a nervous breakdown any day now—maybe
any minute."
"Ohmigod. Is it that bad?"
Harris nodded, grim-faced. "I will give you medication
to calm your nerves. The ideal thing would be to find the
cause of your distress and eliminate it."
"I know what the cause is. Avatars are harassing me.
But I don't know how to get rid of them."
Harris held up the vial Bondurant had given him.
"Take this medication to calm your nerves. If you don't
take it, you will suffer a breakdown."
Ivy stared at him, nonplussed.
"I wish I was exaggerating, but your condition is
grave," he said.
Ivy accepted the vial and inspected it. "What is it?
There's no label on it."
"That's a free sample the pharmaceutical company
gave me. It will save you the cost of a prescription—which
is very expensive."
"Do they always hand out bottles with no labels on
them? How does anyone know what company
manufactured the product?"
"I'm not supposed to give the sample to my patients.
But in your case, this is an emergency, and you need to take
it right away."
"You mean, here in the office?" said Ivy, cocking an
eyebrow.
Harris nodded yes. "Believe me, you need it."

Ivy inspected the bottle. "What's in it?"

"In layman's terms, it's a sedative. It will settle your nerves and help your mind cope with your problems."

"I'd like to know the ingredients."

"The ingredients would mean nothing to you unless you're a chemist.'

Ivy unscrewed the black plastic cap on the vial and sniffed the liquid with a quizzical expression on her face. She couldn't place the unpleasant odor.

"How much do I take?" she said.

"The whole vial."

"Will it make me drowsy? I drove here, and I don't want to fall asleep at the wheel. Maybe I should take it when I get home."

"The sooner you take it, the better. I'll feel a lot better once I know you've taken your medicine. Are you allergic to anything?"

"No."

"Then down the hatch."

Ivy hesitated. "I've never taken a medicine I didn't know the name of."

Harris folded his hands on the desktop. "Look. I'm your doctor. Have I ever given you anything bad for you?"

"Of course not." Ivy glanced at the couch. "Don't you want me to lie down on the couch for our session?"

"The best thing for you at this time is to take your medicine."

Ivy held the vial up to her lips and drank the contents. She made a face.

"It tastes bitter, sort of metallic like copper pennies," she said.

Harris watched her apprehensively.

"What's wrong?" she said.

"Nothing."

"You look worried."

"Not at all. You should start feeling better soon," said Harris, uncertainly.

"Did you think I was gonna have a bad reaction to the medicine?" said Ivy, unsettled by his nervousness.

"Some people do, but it would happen right away. If you feel fine now, everything will be OK."

"You're starting to worry me," said Ivy, biting her lower lip.

"You can relax. Everything is good."

"Except the avatars are harassing me. And I'm accused of murder."

"I'm a psychiatrist. I can only help the state of your mind. I can't eliminate what causes your ailment. I have noticed you have trouble distinguishing between reality and your imagination. Everything isn't as bad as it seems."

"I threw up before I came here."

Harris did a double take. "That's a symptom of stress. Stay calm and you'll feel better."

"I dunno."

"Maybe you should go to your doctor and have a physical to prove to yourself you're in good health."

Ivy twisted her mouth. "I guess you know what's best. I haven't thrown up in a long time."

Chapter 81

Ivy had just walked into her house when she felt the overpowering urge to vomit. The blood draining from her face, she ran to the bathroom and tossed her cookies.

What the hell was going on? she wondered, on her knees hunched over the toilet

After voiding her stomach she felt weak. She flushed the toilet to get rid of the rancid reek of the vomit.

She shambled to the living room and plumped herself down on the sofa. Why did she keep getting nauseated? she wondered. Did that copper-tasting medicine she drank at Harris's have anything to do with it? But the medicine had nothing to do with the previous time she had vomited. On the other hand, why did Harris refuse to tell her its name?

Becoming paranoid she wondered if Harris was trying to poison her. Why would he? she asked herself. Did he think she suspected he had killed Orion? Maybe he *had* killed Orion.

Ivy produced her cell phone and called Brody.

"Harris might be trying to poison me," she said.

"What?" said Brody, taken aback. "Why do you say that?"

"He gave me some medicine at his office and refused to tell me what's in it."

"Didn't the medicine bottle have a label?"

"It was an unlabeled vial. I asked him what was in it. He said it was a sedative without giving me its name."

"Why would he poison you?"

"Maybe he thinks I suspect he killed Orion and he doesn't want me to tell anyone."

Brody cleared his throat. "Um, if he poisoned you, why are you alive?"

Ivy thought about it. "Maybe he didn't give me enough. Or maybe it takes a while for it to spread through my system. Who knows?"

"Did he watch you leave his office after you drank the medicine?"

"He did."

"Did he look astonished that you were in any condition to leave?"

"I didn't pay attention to him when I left. I can't tell you how he looked."

"So you don't believe it was the avatars that killed Orion, anymore?"

"I'll ask you a question. If he was innocent of Orion's murder, why would he poison me?"

"Do you feel like you're dying?"

"I threw up when I came back from his office," said Ivy, wincing. "I feel weak."

"Think carefully. Did he know you had my pistol in your purse?"

Ivy shook her head, uncertain. "I can't say for sure he did or didn't."

"If we accuse him of killing Orion, we need proof. All we have is motive, at this point."

"What should I do?"

"If you believe he poisoned you, you should go to the hospital and have your stomach pumped."

Ivy wanted to scream. "I don't know what's going on. I don't feel like I'm dying. I just feel weak—and this isn't the first time I felt nauseous today. I was sick before I went to his office."

"Then the medicine you took at Harris's office might not have made you sick."

"It sure didn't make me well."

Chapter 82

When Brody got off the phone in his apartment, he
didn't know what to think. Was Ivy going nuts, thinking
her psychiatrist was out to kill her? Brody had suspected
she might be losing it when she had told him about the
avatars attacking her in the real world. Nobody had yet
corroborated her claim that avatars were walking around in
the real world harassing her.

Maybe she had gone off her rocker into paranoia land
and murdered Orion thinking he was trying to kill her.
After all, her fingerprints were found on the murder
weapon. And now she had got into her head that her
psychiatrist was plotting to kill her.

When Brody had gone to her house while she said she
was being attacked by avatars, he hadn't seen any avatars
near her house nor inside it. She could have imagined them.

He wanted to believe her side of the story about
everything, but it was becoming difficult. If, indeed, she
was a homicidal paranoid schizophrenic who had hired
him, he was going around in circles chasing figments of her
imagination. If she was a psychotic liar who believed her
own lies, how could he tell if she was lying? He was giving
himself a headache thinking about it.

He decided to talk to Liz. He called her up and
arranged to have lunch with her. He wanted to get her take
on Ivy, since they were best friends.

He drove his Mini to a Chinese restaurant in
Brentwood, where he parked at a meter on San Vicente
Boulevard.

When he got out of his car and struck out for the
restaurant on foot, he noticed a guy with a missing finger
limping past him. The guy was wearing a mask, which
wasn't strange since a lot of people continued to wear
masks because of the Covid pandemic. The missing finger

rang a bell in Brody's mind. Bondurant. The fed who had hassled him at the mall. Why was Bondurant limping? He hadn't been limping at the mall, recalled Brody.

As Brody turned around to see where Bondurant was heading, he caught sight of Bondurant pulling out a knife and getting ready to stab him in the kidney. His heartbeat hammering with a shot of adrenaline, Brody thrust his elbow backward into Bondurant's hand to deflect the knife. As Brody elbowed the knife, he wheeled around to confront Bondurant.

Bondurant got ready to repeat his thrust after Brody had thwarted his initial attack. Bondurant wasn't worried about witnesses because there weren't any other pedestrians on the sidewalk. People rarely got out of their cars to walk in LA.

Brody didn't have time to reach for his SIG in his ankle holster without getting knifed by Bondurant. Brody had to contend with the knife first. He pulled off his polo shirt and, bare-chested, backed away from Bondurant's underhanded knife thrust to his abdomen in the nick of time. Wrapping his left arm in his shirt for protection, Brody used the arm to ward off Bondurant's thrusts. The blade sliced into Brody's shirt, as Bondurant tried to stab beneath it and disembowel Brody, who hammered down on the blade to deflect it. Bondurant tried to jam the knife upward, but Brody fended off the thrust, forcing the knife down with his shirt-wrapped arm.

Brody could see Bondurant was having trouble maneuvering in the knife fight thanks to his bum leg. Brody's footwork was quicker, enabling him to dodge Bondurant's knife thrusts. Bondurant had lost the advantage of surprise because Brody had recognized him before Bondurant had been able to wield his knife.

They both started when they heard a scream and turned to look where it was coming from.

Wearing a backpack Liz was standing in front of the Chinese restaurant screaming as she watched them in horror.

Bondurant made use of the distraction to duck into a sedan that had been idling near the curb. The driver, who wore his hair in a mullet, peeled away from the curb, as Bondurant yanked shut the passenger's-side door behind him. His face a contorted mask of rage, the irate driver of an SUV leaned on his horn after Bondurant's car cut him off.

Brody had no time to reach for his SIG and shoot at Bondurant. Brody sprinted over to Liz, concerned Bondurant might have a gun in the car and try to shoot her. However, Bondurant's car sped off, its tires shrieking.

"Are you OK?" said Brody, reaching Liz.

"I'm OK. The question is, what about you?" she said, holding her chest, taking deep breaths, her eyes wide. "I saw that guy trying to knife you."

Brody eyed his shredded shirt encasing his arm.

"I'll have to buy a new shirt," he said with dismay.

"He could have killed you."

"That was his intent."

"Do you know who he was?"

"He told me he's a fed. But feds don't go around ambushing people with knives," said Brody, watching Bondurant's car careen around a corner out of sight.

"He's a fucking killer."

"Let's get lunch."

They made for the Chinese restaurant.

Realizing the restaurant wouldn't let him in bare-chested, he put on his ripped polo. Not much of an improvement, he decided, looking down at his tattered shirt.

"It's a new style," said Liz, following his gaze, smiling. "Like stressed jeans. A stressed shirt."

"I hope the restaurant management agrees with you."

"If they don't, we'll do takeout. Your arm's bleeding."

Brody noticed the knife cuts on his arm. The blade must have penetrated his shirt and scored his flesh. The cuts weren't deep.

He withdrew a handkerchief from his rear trouser pocket and wiped off the blood.

"It's nothing," he said.

"Are you gonna call the cops?"

"Not now. I want to talk to you first."

Brody wasn't sure he was going to tell the cops. They would blame him for the attack like they always did.

"It's the end of the world, I'm telling you," said Liz. "Like a zombie apocalypse. People going nuts and rioting in the streets, ripping each other apart for no reason. This is only the beginning."

"Bondurant has a reason, but I don't know what it is."

"Bondurant? Is that the guy who tried to knife you?"

"Yeah."

"What's his problem?"

"He says he's working for the FBI. I have my doubts."

"I hope you have your go-bag ready," said Liz, hunching her shoulders, shifting the leather straps on her backpack for a more comfortable fit. "It's as necessary as a cell phone these days. Any day now. Any *minute* now . . . the whole house of cards comes tumbling down. Riots like you wouldn't believe. Blood streaming in the gutters. Death and destruction on every square inch of earth."

"I'm losing my appetite."

Liz chuckled. "My friends call me Apocalyptic Liz. It takes a while to get used to me."

Chapter 83

Brody and Liz sat at a table in the Chinese restaurant, which had red paper lanterns hanging from the ceiling. The waiters gave Brody's shirt dirty looks, but they didn't tell him to leave. Maybe because it was a slow day, decided Brody. Or maybe because it was LA, where anything goes in terms of fashion. Or maybe because Brody was a big guy nobody on the staff wanted to tussle with.

Brody and Liz sat in a booth upholstered in scarlet leather near the window. Liz removed her backpack and placed it at her side on her seat so she could sit.

Brody ordered wonton soup and chicken chow mein. Liz ordered kung pao chicken.

"You're Brody the PI, right?" said Liz, wearing jeans and a T with horizontal blue and white stripes.

"Right."

"Ivy told me about you."

"How did you two first meet?"

"At a twelve-step get-together. We were both hitting the juice too hard. My mother was an alcoholic who slapped me around when she got drunk. I left my home in Idaho. I couldn't find a job I liked when I got to LA. My life was in a tailspin, and I was drinking hard to drown my troubles. At last I decided the drinking wasn't helping, so I attended the twelve-step meeting where I met Ivy."

"Why was Ivy drinking too much?"

"She thought her marriage was falling apart, and she didn't know how to save it. She also had daddy issues. He was wealthy and successful. She felt inferior to him. His overpowering personality prevented her from developing her own."

"You sound like a psychiatrist."

"You have to understand we both come from messed-up families and were damaged psychologically by them. In her case, she came from a rich family, while I came from a poor one, but the bottom line was the same—our families were dysfunctional. And we were the by-products— damaged goods. So Ivy and me can relate."

Brody became pensive. "What's your take on Ivy?"

"She has issues. Her father and her husband are crushing her spirit. They're not allowing her to develop."

"How do you feel about her?"

"Ivy's my best friend. She's the greatest."

"Do you think her psychological issues are becoming worse?"

"She'd be the first to admit it. She must have told you about the vicious attack she suffered in Rabbit World. Isn't that why she hired you?"

"You've known her a while. Has the attack changed her psychologically?"

Liz rubbed her chin. "I don't know if *changed* is the right word. It upset her. It would upset anyone. How would you feel if it happened to you?"

"Then you believe she was actually assaulted in Rabbit World?"

"Of course, she was. Do you think she made it all up?" asked Liz in disbelief.

"I'm having a hard time verifying that avatars are harassing her in the real world. Nobody has witnessed them, except her."

"You think she's losing her mind?"

"You're her best friend. You know her better than anyone. What do you think?"

Liz was in the process of leaning over the tabletop toward him, when the waiter served their meals. Liz backed away. She waited for the waiter to leave and leaned toward Brody again.

"Her husband Orion was gaslighting her, you know," she whispered, holding her hand at the side of her mouth.

"You think he drove her crazy?"

"He was trying to. The guy was evil and greedy. He wanted to have her committed so he could get his grubby little hands on her money."

"Are you sure?"

"Positive," said Liz, and tapped the tabletop with her knuckles with authority. "He knew Ivy is very sensitive and has self-esteem problems and would suffer a breakdown if he gaslighted her. She was putty in his hands."

Maybe she had a point, decided Brody. If Orion was gaslighting Ivy, it would explain the driverless cars crashing into Ivy. XBY Systems was helping fund Orion's Rabbit World. It was a good bet Orion owned XBY Systems. His sending driverless cars to harass and crash into Ivy would help drive her over the edge. It made more sense than any other explanation of her harassment by driverless cars.

"Do you think she killed him in retaliation?" said Brody.

"I can't blame her if she did. I can't believe she did it, though. It doesn't fit her personality. Not the Ivy I know."

"Who do *you* think killed Orion?"

Liz shook her head. "I have no idea."

"Do you think she's really seeing these avatars stalking her?"

Liz removed her wire-rim glasses and rubbed her closed eyes. "She's under a lot of stress. I can understand how she would think avatars are stalking her after they assaulted her in the metaverse."

"Do you think she's imagining them?"

"I don't know what to think," said Liz, putting her glasses back on. "She's going through a tough time. There's no question of that. And Orion was gaslighting her. When you add it all together, I can see how it could drive anyone nuts."

"Then you think she's insane now?"

"Orion was an asshole. He did this to her."

"You didn't answer my question."

308

"I'm not a psychiatrist."

Brody mulled it over. "You must have really hated Orion."

"How can you tell?" she said, dryly.

"Did you know she was carrying a gun in her purse for self-protection?"

"Uh—what? A gun? Ivy? That's hard to believe."

"She never told you about it?" said Brody, searching her face.

Cocking her head Liz frowned in thought. "Not that I recall."

Brody thought she might be lying. He had spotted a tell, a slight tic near her left eye when she had denied knowing Ivy had a gun in her purse. Why would she lie about it?

"What do you think about Ivy getting blamed for Orion's murder?" he said.

"There's no way she did it. She wouldn't harm a fly," said Liz, worked up. She ground her teeth. "It's so wrong. This never should have happened."

"I thought you were glad Orion's dead."

"I'm not talking about him. I'm talking about Ivy getting blamed for his murder. How could the cops make such an egregious mistake? I can't stand seeing Ivy take the blame for this. Hasn't she been through enough misery with the avatars harassing her?"

"We could get her off, if we knew who the real killer is."

"Why did it have to come to this?" said Liz, contorting her face with anguish.

Brody got the impression she knew more than she was letting on.

"The killer must've really hated Orion," he said, narrowing his eyes.

"You bet. That evil bastard. My vote for worst husband in the world."

"*You* hated him." Brody paused for effect. "Enough to kill him?"

But why would she frame Ivy if she liked Ivy so much? he wondered.

Liz's face turned ashen. She looked like she was at war with herself. She broke down, weeping.

"Oh God," she sobbed. "I can't let this go on."

"Let what go on?"

"All right. I've been racked with guilt ever since they arrested Ivy. I can't take it anymore. I did it. I shot the prick. I can't stand the idea of Ivy going to prison for the rest of her life because of me. How was I supposed to know her prints were on the gun?" Liz wrung her hands in agitation. "He was gaslighting her. I couldn't let it go on. She was changing into a different person under my very eyes with him working on her, driving her over the edge with his dirty brainwashing games."

"Are you willing to confess to the cops?"

"How did she ever get mixed up with him?"

"You don't want her to go to jail for your crime, do you?"

"Not at all. That was never my plan. I *did* use her gun. I saw it in her purse when we were having lunch on the pier and I slipped it into my purse when she used the restroom. I wiped the gun's handle with a handkerchief, but I never thought she had left her fingerprints on the gun barrel. I used gloves when I fired the gun. The last thing I wanted was for her to be blamed for the murder. I wanted to save her from that monster for Chrissake." Clutching her forehead in anguish, Liz sobbed uncontrollably. "I wanted to die when I heard they had put her in jail for his murder."

Chapter 84

Feeling ill, Ivy made an emergency appointment to see her private physician, Dr. Pond.

Pushing sixty, clad in a navy blue suit sans necktie, his white shirt open at the collar, Walter Pond had a receding hairline with curly, unruly white hair on his temples that tumbled over his ears like mop yarn. He had a ruddy complexion. Of average height he had pudgy fingers, short arms, and the beginnings of a paunch.

Ivy sat on the examination table in his Beverly Hills patient room, which had a picture window with an enviable view of Los Angeles.

"Thank you for seeing me on such short notice," she said.

"You said it was an emergency," said Pond, with a concerned expression.

"I'm feeling sick. I've thrown up several times today."

"Was it something you ate?"

Ivy grimaced. "I think my psychiatrist poisoned me."

Pond stared at her, dumbfounded.

"Why would he poison you?" he said.

"I have no idea. Except—uh—maybe my husband told him to."

"This is a serious accusation. Doctors take an oath. They don't go around poisoning their patients."

"He made me drink something and refused to tell me what it was."

Pond raised his white eyebrows. "Odd. Did he tell you what it was for?"

"A medicine to relax me, because I'm under a lot of stress. Somebody murdered my husband, and I'm being harassed."

Pond commiserated with her. "I heard on the news about your husband. I'm sorry for your loss. Why would your psychiatrist poison you?"

"I think he was telling my husband about my therapy sessions."

"That's highly irregular and flies in the face of the medical code of ethics—if true," said Pond with a stern visage.

"I want you to examine me to see what medicine he gave me. Can you do that?"

"I would need a lab to do that. And it could take a week or so."

"I could be dead by then," said Ivy, chewing her lower lip.

"I can give you a quick physical, if you'd like."

Ivy nodded yes.

Pond told her to remove her blouse.

He retrieved his stethoscope from a desk drawer and listened to Ivy's heartbeat. He told her to take deep breaths, thumped on her back, and listened to her lungs. He glanced at her stomach.

"Putting on a little weight, I see," he said.

"I hadn't noticed. I've been too preoccupied."

"Have you been eating a lot lately?"

"I have a weird craving for strange foods that I ordinarily don't eat. Like pickles with pistachio ice cream."

Pond harrumphed. "Strange."

He applied the stethoscope to her stomach.

"Not so strange," he said, stepping back from her with a smile.

Ivy gave him a baffled expression.

"You're pregnant," he said, chortling.

"That's—that's impossible," said Ivy, dumbfounded.

"Why? You're not too old to have children."

"My stomach isn't bulging."

"Some women have smaller bulges. Perfectly normal."

"Are you sure I'm pregnant?"

"I detected a heartbeat in your womb."

"Orion was impotent for over a year. I haven't had sex for that long."

Pond knitted his brow. "Impossible. Have you been seeing someone else?"

"No way." Ivy paused in confusion. "Oh no It can't be."

"What?"

"I was assaulted by two avatars in the metaverse a few days ago."

Pond shook his head. "You couldn't get pregnant from that. It takes nine months to conceive. Wait a minute. Avatars, you said? Impossible."

"Then how do you explain it?"

"I can't explain it. Unless your memory is faulty. You said you've been having psychiatric issues."

"Yes."

"Maybe your memory is playing tricks on you. Maybe Orion wasn't impotent for a year. Maybe it was for only a few months."

Grimacing, Ivy massaged her forehead. "I've been under tremendous stress lately. I guess that could affect my memory."

"It certainly could. You should be quite happy soon. You're about to become a mother."

"Is that why I've had nausea and cravings for weird food?"

"It would explain it. I doubt very much your psychiatrist would poison you. What is his name?"

"Dr. Jamal Harris."

Recognizing the name Pond smiled. "He's a brilliant psychiatrist. He would never do anything to harm one of his patients. Rest easy. You're in good hands with Dr. Harris."

Ivy felt shellshocked. How could she be pregnant?

"Are you positive I'm pregnant?" she said.

"I am, indeed."

Ivy couldn't get her head around it. What was happening to her? Was this part of losing her mind? Was she even here in Pond's office, or was she imagining it? This couldn't be happening.

If it was a dream, why couldn't she wake up and snap out of it?

Chapter 85

Bondurant used his cell phone to call Nieman from a pocket park in Santa Monica, which had a pond filled with muddy water. The mud was so thick you couldn't see a thing below the surface. If fish were swimming in the water, nobody could see them. Ducks did not mind the mud. They floated idly in the pond and pecked at the ruffled feathers on their backs. Maybe they had lice or fleas, decided Bondurant.

He sat at an empty redwood picnic table stippled with bird droppings under a stand of firs and eucalyptuses and put down his cell on the tabletop. Waiting for Nieman to pick up, Bondurant withdrew an open package of cigarettes from his breast pocket, tapped out a cigarette, inserted it between his lips, produced a lighter, and lit up.

An old lady with a wizened face scowled at him from a table where she sat thirty feet away and waved her hand in front of her face like she was clearing the air of smoke.

"You're thirty feet away, you old bat," muttered Bondurant, and took a deep drag on his cigarette.

"Hello," said Nieman, as he picked up, his voice on speaker.

"It's me," said Bondurant.

"Are you calling to tell me what I want to hear?" said Nieman.

"I believe so," said Bondurant, lifting his mobile to his face with one hand and plucking the cigarette from his mouth with the other.

"Well?"

"I gave the medicine to Harris. He agreed to give it to Ivy."

"I knew he would for the amount of cash I gave him."

"He wanted to know the name of the medicine."

"Tough titty."

315

"That's what I said," said Bondurant with amusement.

"It's none of his business, but it will help Ivy with her pregnancy."

"I didn't know she was pregnant," said Bondurant in surprise. "She doesn't look pregnant."

"My avatars, you know . . ."

Bondurant wasn't sure what Nieman was talking about. It must have had something to do with the avatars Nieman had used to gang-rape Ivy in Rabbit World. Nieman had wanted her to report the assault to the cops, so it would reflect badly on the Rabbit World metaverse and torpedo its IPO next week. But Ivy hadn't done what she was supposed to do. She hadn't gone to the cops. Nieman had sent his avatars to harass her to get her to change her mind. It hadn't worked. In order to save his IPO, Orion had talked Ivy out of telling the cops, which would have given Rabbit World a black eye for all the world to see.

What did Ivy's pregnancy have to do with the IPO? wondered Bondurant. She hadn't looked pregnant, from what he had seen of her. He knew Nieman couldn't have knocked her up, because he was a homosexual. Why would Nieman care about Ivy's pregnancy? He had just said something about his avatars. What the hell did that mean?

"Your avatars?" said Bondurant, bewildered. "What about them?"

"Never mind. They'll take care of her tonight."

Tonight? wondered Bondurant. What was supposed to happen tonight?

"I don't understand," said Bondurant.

"Gays can't reproduce among themselves."

Nah, I guess they can't shit babies.

"You don't say," said Bondurant.

"Don't be an ass. I sent my avatars to her to do the job. I picked Ivy because she's my worst rival's beautiful wife, and she would make fine breeding material. I was rubbing his nose in the dirt, because I knew he was impotent."

A psycho. Fine breeding material? Am I missing something?

"How could you know he couldn't get it up?" said Bondurant.

"Ivy's psychiatrist told me. Jamal Harris would sell his soul for a buck. You can't blame him. His girlfriend is a gold digger."

"Your worst rival is dead. Did you have something to do with that, too?"

"That's not my doing. The algorithms said it wasn't necessary."

"Well, they're never wrong," said Bondurant, rolling his eyes.

"My plan was a stroke of genius. I sent my avatars to rape Ivy, which served two purposes. First, she was supposed to tell the cops. The ensuing bad PR would tank Rabbit World's IPO next week. Second, she would bear my child, courtesy of my avatars."

If Bondurant didn't think Nieman was crazy before, he knew it for certain now.

"Then why did they almost kill her when they ran her off the road into Topanga Canyon?" said Bondurant. "How could she have a baby if they wasted her?"

"She wasn't supposed to crash. They were trying to get her to go to the cops and tell them avatars were stalking her and had raped her in Rabbit World. She wasn't acting according to the algorithms by not going to the cops. And . . ."

"And what?"

"And they were supposed to rape her again in the real world to make sure she was pregnant."

"So much for the track record of your almighty algorithms," said Bondurant with a snicker.

Nieman ignored the sarcasm. "What about Brody? Did you take him out?"

"Uh—not—"

"The algorithms say he has to go," cut in Nieman, losing his temper.

"He's gone. Just not yet."

"The algorithms are never wrong," yelled Nieman.

"Of course not. He's a lucky guy. Otherwise, he'd be dead by now."

The more Bondurant talked to Nieman, the more he thought Nieman was nuts. The guy had to be intelligent because he had graduated from Stanford, one of the best universities in the country. But being smart didn't mean you weren't nuts, was Bondurant's experience. Using avatars to impregnate Ivy? The guy had to be bonkers. Any guy who had blue hair was out there . . .

"You failed your assignment," said Nieman. "It's time for you to face the music."

Bondurant didn't take kindly to threats.

"You should rephrase that," he snarled.

"The algorithms don't lie. They say you're dead."

Bondurant wanted to laugh. *Me dead? Ha. Think again.*

He was about to reply, when Nieman cut him off.

"We're entering a new phase of life," said Nieman. "It's only just begun. I am the alpha and the omega. I will be the father of millions."

Jesus, I hope not.

"Huh?" said Bondurant.

Nieman hung up.

Blue-haired whack job. Bondurant pocketed his cell phone. How do lunatics like Nieman make so much money? The guy was worth billions. Go figure. *Fortune favors the nutbags.*

Bondurant glared at the wizened old hag who persisted in waving her hand in front of her scowling face as she watched him smoke. *Like you can smell it from there.*

He took a deep draft and blew a cone of smoke in her direction. He grinned at her.

And felt weak.

318

He heard a dripping sound. Looking down he saw blood dripping from his blood-drenched pant leg onto the dirt beside his shoe. The superglue must not have held, he decided with dismay. Maybe Brody's bullet had hit his femoral artery after all, or maybe he had nicked it with his tweezers when he was poking around for the slug.

I'm gonna die.

He had one more thing to do before he died. He had failed his mission to take out Brody. He withdrew a jackknife from his trouser pocket, flicked open the blade, splayed the fingers of his left hand on the picnic tabletop, and hacked his forefinger off. Blood spurted from his forefinger's stub.

He didn't feel pain. He felt warm fluid flowing down the remnants of his forefinger.

The old woman sitting at the table thirty feet away screamed in horror as she saw the blood spurting from what was left of his severed finger.

Failure, decided Bondurant. Failure was unacceptable.

A mallard flew out of the pond and, flapping its brown wings, soared over Bondurant's head.

Dropping his cigarette from his lips, Bondurant slouched forward and hit his head on the tabletop, exhaling a last draft of cigarette smoke.

Fucking algorithms. They're never wrong.

Chapter 86

Ivy returned home in a state of stunned disbelief. She couldn't be pregnant. Could Dr. Pond be wrong? She doubted it.

She knew for a fact she hadn't had sex with Orion for the last nine months. She couldn't be having a baby.

Maybe none of this was really happening. Had she gone mad? Was she going mad because her life had become so unbearable that madness was the only escape? It terrified her to think about it. How could you know if you were insane or not?

Should she go back to Dr. Harris and ask him? But he had given her some weird potion to drink. How could she trust him? What would she say to him? *Doctor, am I insane? My personal physician says I'm pregnant when I know it's impossible. Does that mean I'm insane? Did you give me a drug that causes insanity? Is that why you didn't tell me its name?*

Orion had tried to drive her insane. Was Harris doing the same thing? she wondered. She sounded paranoid. Why would Harris want to drive her insane? Orion wanted her money, but what could Harris want?

She felt exhausted. Maybe fatigue was skewing her thinking.

Feeling groggy she dragged herself up the stairs and entered her bedroom. Had she locked the front door? She couldn't remember. She didn't have enough energy to go downstairs and check. Did it even matter if the door was locked? Nothing mattered to her at the moment other than sleep.

She was alone in the world. Orion was gone.

She lay down in bed without changing her clothes and nodded off.

She woke up to the sound of chanting.

320

"We will protect our baby," the voices chanted. "We will protect our baby."

What was going on? she wondered.

The chanting became louder.

She opened her eyes.

At first, everything was blurry. Her vision cleared. She couldn't believe the horrifying sight she beheld.

Her bed was surrounded by chanting avatars, including her rapists Joe Cohan and Ed Vidor.

"We will protect our baby," they all chanted. "We will protect our baby."

The chanting was so loud it sounded like thousands of avatars were outside the house surrounding it and joining in the chorus.

This couldn't be real, she told herself. She needed to wake up. She pinched her arm. Nothing changed. She pinched harder. If she was dreaming, she should wake up. The avatars were still surrounding her bed chanting. Was she dreaming she was pinching her arm?

She closed her eyes and opened them again.

Terrified, she realized nothing had changed. The avatars stood around her bed and kept chanting. Their chanting crescendoed.

Ivy felt a stab of pain in her gut.

She heard a baby scream. Face sweaty, she looked down at her supine body.

A blood-shrouded form like a baby with enormous blue eyes was wriggling and crying between her open legs.

ABOUT THE AUTHOR

Award-winning author Bryan Cassiday writes thrillers and horror fiction. His postapocalyptic horror thriller *Horde (Zombie Apocalypse: The Chad Halverson Series Book 6)* won the Independent Press Award for Best Horror Novel 2022 and the American Fiction Award for Best Horror Novel 2021. He has written four other Scott Brody thrillers. He lives in Southern California.